THE MAN-WOLF
AND OTHER TALES
(EXPANDED EDITION)

THE MAN-WOLF
AND OTHER TALES
(EXPANDED EDITION)

BY ERCKMANN-CHATRIAN

(Émile Erckmann & Alexandre Chatrian)

WILDSIDE PRESS

THE MAN-WOLF AND OTHER TALES

Translated from the French.

Note from the Editor.

The Wildside Press edition includes the complete 1876 text of the collection "The Man-Wolf and Other Tales" and adds four additional stories (the last four in this book)

CONTENTS.

PRELIMINARY NOTE BY THE TRANSLATOR 7

THE MAN-WOLF 10

MYRTLE 99

UNCLE CHRISTIAN'S INHERITANCE 108

THE BEAR-BAITING 118

THE SCAPEGOAT 129

A NIGHT IN THE WOODS 136

THE QUEEN OF THE BEES 148

THE INVISIBLE EYE 159

THE MURDERER'S VIOLIN 173

THE SPIDER OF GUYANA 179

THE WHITE AND BLACK 188

PRELIMINARY NOTE BY THE TRANSLATOR

It has often been remarked, with perfect justice, that the eminent French writers, a translation of one of whose works is here attempted, are singularly faithful in their adherence to historic truth. Remove the thread of obvious fiction which is indispensable to make these admirable productions romances or tales, and what we have left is perfectly reliable history. It is this feature mainly which gives the indescribable charm to their historical tales — a charm powerfully realised in the original, though less appreciable in an imperfect translation.

The same claim to perfect truthfulness in all essential points may be placed to the credit of the following "Roman Populaire," notwithstanding the startling supernatural element on which the story is founded. Erckmann-Chatrian have not thought it right or necessary to depart in this case from their practice of abstaining from all prefaces or notes in every edition of their works. Yet perhaps the translator may be forgiven, and even condoned with thanks, if he ventures upon an explanation tending to show that the tale of *Hugh the Wolf* is not entirely founded upon superstition and the supernatural.

"Let his heart be changed from man's, and let a beast's heart be given unto him!" Such was the sentence pronounced and executed upon him of Babylon whose pride called for abasement from the Lord. Dr. Mead (*Medica Sacra*, p. 59) observes that there was known among the ancients a mental disorder called lycanthropy, the victims of which fancied themselves wolves, and went about howling and attacking and tearing sheep and young children (*Aetius, Lib. Med.* vi., *Paul Ægineta*, iii. 16). So, again, Virgil tells of the daughters of Prætus, who fancied themselves to be cows, and running wildly about the pastures, "*implêrunt falsis mugitibus agros.*" — Ecl. vi. 48. This horrible disease appears happily to have been a rare one, and recoveries from it have taken place, for it is not destructive of the sufferer's life. It has even been thoroughly cured after a lapse of many years.

Dr. Pusey (*Notes on Daniel*, p. 425), in a disquisition of great fulness upon the disease of Nebuchadnezzar, refers to a communication which he received from Dr. Browne, a Commissioner of the Board of Lunacy for Scotland, in which he says, "My opinion is that in all mental powers or conditions the idea of personal identity is but rarely enfeebled, and that it is never extinguished. The ego and non-ego may be confused; the ego, however, continues to preserve the personality. All the angels, devils, dukes, lords, kings, 'gods many' that I have had under my care remained what they were before they became angels, dukes, etc., in a sense, and even nominally. I have seen a man declaring himself the Saviour or St. Paul sign himself *James Thomson,* and attend worship as regularly as if the notion of divinity had never entered into his head."

Esquirol, a very trustworthy writer, has a description of an extraordinary outbreak of lycanthropy in France (in the Jura, at Dole, and other places in Eastern France) in the 16th century.

"This terrible affliction began to manifest itself in France in the 15th century, and the name of '*loups-garous*' has been given to the sufferers. These unhappy beings fly from the society of mankind and live in the woods, the cemeteries, or old ruins, prowling about the open country only by night, howling as they go. They let their beard and nails grow, and then seeing themselves armed with claws and covered with shaggy hair, they become confirmed in the belief that they are wolves. Impelled by ferocity or want, they throw themselves upon young children and tear, kill, and devour them." (Esquiról, *Des Maladies Mentales*, Paris, 1838, vol i., p. 521.) Those whom the French called *loups-garous* were in German termed *werewolves.*

It may be observed on this that when the nails of the fingers and toes are cut they grow indefinitely; but if they are allowed to grow unchecked they soon curve over the extremities, form talons or claws, and cease to grow — answering to the Scriptural account of the effects of the mental disorder of Nebuchadnezzar.

Of course for every case of real malady many were imputed or charged upon poor creatures, who were driven to madness by groundless charges of witchcraft and sorcery, and being *loups-garous* in secret. Many innocent people were in the fifteenth and sixteenth centuries burnt at the stake as wolves in human form.

A correspondent has kindly supplied the following information: "When in Oude in India, twenty-six years ago, we heard of several instances of native babies being carried off out of the villages by she-wolves, and placed with their whelps, and brought up wild there; there was one about when we were there, partially reclaimed, but retaining much of the savage nature imbibed with the wolf's milk, and having been accustomed to go on all-fours — *i.e.,* knees and elbows; but I conclude these were not affected with 'Lycanthropy.'"

With a few touches of his magic pencil the Laureate has

drawn a powerful picture of such a state of things in ancient Britain, of which we can scarcely deny the literal faithfulness. It is not a poetic conception; it is historic truth:

> *"And ever and anon the wolf would steal*
> *The children and devour; but now and then,*
> *Her own brood lost or dead, lent her fierce teat*
> *To human sucklings; and the children, housed*
> *In her foul den, there at their meat would growl,*
> *And mock their foster-mother on four feet,*
> *Till, straightened, they grew up to wolf-like men,*
> *Worse than the wolves."*

The following tale, in which the lycanthropy is far from being altogether a mere effort of the imagination, appears to be founded upon the belief in the continued existence of this rare species of madness down to our own day — or near it — for the story seems to belong to the year 1832.

The English reader will not fail to notice the correspondence between the title and the well-known designation of the illustrious head of the noble house of Grosvenor. Whatever connection there may or may not be between that German Hugh Lupus of a thousand years ago and the truly British Hugh Lupus of our day, all the base qualities of his supposed progenitor have disappeared in him who is adorned with all the qualities which make the English nobility rank as the pride and the flower of our land.

F. A. M.
The Vicaraqe,
Broughton-in-Furness.

THE MAN-WOLF.

CHAPTER I.

About Christmas time in the year 18 —, as I was lying fast asleep at the Cygne at Fribourg, my old friend Gideon Sperver broke abruptly into my room, crying —

"Fritz, I have good news for you; I am going to take you to Nideck, two leagues from this place. You know Nideck, the finest baronial castle in the country, a grand monument of the glory of our forefathers?"

Now I had not seen Sperver, who was my foster-father, for sixteen years; he had grown a full beard in that time, a huge fox-skin cap covered his head, and he was holding his lantern close under my nose. It was, therefore, only natural that I should answer —

"In the first place let us do things in order. Tell me who you are."

"Who I am? What! Don't you remember Gideon Sperver, the Schwartzwald huntsman? You would not be so ungrateful, would you? Was it not I who taught you to set a trap, to lay wait for the foxes along the skirts of the woods, to start the dogs after the wild birds? Do you remember me now? Look at my left ear, with a frost-bite."

"Now I know you; that left ear of yours has done it; Shake hands."

Sperver, passing the back of his hand across his eyes, went on —

"You know Nideck?"

"Of course I do — by reputation; what have you to do there?"

"I am the count's chief huntsman."

"And who has sent you?"

"The young Countess Odile."

"Very good. How soon are we to start?"

"This moment. The matter is urgent; the old count is very ill, and his daughter has begged me not to lose a moment. The horses are quite ready."

"But, Gideon, my dear fellow, just look out at the weather; it has been snowing three days without cessation."

"Oh, nonsense; we are not going out boar-hunting; put on your thick coat, buckle on your spurs, and let us prepare to start. I will order something to eat first." And he went out, first adding,

"Be sure to put on your cape."

I could never refuse old Gideon anything; from my childhood he could do anything with me with a nod or a sign; so I equipped myself and came into the coffee-room.

"I knew," he said, "that you would not let me go back without you. Eat every bit of this slice of ham, and let us drink a stirrup cup, for the horses are getting impatient. I have had your portmanteau put in."

"My portmanteau! What is that for?"

"Yes, it will be all right; you will have to stay a few days at Nideck, that is indispensable, and I will tell you why presently."

So we went down into the courtyard.

At that moment two horsemen arrived, evidently tired out with riding, their horses in a perfect lather of foam. Sperver, who had always been a great admirer of a fine horse, expressed his surprise and admiration at these splendid animals.

"What beauties! They are of the Wallachian breed, I can see, as finely formed as deer, and as swift. Nicholas, throw a cloth over them quickly, or they will take cold."

The travellers, muffled in Siberian furs, passed close by us just as we were going to mount. I could only discern the long brown moustache of one, and his singularly bright and sparkling eyes.

They entered the hotel.

The groom was holding our horses by the bridle. He wished us *bon voyage*, removed his hand, and we were off.

Sperver rode a pure Mecklemburg. I was mounted on a stout cob bred in the Ardennes, full of fire; we flew over the snowy ground. In ten minutes we had left Fribourg behind us.

The sky was beginning to clear up. As far as the eye could reach we could distinguish neither road, path, nor track. Our only company were the ravens of the Black Forest spreading their hollow wings wide over the banks of snow, trying one place after another unsuccessfully for food, and croaking, "Misery! Misery!"

Gideon, with his weather-beaten countenance, his fur cloak and cap, galloped on ahead, whistling airs from the *Freyschütz*; sometimes as he turned I could see the sparkling drops of moisture hanging from his long moustache.

"Well, Fritz, my boy, this is a fine winter's morning."

"So it is, but it is rather severe; don't you think so?"

"I am fond of a clear hard frost," he replied; "it promotes circulation. If our old minister Tobias had but the courage to start out in weather like this he would soon put an end to his rheumatic pains."

I smiled, I am afraid, involuntarily.

After an hour of this rapid pace Sperver slackened his speed and let me come abreast of him.

"Fritz, I shall have to tell you the object of this journey at some time, I suppose?"

"I was beginning to think I ought to know what I am going about."

"A good many doctors have already been consulted."

"Indeed!"

"Yes, some came from Berlin in great wigs who only asked to see the patient's tongue. Others from Switzerland examined him another way. The doctors from Paris stared at their patient through magnifying glasses to learn something from his physiognomy. But all their learning was wasted, and they got large fees in reward of their ignorance."

"Is that the way you speak of us medical gentlemen?"

"I am not alluding to you at all. I have too much respect for you, and if I should happen to break my leg I don't know that there is another that I should prefer to yourself to treat me as a patient, but you have not discovered an optical instrument yet to tell what is going on inside of us."

"How do you know that?"

At this reply the worthy fellow looked at me doubtfully as if he thought me a quack like the rest, yet he replied —

"Well, Fritz, if you have indeed such a glass it will be wanted now, for the count's complaint is internal; it is a terrible kind of illness, something like madness. You know that madness shows itself in either nine hours, nine days, or nine weeks?"

"So it is said; but not having noticed this myself, I cannot say that it is so."

"Still you know there are agues which return at periods of either three, six, or nine years. There are singular works in this machinery of ours. Whenever this human clockwork is wound up in some particular way, fever, or indigestion, or toothache returns at the very hour and day."

"Why, Gideon, I am quite aware of that; those periodical complaints are the greatest trouble we have."

"I am sorry to hear it, for the count's complaint is periodical; it comes back every year, on the same day, at the same hour; his mouth runs over with foam, his eyes stand out white and staring, like great billiard-balls; he shakes from head to foot, and he gnashes with his teeth."

"Perhaps this man has had serious troubles to go through?"

"No, he has not. If his daughter would but consent to be married he would be the happiest man alive. He is rich and powerful and full of honours. He possesses everything that the rest of the world is coveting. Unfortunately his daughter persists in refusing every offer of marriage. She consecrates her life to God, and it harasses him to think that the ancient house of Nideck will become extinct."

"How did his illness come on?" I asked.

"Suddenly, ten years ago," was the reply.

All at once the honest fellow seemed to be recollecting himself. He took from his pocket a short pipe, filled it, and having lighted it —

"One evening," said he, "I was sitting alone with the count in the armoury of the castle. It was about Christmas time. We had been hunting wild boars the whole day in the valleys of the Rhéthal, and had returned at night bringing home with us two of our boar-hounds ripped open from head to tail. It was just as cold as it is tonight, with snow and frost. The count was pacing up and down the room with his chin upon his breast and his hands crossed behind him, like a man in profound thought. From time to time he stopped to watch the gathering snow on the high windows, and I was warming myself in the chimney corner, bewailing my dead hounds, and bestowing maledictions on all the wild boars that infest the Schwartzwald. Everybody at Nideck had been asleep a couple of hours, and not a sound could be heard but the tread and the clank of the count's heavy spurred boots upon the flags. I remember well that a crow, no doubt driven by a gust of wind, came flapping its wings against the windowpanes, uttering a discordant shriek, and how the sheets of snow fell from the windows, and the windows suddenly changed from white to black —"

"But what has all this to do with your master's illness?" I interrupted.

"Let me go on — you will soon see. At that cry the count suddenly gathered himself together with a shuddering movement, his eyes became fixed with a glassy stare, his cheeks were bloodless, and he bent his head forward just like a hunter catching the sound of his approaching game. I went on warming myself, and I thought, 'Won't he soon go to bed now?' for, to tell you the truth, I was overcome with fatigue. All these details, Fritz, are still present in my memory. Scarcely had the bird of ill omen croaked its unearthly cry when the old clock struck eleven. At that moment the count turns on his heel — he listens, his lips tremble,

I can see him staggering like a drunken man. He stretches out his hands, his jaws are tightly clenched, his eyes staring and white. I cried, 'My lord, what is the matter?' but he began to laugh discordantly like a madman, stumbled, and fell upon the stone floor, face downwards. I called for help; servants came round. Sébalt took the count by the shoulders; we removed him to a bed near the window; but just as I was loosening the count's neckerchief — for I was afraid it was apoplexy — the countess came and flung herself upon the body of her father, uttering such heartrending cries that the very remembrance of them makes me shudder."

Here Gideon took his pipe from his lips, knocked the ashes out upon the pommel of his saddle, and pursued his tale in a saddened voice.

"From that day, Fritz, none but evil days have come upon Nideck, and better times seem to be far off. Every year at the same day and hour the count has shuddering fits. The malady lasts from a week to a fortnight, during which he howls and yells so frightfully that it makes a man's blood run cold to hear him. Then he slowly recovers his usual health. He is still pale and weak, and moves trembling from one chair to another, starting at the least noise or movement, and fearful of his own shadow. The young countess, the sweetest creature in the world, never leaves his side; but he cannot endure her while the fit is upon him. He roars at her, 'Go, leave me this moment! I have enough to endure without seeing you hanging about me!' It is a horrible sight. I am always close at his heels in the chase, I who sound the horn when he has killed the forest beasts; I am at the head of all his retainers, and I would give my life for his sake; yet when he is at his worst I can hardly keep off my hands from his throat, I am so horrified at the way in which he treats his beautiful daughter."

Sperver looked dangerously wroth for a moment, clapped both his spurs to his mount, and we rode on at a hard gallop.

I had fallen into a reverie. The cure of a complaint of this description appeared to me more than doubtful, even impossible. It was evidently a mental disorder. To fight against it with any hope of success it would be needful to trace it back to its origin, and this would, no doubt, be too remote for successful investigation.

All these reflections perplexed me greatly. The old huntsman's story, far from strengthening my hopes, only depressed me — not a very favourable condition to insure success. At about three we came in sight of the ancient castle of Nideck on the verge of the horizon. In spite of the great distance we could distinguish the projecting turrets, apparently suspended from the angles of the edifice. It was but a dim outline barely distinguishable from the blue sky, but soon the red points of the Vosges became visible.

At that moment Sperver drew in his bridle and said —

"Fritz, we shall have to get there before night — onward!"

But it was in vain that he spurred and lashed. The horse stood rooted to the ground, his ears thrown back, his nostrils dilated, his sides panting, his legs firmly planted in an attitude of resistance.

"What is the matter with the beast?" cried Gideon in astonishment. "Do you see anything, Fritz? Surely —"

He broke off abruptly, pointing with his whip at a dark form in the snow fifty yards off, on the slope of the hill.

"The Black Plague!" he exclaimed with a voice of distress which almost robbed me of my self-possession.

Following the indication of his outstretched whip I discerned with astonishment an aged woman crouching on the snowy ground, with her arms clasped about her knees, and so tattered that her red elbows came through her tattered sleeves. A few ragged locks of grey hung about her long, scraggy, red, and vulture-like neck.

Strange to say, a bundle of some kind lay upon her knees, and her haggard eyes were directed upon distant objects in the white landscape.

Spencer drew off to the left, giving the hideous object as wide a berth as he could, and I had some difficulty in following him.

"Now," I cried, "what is all this for? Are you joking?"

"Joking? — assuredly not! I never joke about such serious matters. I am not given to superstition, but I confess that I am alarmed at this meeting!"

Then turning his head, and noticing that the old woman had not moved, and that her eyes were fixed upon the same one spot, he appeared to gather a little courage.

"Fritz," he said solemnly, "you are a man of learning — you know many things of which I know nothing at all. Well, I can tell you this, that a man is in the wrong who laughs at a thing because he can't understand it. I have good reasons for calling this woman the Black Plague. She is known by that name in the whole Black Forest, but here at Nideck she has earned that title by supreme right."

And the good man pursued his way without further observation.

"Now, Sperver, just explain what you mean," I asked, "for I

don't understand you."

"That woman is the ruin of us all. She is a witch. She is the cause of it all. It is she who is killing the count by inches."

"How is that possible?" I exclaimed. "How could she exercise such a baneful influence?"

"I cannot tell how it is. All I know is, that on the very day that the attack comes on, at the very moment, if you will ascend the beacon tower, you will see the Black Plague squatting down like a dark speck on the snow just between the Tiefenbach and the castle of Nideck. She sits there alone, crouching close to the snow. Every day she comes a little nearer, and every day the attacks grow worse. You would think he hears her approach. Sometimes on the first day, when the fits of trembling have come over him, he has said to me, 'Gideon, I feel her coming.' I hold him by the arms and restrain the shuddering somewhat, but he still repeats, stammering and struggling with his agony, and his eyes staring and fixed, 'She is coming — nearer — oh — oh — she comes!' Then I go up Hugh Lupus's tower; I survey the country. You know I have a keen eye for distant objects. At last, amidst the grey mists afar off, between sky and Earth, I can just make out a dark speck. The next morning that black spot has grown larger. The Count of Nideck goes to bed with chattering teeth. The next day again we can make out the figure of the old hag; the fierce attacks begin; the count cries out. The day after, the witch is at the foot of the mountain, and the consequence is that the count's jaws are set like a vice; his mouth foams; his eyes turn in his head. Vile creature! Twenty times I have had her within gunshot, and the count has bid me shed no blood. 'No, Sperver, no; let us have no bloodshed.' Poor man, he is sparing the life of the wretch who is draining his life from him, for she is killing him, Fritz; he is reduced to skin and bone."

My good friend Gideon was in too great a rage with the unhappy woman to make it possible to bring him back to calm reason. Besides, who can draw the limits around the region of possibility? Every day we see the range of reality extending more widely. Unseen and unknown influences, marvellous correspondences, invisible bonds, some kind of mysterious magnetism, are, on the one hand, proclaimed as undoubted facts, and denied on the other with irony and scepticism, and yet who can say that after a while there will not be some astonishing revelations breaking in in the midst of us all when we least expect it? In the midst of so much ignorance it seems easy to lay a claim to wisdom and shrewdness.

I therefore only begged Sperver to moderate his anger, and by no means to fire upon the Black Plague, warning him that such a proceeding would bring serious misfortune upon him.

"Pooh!" he cried; "at the very worst they could but hang me."

But that, I remarked, was a good deal for an honest man to suffer.

"Not at all," he cried; "it is but one kind of death out of many. You are suffocated, that is all. I would just as soon die of that as of a hammer falling on my head, as in apoplexy, or not to be able to sleep, or smoke, or swallow, or digest my food."

"You, Gideon, with your grey beard, you have learnt a peculiar mode of reasoning."

"Grey beard or not, that is my way of seeing things. I always keep a ball in my double-barrelled gun at the witch's service; from time to time I put in a fresh charge, and if I get the chance —"

He only added an expressive gesture.

"Quite wrong, Sperver, quite wrong. I agree with the Count of Nideck, and I say no bloodshed. Oceans cannot wipe away blood shed in anger. Think of that, and discharge that barrel against the first boar you meet."

These words seemed to make some impression upon the old huntsman; he hung down his head and looked thoughtful.

We were then climbing the wooded steeps which separate the poor village of Tiefenbach from the Castle of Nideck.

Night had closed in. As it always happens with us after a bright clear winter's day, snow was again beginning to fall, heavy flakes dropped and melted upon our horses' manes, who were beginning now to pluck up their spirits at the near prospect of the comfortable stable.

Now and then Sperver looked over his shoulder with evident uneasiness; and I myself was not altogether free from a feeling of apprehension in thinking of the strange account which the huntsman had given me of his master's complaint.

Besides all this, there is a certain harmony between external nature and the spirit of a man, and I know of nothing more depressing than a gloomy forest loaded in every branch with thick snow and hoar frost, and moaning in the north wind. The gaunt and weird-looking trunks of the tall pines and the gnarled and massive oaks look mournfully upon you, and fill you with melancholy thoughts.

As we ascended the rocky eminence the oaks became fewer, and scattered birches, straight and white as marble pillars, divided the dark green of the forest pines, when in a moment, as we issued from a thicket, the ancient stronghold stood before us in a heavy mass, its dark surface studded with brilliant points of light.

Sperver had pulled up before a deep gateway between two towers, barred in by an iron grating.

"Here we are," he cried, throwing the reins on the horses' necks.

He laid hold of the deer's-foot bell-handle, and the clear sound of a bell broke the stillness.

After waiting a few minutes the light of a lantern flickered in the deep archway, showing us in its semicircular frame of ruddy light the figure of a humpbacked dwarf, yellow-bearded, broad-shouldered, and wrapped in furs from head to foot.

You might have thought him, in the deep shadow, some gnome or evil spirit of earth realised out of the dreams of the Niebelungen Lieder.

He came towards us at a very leisurely pace, and laid his great flat features close against the massive grating, straining his eyes, and trying to make us out in the darkness in which we were standing.

"Is that you, Sperver?" he asked in a hoarse voice.

"Open at once, Knapwurst," was the quick reply. "Don't you know how cold it is?"

"Oh! I know you now," cried the little man; "there's no mis-taking you. You always speak as if you were going to gobble people up."

The door opened, and the dwarf, examining me with his lan-tern, with an odd expression in his face, received me with "*Will-kommen, herr doktor,*" but which seemed to say besides, "Here is another who will have to go away again as others have done." Then he quietly closed the door, whilst we alighted, and came to take our horses by the bridle.

CHAPTER II.

Following Sperver, who ascended the staircase with rapid steps, I was still able to convince myself that the Castle of Nideck had not an undeserved reputation.

It was a true stronghold, partly cut out of the rock, such as used formerly to be called a *château d'ambuscade.* Its lofty vaulted arches re-echoed afar with our steps, and the outside air blowing with sharp gusts through the loopholes — narrow slits made for the archers of former days — caused our torches to flare and flicker from space to space over the faintly-illuminated protruding lines of the arches as they caught the uncertain light.

Sperver knew every nook and corner of this vast place. He turned now to the right and now to the left, and I followed him breathless. At last he stopped on a spacious landing, and said to me —

"Now, Fritz, I will leave you for a minute with the people of the castle to inform the young Countess Odile of your arrival."

"Do just what you think right."

"Then you will find the head butler, Tobias Offenloch, an old soldier of the regiment of Nideck. He campaigned in France under the count; and you will see his wife, a Frenchwoman, Marie Lagoutte, who pretends that she comes of a high family."

"And why should she not?"

"Of course she might; but, between ourselves, she was nothing but a *cantinière* in the Grande Armée. She brought in Tobias Offenloch upon her cart, with one of his legs gone, and he has married her out of gratitude. You understand?"

"That will do, but open, for I am numb with cold."

And I was about to push on; but Sperver, as obstinate as any other good German, was not going to let me off without edifying me upon the history of the people with whom my lot was going to be cast for awhile, and holding me by the frogs of my fur coat he went on —

"There's, besides, Sébalt Kraft, the master of the hounds; he is rather a dismal fellow, but he has not his equal at sounding the horn; and there will be Karl Trumpf, the butler, and Christian Becker, and everybody, unless they have all gone to bed."

Thereupon Sperver pushed open the door, and I stood in some surprise on the threshold of a high, dark hall, the guard room of the old lords of Nideck.

My eyes fell at first upon the three windows at the farther end, looking out upon the sheer rocky precipice. On the right stood an old sideboard in dark oak, and upon it a cask, glasses, and bottles; on the left a Gothic chimney overhung with its heavy massive mantelpiece, empurpled by the brilliant roaring fire underneath, and ornamented on both front and sides with wood-carvings representing scenes from boar-hunts in the Middle Ages, and along the centre of the apartment a long table, upon which stood a huge lamp throwing its light upon a dozen pewter tankards.

At one glance I saw all this; but the human portion of the scene interested me most.

I recognised the major-domo, or head butler, by his wooden

leg, of which I had already heard; he was of low stature, round, fat, and rosy, and his knees seldom coming within an easy range of his eyesight; a nose red and bulbous like a ripe raspberry; on his head he wore a huge hemp-coloured wig, bulging out over his fat poll; a coat of light green plush, with steel buttons as large as a five-franc piece; velvet breeches, silk stockings, and shoes garnished with silver buckles. He was just with his hand upon the top of the cask, with an air of inexpressible satisfaction beaming upon his ruddy features, and his eyes glowing in profile, from the reflection of the fire, like a couple of watch-glasses.

His wife, the worthy Marie Lagoutte, her spare figure draped in voluminous folds, her long and sallow face like a skin of chamois leather, was playing at cards with two servants who were gravely seated on straight-backed armchairs. Certain small split pegs were seated astride across the nose of the old woman and that of another player, whilst the third was significantly and cunningly winking his eye and seeming to enjoy seeing them victimised upon these new Caudine Forks.

"How many cards?" he was asking.

"Two," answered the old woman.

"And you, Christian?"

"Two."

"Aha! Now I have got you, then. Cut the king — now the ace — here's one, here's another. Another peg, mother! This will teach you once more not to brag about French games."

"Monsieur Christian, you don't treat the fair sex with proper respect."

"At cards you respect nobody."

"But you see I have no room left!"

"Pooh, on a nose like yours there's always room for more!"

At that moment Sperver cried —

"Mates, here I am!"

"Ha! Gideon, back already?"

Marie Lagoutte shook off her numerous pegs with a jerk of her head. The big butler drank off his glass. Everybody turned our way.

"Is monseigneur better?"

The butler answered with a doubtful ejaculation.

"Is he just the same?"

"Much about," answered Marie Lagoutte, who never took her eyes off me.

Sperver noticed this.

"Let me introduce to you my foster-son, Doctor Fritz, from

the Black Forest," he answered proudly. "Now we shall see a change, Master Tobie. Now that Fritz has come the abominable fits will be put an end to. If I had but been listened to earlier — but better late than never."

Marie Lagoutte was still watching us, and her scrutiny seemed satisfactory, for, addressing the major-domo, she said —

"Now, Monsieur Offenloch, hand the doctor a chair; move about a little, do! There you stand with your mouth wide open, just like a fish. Ah, sir, these Germans!"

And the good man, jumping up as if moved by a spring, came to take off my cloak.

"Permit me, sir."

"You are very kind, my dear lady."

"Give it to me. What terrible weather! Ah, monsieur, what a dreadful country this is!"

"So monseigneur is neither better nor worse," said Sperver, shaking the snow off his cap; "we are not too late, then. Ho, Kasper! Kasper!"

A little man, who had one shoulder higher than the other, and his face spotted with innumerable freckles, came out of the chimney corner.

"Here I am!"

"Very good; now get ready for this gentleman the bedroom at the end of the long gallery — Hugh's room; you know which I mean."

"Yes, Sperver, in a minute."

"And you will take with you, as you go, the doctor's knapsack. Knapwurst will give it you. As for supper —"

"Never you mind. That is my business."

"Very well, then. I will depend upon you."

The little man went out, and Gideon, after taking off his cape, left us to go and inform the young countess of my arrival.

I was rather overpowered with the attentions of Marie Lagoutte.

"Give up that place of yours, Sébalt," she cried to the kennel-keeper. "You are roasted enough by this time. Sit near the fire, monsieur le docteur; you must have very cold feet. Stretch out your legs; that's the way."

Then, holding out her snuffbox to me —

"Do you take snuff?"

"No, dear madam, with many thanks."

"That is a pity," she answered, filling both nostrils. "It is the most delightful habit."

She slipped her snuffbox back into her apron pocket, and went on —

"You are come not a bit too soon. Monseigneur had his second attack yesterday; it was an awful attack, was it not, Monsieur Offenloch?"

"Furious indeed," answered the head butler gravely.

"It is not surprising," she continued, "when a man takes no nourishment. Fancy, monsieur, that for two days he has never tasted broth!"

"Nor a glass of wine," added the major-domo, crossing his hands over his portly, well-lined person.

As it seemed expected of me, I expressed my surprise, on which Tobias Offenloch came to sit at my right hand, and said —

"Doctor, take my advice; order him a bottle a day of Marcobrunner."

"And," chimed in Marie Lagoutte, "a wing of a chicken at every meal. The poor man is frightfully thin."

"We have got Marcobrunner sixty years in bottle," added the major-domo, "for it is a mistake of Madame Offenloch's to suppose that the French drank it all. And you had better order, while you are about it, now and then, a good bottle of Johannisberg. That is the best wine to set a man up again."

"Time was," remarked the master of the hounds in a dismal voice — "time was when monseigneur hunted twice a week; then he was well; when he left off hunting, then he fell ill."

"Of course it could not be otherwise," observed Marie Lagoutte. "The open air gives you an appetite. The doctor had better order him to hunt three times a week to make up for lost time."

"Two would be enough," replied the man of dogs with the same gravity; "quite enough. The hounds must have their rest. Dogs have just as much right to rest as we have."

There was a few moments' silence, during which I could hear the wind beating against the windowpanes, and rush, sighing and wailing, through the loopholes into the towers.

Sébalt sat with legs across, and his elbow resting on his knee, gazing into the fire with unspeakable dolefulness. Marie Lagoutte, after having refreshed herself with a fresh pinch, was settling her snuff into shape in its box, while I sat thinking on the strange habit people indulge in of pressing their advice upon those who don't want it.

At this moment the major-domo rose.

"Will you have a glass of wine, doctor?" said he, leaning over the back of my armchair.

"Thank you, but I never drink before seeing a patient."

"What! Not even one little glass?"

"Not the smallest glass you could offer me."

He opened his eyes wide and looked with astonishment at his wife.

"The doctor is right," she said. "I am quite of his opinion. I prefer to drink with my meat, and to take a glass of cognac afterwards. That is what the ladies do in France. Cognac is more fashionable than kirschwasser!"

Marie Lagoutte had hardly finished with her dissertation when Sperver opened the door quietly and beckoned me to follow him.

I bowed to the "honourable company," and as I was entering the passage I could hear that lady saying to her husband —

"That is a nice young man. He would have made a good-looking soldier."

Sperver looked uneasy, but said nothing. I was full of my own thoughts.

A few steps under the darkling vaults of Nideck completely effaced from my memory the queer figures of Tobias and Marie Lagoutte, poor harmless creatures, existing like bats under the mighty wing of the vulture.

Soon Gideon brought me into a sumptuous apartment hung with violet-coloured velvet, relieved with gold. A bronze lamp stood in a corner, its brightness toned down by a globe of ground crystal; thick carpets, soft as the turf on the hills, made our steps noiseless. It seemed a fit abode for silence and meditation.

On entering Sperver lifted the heavy draperies which fell around an ogee window. I observed him straining his eyes to discover something in the darkened distance; he was trying to make out whether the witch still lay there crouching down upon the snow in the midst of the plain; but he could see nothing, for there was deep darkness over all.

But I had gone on a few steps, and came in sight, by the faint rays of the lamp, of a pale, delicate figure seated in a Gothic chair not far from the sick man. It was Odile of Nideck. Her long black silk dress, her gentle expression of calm self-devotion and complete resignation, the ideal angellike cast of her sweet features, recalled to one's mind those mysterious creations of the pencil in the Middle Ages when painting was pursued as a true art, but which modern imitators have found themselves obliged to give up in despair, while at the same time they never can forget them.

I cannot say what thoughts passed rapidly through my mind

at the sight of this fair creature, but certainly much of devotion mingled with my sentiments. A sense of music and harmony swept sadly through by soul, with faint impressions of the old ballads of my childhood — of those pious songs with which the kind nurses of the Black Forest rock to peaceful sleep our infant sorrows.

At my approach Odile rose.

"You are very welcome, monsieur le docteur," she said with touching kindness and simplicity; then, pointing with her finger to a recess where lay the count, she added, "There is my father."

I bowed respectfully and without answering, for I felt deeply affected, and drew near to my patient.

Sperver, standing at the head of the bed, held up the lamp with one hand, holding his far cap in the other. Odile stood at my left hand. The light, softened by the subdued light of the globe of ground crystal, fell softly on the face of the count.

At once I was struck with a strangeness in the physiognomy of the Count of Nideck, and in spite of all the admiration which his lovely daughter had at once obtained from me, my first conclusion was, "What an old wolf!"

And such he seemed to be indeed. A grey head, covered with short, close hair, strangely full behind the ears, and drawn out in the face to a portentous length, the narrowness of his forehead up to its summit widening over the eyebrows, which were shaggy and met, pointing downwards over the bridge of the nose, imperfectly shading with their sable outline the cold and inexpressive eyes; the short, rough beard, irregularly spread over the angular and bony outline of the mouth — every feature of this man's dreadful countenance made me shudder, and strange notions crossed my mind about the mysterious affinities between man and the lower creation.

But I resisted my first impressions and took the sick man's hand. It was dry and wiry, yet small and strong; I found the pulse quick, feverish, and denoting great irritability.

What was I to do?

I stood considering; on the one side stood the young lady, anxiously trying to read a little hope in my face; on the other Sperver, equally anxious and watching my every movement. A painful constraint lay, therefore, upon me, yet I saw that there was nothing definite that could be attempted yet.

I dropped the arm and listened to the breathing. From time to time a convulsive sob heaved the sick man's heart, after which followed a succession of quick, short respirations. A kind of nightmare was evidently weighing him down — epilepsy, perhaps, or tetanus. But what could be the cause or origin?

I turned round full of painful thoughts.

"Is there any hope, sir?" asked the young countess.

"Yesterday's crisis is drawing to its close," I answered; "we must see if we can prevent its recurrence."

"Is there any possibility of it, sir?"

I was about to answer in general medical terms, not daring to venture any positive assertions, when the distant sound of the bell at the gate fell upon our ears.

"Visitors," said Sperver.

There was a moment's silence.

"Go and see who it is," said Odile, whose brow was for a minute shaded with anxiety. "How can one be hospitable to strangers at such a time? It is hardly possible!"

But the door opened, and a rosy face, with golden hair, appeared in the shadow, and said in a whisper —

"It is the Baron of Zimmer-Bluderich, with a servant, and he asks for shelter in the Nideck. He has lost his way among the mountains."

"Very well, Gretchen," answered the young countess, kindly; "go and tell the steward to attend to the Baron de Zimmer. Inform him that the count is very ill, and that this alone prevents him from doing the honours as he would wish. Wake up some of our people to wait on him, and let everything be done properly."

Nothing could exceed the sweet and noble simplicity of the young châtelaine in giving her orders. If an air of distinction seems hereditary in some families it is surely because the exercise of the duties conferred by the possession of wealth has a natural tendency to ennoble the whole character and bearing.

These thoughts passed through my mind whilst admiring the grace and gentleness in every movement of Odile of Nideck, and that clearness and purity of outline which is only found marked in the features of the higher aristocracy, and I could recall nothing to my recollection equal to this ideal beauty.

"Go now, Gretchen," said the young countess, "and make haste."

The attendant went out, and I stood a few seconds under the influence of the charm of her manner.

Odile turned round, and addressing me, "You see, sir," said she with a sad smile, "one may not indulge in grief without a pause; we must divide ourselves between our affection within and the world without."

"True, madam," I replied; "souls of the highest order are for the common property and advantage of the unhappy — the lost wayfarer, the sick, the hungry poor — each has his claim for a share, for God has made them like the stars of Heaven to give light and pleasure to all."

The deep-fringed eyelids veiled the blue eyes for a moment, while Sperver pressed my hand.

Presently she pursued —

"Ah, if you could but restore my father's health!"

"As I have had the pleasure to inform you, madam, the crisis is past; the return must be anticipated, if possible."

"Do you hope that it may?"

"With God's help, madam, it is not impossible; I will think carefully over it."

Odile, much moved, came with me to the door. Sperver and I crossed the anteroom, where a few servants were waiting for the orders of their mistress. We had just entered the corridor when Gideon, who was walking first, turned quickly round, and, placing both his hands on my shoulders, said —

"Come, Fritz; I am to be depended upon for keeping a secret; what is your opinion?"

"I think there is no cause of apprehension for tonight."

"I know that — so you told the countess — but how about tomorrow?"

"Tomorrow?"

"Yes; don't turn round. I suppose you cannot prevent the return of the complaint; do you think, Fritz, he will die of it?"

"It is possible, but hardly probable."

"Well done!" cried the good man, springing from the ground with joy; "if you don't think so, that means that you are sure."

And taking my arm, he drew me into the gallery. We had just reached it when the Baron of Zimmer-Bluderich and his groom appeared there also, marshalled by Sébalt with a lighted torch in his hand. They were on their way to their chambers, and those two figures, with their cloaks flung over their shoulders, their loose Hungarian boots up to the knees, the body closely girt with long dark-green laced and frogged tunics, and the bearskin cap closely and warmly covering the head, were very picturesque objects by the flickering light of the pine-torch.

"There," whispered Sperver, "if I am not very much mistaken, those are our Fribourg friends; they have followed very close upon our heels."

"You are quite right: they are the men; I recognise the

younger by his tall, slender figure, his aquiline nose, and his long, drooping moustache."

They disappeared through a side passage.

Gideon took a torch from the wall, and guided me through quite a maze of corridors, aisles, narrow and wide passages, under high vaulted roofs and under low-built arches; who could remember? There seemed no end.

"Here is the hall of the margraves," said he; "here is the portrait-gallery, and this is the chapel, where no mass has been said since Louis the Bold became a Protestant."

All these particulars had very little interest for me.

After reaching the end we had again to go down steps; at last we happily came to the end of our journey before a low massive door. Sperver took a huge key out of his pocket, and handing me the torch, said —

"Mind the light — look out!"

At the same time he pushed open the door, and the cold outside air rushed into the narrow passage. The torch flared and sent out a volley of sparks in all directions. I thought I saw a dark abyss before me, and recoiled with fear.

"Ha, ha, ha!" cried the huntsman, opening his mouth from ear to ear, "you are surely not afraid, Fritz? Come on; don't be frightened! We are upon the parapet between the castle and the old tower."

And my friend advanced to set me the example.

The narrow granite-walled platform was deep in snow, swept in swirling banks by the angry winds. Any one who had seen our flaring torch from below would have asked, "What are they doing up there in the clouds? what can they want at this time of the night?"

Perhaps, I thought within myself, the witch is looking up at us, and that idea gave me a fit of shuddering. I drew closer together the folds of my horseman's cloak, and with my hand upon my hat, I set off after Sperver at a run; he was raising the light above his head to show me the road, and was moving forward rapidly.

We rushed into the tower and then into Hugh Lupus's chamber. A bright fire saluted us here with its cheerful rays; how delightful to be once more sheltered by thick walls!

I had stopped while Sperver closed the door, and contemplating this ancient abode, I cried —

"Thank God! We shall rest now!"

"With a well-furnished table before us," added Gideon. "Don't stand there with your nose in the air, but rather consider what is before you — a leg of a kid, a couple of roast fowls, a pike fresh caught, with parsley sauce; cold meats and hot wines, that's what I like. Kasper has attended to my orders like a real good fellow."

Gideon spoke the truth. The meats were cold and the wines were warm, for in front of the fire stood a row of small bottles under the gentle influence of the heat.

At the sight of these good things my appetite rose in me wonderfully. But Sperver, who understood what is comfortable, stopped me.

"Fritz," said he, "don't let us be in too great a hurry; we have plenty of time; the fowls won't fly away. Your boots must hurt you. After eight hours on horseback it is pleasant to take off one's boots, that's my principle. Now sit down, put your boot between my knees; there goes one off, now the other, that's the way; now put your feet into these slippers, take off your cloak and throw this lighter coat over your shoulders. Now we are ready."

And with his cheery summons I sat down with him to work, one on each side of the table, remembering the German proverb — "Thirst comes from the evil one, but good wine from the Powers above."

CHAPTER III.

We ate with the vigorous appetite which ten hours in the snows of the Black Forest would be sure to provoke.

Sperver making indiscriminate attacks upon the kid, the fowls, and the fish, murmured with his mouth full —

"The woods, the lakes and rivers, and the heathery hills are full of good things!"

Then he leaned over the back of his chair, and laying his hand on the first bottle that came to hand, he added —

"And we have hills green in spring, purple in autumn when the grapes ripen. Your health, Fritz!"

"Yours, Gideon!"

We were a wonder to behold. We reciprocally admired each other.

The fire crackled, the forks rattled, teeth were in full activity, bottles gurgled, glasses jingled, while outside the wintry blast, the high moaning mountain winds, were mournfully chanting the dirge of the year, that strange wailing hymn with which they accompany the shock of the tempest and the swift rush of the grey clouds charged with snow and hail, while the pale moon lights up the grim and ghastly battle scene.

But we were snug under cover, and our appetite was fading away into history. Sperver had filled the "wieder komm," the "come again," with old wine of Brumberg; the sparkling froth fringed its ample borders; he presented it to me, saying —

"Drink the health of Yeri-Hans, lord of Nideck. Drink to the last drop, and show them that you mean it!"

Which was done.

Then he filled it again, and repeating with a voice that re-echoed among the old walls, "To the recovery of my noble master, the high and mighty lord of Nideck," he drained it also.

Then a feeling of satisfied repletion stole gently over us, and we felt pleased with everything.

I fell back in my chair, with my face directed to the ceiling, and my arms hanging lazily down. I began dreamily to consider what sort of a place I had got into.

It was a low vaulted ceiling cut out of the live rock, almost oven-shaped, and hardly twelve feet high at the highest point. At the farther end I saw a sort of deep recess where lay my bed on the ground, and consisting, as I thought I could see, of a huge bear-skin above, and I could not tell what below, and within this yet another smaller niche with a figure of the Virgin Mary carved out of the same granite, and crowned with a bunch of withered grass.

"You are looking over your room," said Spencer. "*Parbleu!* It is none of the biggest or grandest, not quite like the rooms in the castle. We are now in Hugh Lupus's tower, a place as old as the mountain itself, going as far back as the days of Charlemagne. In those days, as you see, people had not yet learned to build arches high, round, or pointed. They worked right into the rock."

"Well, for all that, you have put me in strange lodgings."

"Don't be mistaken, Fritz; it is the place of honour. It is here that the count put all his most distinguished friends. Mind that: Hugh Lupus's tower is the most honourable accommodation we have."

"And who was Hugh Lupus?"

"Why, Hugh the Wolf, to be sure. He was the head of the family of Nideck, a rough-and-ready warrior, I can tell you. He came to settle up here with a score of horsemen and halberdiers of his following. They climbed up this rock — the highest rock amongst these mountains. You will see this tomorrow. They constructed this tower, and proclaimed, 'Now we are the masters! Woe befall the miserable wretches who shall pass without paying toll to us! We will tear the wool off their backs, and their hide too, if need be. From this watch-tower we shall command a view of the far distance all round. The passes of the Rhéthal, of Steinbach, Koche Plate, and of the whole line of the Black Forest are under our eye. Let the Jew pedlars and the dealers beware!' And the noble fellows did what they promised. Hugh the Wolf was at their head. Knapwurst told me all about it sitting up one night."

"Who is Knapwurst?"

"That little humpback who opened the gate for us. He is an odd fellow, Fritz, and almost lives in the library."

"So you have a man of learning at Nideck?"

"Yes, we have, the rascal! Instead of confining himself to the porter's lodge, his proper place, all the day over he is amongst the dusty books and parchments belonging to the family. He comes and goes along the shelves of the library just like a big cat. Knapwurst knows our story better than we know it ourselves. He would tell you the longest tales, Fritz, if you would only let him. He calls them chronicles — ha, ha!"

And Sperver, with the wine mounting a little into his head, began to laugh, he could hardly say why.

"So then, Gideon, you call this tower, Hugh's tower the Hugh Lupus tower?"

"Haven't I told you so already? What are you so astonished at?"

"Nothing particular."

"But you are. I can see it in your face. You are thinking of something strange. What is it?"

"Oh, never mind! It is not the name of the tower which surprises me. What I am wondering at is, how it is that you, an old poacher, who had never lived anywhere since you were a boy but amongst the fir forests, between the snowy summits of the Wald Horn and the passes of the Rhéthal — you who, during all your prime of life, thought it the finest of fun to laugh at the count's gamekeepers, and to scour the mountain paths of the Schwartz-wald, and boat the bushes there, and breathe the free air, and bask in the bright sunshine amongst the hills and valleys — here I find you, at the end of sixteen years of such a life, shut up in this red granite hole. That is what surprises me and what I cannot understand. Come, Sperver, light your pipe, and tell me all about it."

The old poacher took out of his leathern jacket a bit of a blackened pipe; he filled it at his leisure, gathered up in the hollow of his hand a live ember, which he placed upon the bowl of his pipe; then with his eyes dreamily cast up to the ceiling he answered meditatively —

"Old falcons, gerfalcons, and hawks, when they have long swept the plains, end their lives in a hole in a rock. Sure enough I am fond of the wide expanse of sky and land. I always was fond of it; but instead of perching by night upon a high branch of a tall tree, rocked by the wind, I now prefer to return to my cavern, to drink a glass, to pick a bone of venison, and dry my plumage before a warm fire. The Count of Nideck does not disdain Sperver, the old hawk, the true man of the woods. One evening, meeting me by moonlight, he frankly said to me, 'Old comrade, you hunt only by night. Come and hunt by day with me. You have a sharp beak and strong claws. Well, hunt away, if such is your nature; but hunt by my licence, for I am the eagle upon these mountains, and my name is Nideck!'"

Sperver was silent a few minutes; then he resumed —

"That was just what suited me, and now I hunt as I used to do, and I quietly drink along with a friend my bottle of Affenthal or —"

At that moment there was a shock that made the door vibrate; Sperver stopped and listened.

"It is a gust of wind," I said.

"No, it is something else. Don't you hear the scratching of claws? It is a dog that has escaped. Open, Lieverlé, open, Blitzen!" cried the huntsman, rising; but he had not gone a couple of steps when a formidable-looking hound of the Danish breed broke into the tower, and ran to lay his heavy paws on his master's shoulders, licking his beard and his cheeks with his long rose-coloured tongue, uttering all the while short barks and yelps expressive of his joy.

Sperver had passed his arm round the dog's neck, and, turning to me, said —

"Fritz, what man could love me as this dog does? Do look at this head, these eyes, these teeth!"

He uncovered the animal's teeth, displaying a set of fangs that would have pulled down and rent a buffalo. Then repelling him with difficulty, for the dog was redoubling his caresses —

"Down, Lieverlé. I know you love me. If you did not, who would?"

Never had I seen so tremendous a dog as this Lieverlé. His height attained two feet and a half. He would have been a most formidable creature in an attack. His forehead was broad, flat, and covered with fine soft hair; his eye was keen, his paws of great length, his sides and legs a woven mass of muscles and nerves, broad over the back and shoulders, slender and tapering towards the hind legs. But he had no scent. If such monstrous and powerful hounds were endowed with the scent of the terrier there would soon be an end of game.

Sperver had returned to his seat, and was passing his hand over Lieverlé's massive head with pride, and enumerating to me his excellent qualities.

Lieverlé seemed to understand him.

"See, Fritz, that dog will throttle a wolf with one snap of his jaws. For courage and strength, he is perfection. He is not five years old, but he is in his prime. I need not tell you that he is trained to hunt the boar. Every time we come across a herd of them I tremble for Lieverlé; his attack is too straightforward, he flies on the game as straight as an arrow. That is why I am afraid of the brutes' tusks. Lie down, Lieverlé, lie on your back!"

The dog obeyed, and presented to view his flesh-coloured sides.

"Look, Fritz, at that long white seam without any hair upon it from under the thigh right up to the chest. A boar did that. Poor creature! He was holding him fast by the ear and would not let go; we tracked the two by the blood. I was the first up with them. Seeing my Lieverlé I gave a shout, I jumped off my horse, I caught him between my arms, flung him into my cloak, and brought him home. I was almost beside myself. Happily the vital parts had not been wounded. I sewed up his belly in spite of his howling and yelling, for he suffered fearfully; but in three days he was already licking his wound, and a dog who licks himself is already saved. You remember that, Lieverlé, hey! And aren't we fonder of each other now than ever?"

I was quite moved with the affection of the man for that dog, and of the dog for his master; they seemed to look into the very depths of each other's souls. The dog wagged his tail, and the man had tears in his eyes.

Sperver went on —

"What amazing strength! Do you see, Fritz, he has burst his cord to get to me — a rope of six strands; he found out my track and here he is! Here, Lieverlé, catch!"

And he threw to him the remains of the leg of kid. The jaws opened wide and closed again with a terrible crash, and Sperver, looking at me significantly, said —

"Fritz, if he were to grip you by your breeches you would not get away so easily!"

"Nor anyone else, I suppose."

The dog went to stretch himself at his ease full length under the mantelshelf with the leg fast between his mighty paws. He began to tear it into pieces. Sperver looked at him out of the corner of his eye with great satisfaction. The bone was fast falling into small fragments in the powerful mill that was crashing it. Lieverlé was partial to marrow!

"Aha! Fritz, if you were requested to fetch that bone away from him, what would you say?"

"I should think it a mission requiring extraordinary delicacy and tact."

Then we broke out into a hearty laugh, and Sperver, seated in his leathern easy chair, with his left arm thrown back over his head, one of his manly legs over a stool, and the other in front of a huge log, which was dripping at its end with the oozing sap, and darted volumes of light grey smoke to the roof.

I was still contemplating the dog, when, suddenly recollecting our broken conversation, I went on —

"Now, Sperver, you have not told me everything. When you left the mountain for the castle was it not on account of the death of Gertrude, your good, excellent wife?"

Gideon frowned, and a tear dimmed his eye; he drew himself up, and shaking out the ashes of his pipe upon his thumbnail, he said —

"True, my wife is dead. That drove me from the woods. I could not look upon the valley of Roche Creuse without pain. I turned my flight in this direction: I hunt less in the woods, and I can see it all from higher up, and if by chance the pack tails off in that direction I let them go. I turn back and try to think of something else."

Sperver had grown taciturn. With his head drooped upon his breast, his eyes fixed on the stone floor, he sat silent. I felt sorry to have awoke these melancholy recollections in him. Then, my thoughts once more returning to the Black Plague grovelling in the snow, I felt a shivering of horror.

How strange! Just one word had sent us into a train of unhappy thoughts. A whole world of remembrances was called up by a chance.

I know not how long this silence lasted, when a growl, deep, long, and terrible, like distant thunder, made us start.

We looked at the dog. The half-gnawed bone was still between his forepaws, but with head raised high, ears cocked up, and flashing eye, he was listening intently — listening to the silence as it were, and an angry quivering ran down the length of his back.

Sperver and I fixed on each other anxious eyes; yet there was not a sound, not a breath outside, for the wind had gone down; nothing could be heard but the deep protracted growl which came from deep down the chest of the noble hound.

Suddenly he sprang up and bounded impetuously against the wall with a hoarse, rough bark of fearful loudness. The walls re-echoed just as if a clap of thunder had rattled the casements.

Lieverlé, with his head low down, seemed to want to see through the granite, and his lips drawn back from his teeth discovered them to the very gums, displaying two close rows of fangs white as ivory. Still he growled. For a moment he would stop abruptly with his nose snuffing close to the wall, next the floor, with strong respirations; then he would rise again in a fresh rage, and with his forepaws seemed as if he would break through the granite.

We watched in silence without being able to understand what caused his excitement.

Another yell of rage more terrible than the first made us spring from our seats.

"Lieverlé! What possesses you? Are you going mad?"

He seized a log and began to sound the wall, which only returned the dead, hard sound of a wall of solid rock. There was no hollow in it; yet the dog stood in the posture of attack.

"Decidedly you must have been dreaming bad dreams," said the huntsman. "Come, lie down, and don't worry us any more with your nonsense."

At that moment a noise outside reached our ears. The door opened, and the fat honest countenance of Tobias Offenloch with his lantern in one hand and his stick in the other, his three-cornered hat on his head, appeared, smiling and jovial, in the opening.

"*Salut! L'honorable compagnie!*" he cried as he entered; "what are you doing here?"

"It was that rascal Lieverlé who made all that row. Just fancy — he set himself up against that wall as if he smelt a thief. What could he mean?"

"Why *parbleu!* He heard the dot, dot of my wooden leg, to be sure, stumping up the tower stairs," answered the jolly fellow, laughing.

Then setting his lantern on the table —

"That will teach you, friend Gideon, to tie up your dogs. You are foolishly weak over your dogs — very foolishly. Those beasts of yours won't be satisfied till they have put us all out of doors. Just this minute I met Blitzen in the long gallery: he sprang at my leg — see there are the marks of his teeth in proof of what I say; and it is quite a new leg — a brute of a hound!"

"Tie up my dogs! That's rather a new idea," said the huntsman. "Dogs tied up are good for nothing at all; they grow too wild. Besides, was not Lieverlé tied up, after all? See his broken cord."

"What I tell you is not on my own account. When they come near me I always hold up my stick and put my wooden leg foremost — that is my discipline. I say, dogs in their kennels, cats on the roof, and the people in the castle."

Tobias sat down after thus delivering himself of his sentiments, and with both elbows on the table, his eyes expanding with delight, he confided to us that just now he was a bachelor.

"You don't mean that!"

"Yes, Marie Anne is sitting up with Gertrude in monseigneur's ante-room."

"Then you are in no hurry to go away?"

"No, none at all. I should like to stay in your company."

"How unfortunate that you should have come in so late!" remarked Sperver; "all the bottles are empty."

The disappointment of the discomfited major-domo excited my compassion. The poor man would so gladly have enjoyed his widowhood. But in spite of my endeavours to repress it a long yawn extended wide my mouth.

"Well, another time," said he, rising. "What is only put off is not given up."

And he took his lantern.

"Good night, gentlemen."

"Stop — wait for me," cried Gideon. "I can see Fritz is sleepy; we will go down together."

"Very gladly, Sperver; on our way we will have a word with Trumpf, the butler. He is downstairs with the rest, and Knapwurst is telling them tales."

"All right. Good night, Fritz."

"Good night, Gideon. Don't forget to send for me if the count is taken worse."

"I will do as you wish. Lieverlé, come."

They went out, and as they were crossing the platform I could hear the Nideck clock strike eleven. I was tired out and soon fell asleep.

CHAPTER IV.

Daylight was beginning to tinge with bluish grey the only window in my dungeon tower when I was roused out of my niche in the granite by the prolonged distant notes of a hunting horn.

There is nothing more sad and melancholy than the wail of this instrument when the day begins to struggle with the night — when not a sigh nor a sound besides comes to molest the solitary reign of silence; it is especially the last long note which spreads in widening waves over the immensity of the plain beneath, awaking the distant, far-off echoes amongst the mountains, that has in it a poetic element that stirs up the depths of the soul.

Leaning upon my elbow in my bearskin I lay listening to the plaintive sound, which suggested something of the feudal ages. The contemplation of my chamber, the ancient den of the Wolf of Nideck, with its low, dark arch, threatening almost to come down to crush the occupant; and further on that small leaden window, just touching the ceiling, more wide than high, and deeply recessed in the wall, added to the reality of the impression.

I arose quickly and ran to open the window wide.

Then presented itself to my astonished eyes such a wondrous spectacle as no mortal tongue, no pen of man, can describe — the wide prospect that the eagle, the denizen of the high Alps, sweeps with his far reaching ken every morning at the rising of the deep purple veil that overhung the horizon by night mountains farther off! Mountains far away! And yet again in the blue distance — mountains still, blending with the grey mists of the morning in the shadowy horizon! — motionless billows that sink into peace and stillness in the blue distance of the plains of Lorraine. Such is a faint idea of the mighty scenery of the Vosges, boundless forests, silver lakes, dazzling crests, ridges, and peaks projecting their clear outlines upon the steel-blue of the valleys clothed in snow. Beyond this, infinite space!

Could any enthusiasm of poet or skill of painter attain the sublime elevation of such a scene as that?

I stood mute with admiration. At every moment the details stood out more clearly in the advancing light of morning; hamlets, farmhouses, villages, seemed to rise and peep out of every undulation of the land. A little more attention brought more and more numerous objects into view.

I had leaned out of my window rapt in contemplation for more than a quarter of an hour when a hand was laid lightly upon my shoulder; I turned round startled, when the calm figure and quiet smile of Gideon saluted me with —

"Guten Tag, Fritz! Good morning!"

Then he also rested his arms on the window, smoking his short pipe. He extended his hand and said —

"Look, Fritz, and admire! You are a son of the Black Forest, and you must admire all that. Look there below; there is Roche Creuse. Do you see it? Don't you remember Gertrude? How far off those times seem now!"

Sperver brushed away a tear. What could I say?

We sat long contemplating and meditating over this grand spectacle. From time to time the old poacher, noticing me with my eyes fixed upon some distant object, would explain —

"That is the Wald Horn; this is the Tiefenthal; there's the fall of the Steinbach; it has stopped running now; it is hanging down in great fringed sheets, like the curtains over the shoulder of the Harberg — a cold winter's cloak! Down there is a path that leads to Fribourg; in a fortnight's time it will be difficult to trace it."

Thus our time passed away.

I could not tear myself away from so beautiful a prospect. A few birds of prey, with wings hollowed into a graceful curve sharp-pointed at each end, the fan-shaped tail spread out, were silently sweeping round the rock-hewn tower; herons flew unscathed above them, owing their safety from the grasp of the sharp claws and the tearing beak to the elevation of their flight.

Not a cloud marred the beauty of the blue sky; all the snow had fallen to Earth; once more the huntsman's horn awoke the echoes.

"That is my friend Sébalt lamenting down there," said Sperver. "He knows everything about horses and dogs, and he sounds the hunter's horn better than any man in Germany. Listen, Fritz, how soft and mellow the notes are! Poor Sébalt! He is pining away over monseigneur's illness; he cannot hunt as he used to do. His only comfort is to get up every morning at sunrise on to the Altenberg and play the count's favourite airs. He thinks he shall be able to cure him that way!"

Sperver, with the good taste of a man who appreciates beautiful scenery, had offered no interruption to my contemplations; but when, my eyes dazzled and swimming with so much light, I turned round to the darkness of the tower, he said to me —

"Fritz, it's all right; the count has had no fresh attack."

These words brought me back to a sense of the realities of life.

"Ah, I am very glad!"

"It is all owing to you, Fritz."

"What do you mean? I have not prescribed yet."

"What signifies? You were there; that was enough."

"You are only joking, Gideon! What is the use of my being present if I don't prescribe?"

"Why, you bring him good luck!"

I looked straight at him, but he was not even smiling!

"Yes, Fritz, you are just a messenger of good; the last two years the lord had another attack the next day after the first, then a third and a fourth. You have put an end to that. What can be clearer?"

"Well, to me it is not so very clear; on the contrary, it is very obscure."

"We are never too old to learn," the good man went on. "Fritz, there are messengers of evil and there are messengers of good. Now that rascal Knapwurst, he is a sure messenger of ill. If ever I meet him as I am going out hunting I am sure of some misadventure; my gun misses fire, or I sprain my ankle, or a dog gets ripped up! — all sorts of mischief come. So, being quite aware of this, I always try and set off at early daybreak, before that author of mischief, who sleeps like a dormouse, has opened his eyes; or else I slip out by a back way by the postern gate. Don't you see?"

"I understand you very well, but your ideas seem to me very strange, Gideon."

"You, Fritz," he went on, without noticing my interruption, "you are a most excellent lad; Heaven has covered your head with innumerable blessings; just one glance at your jolly countenance, your frank, clear eyes, your good-natured smile, is enough to make anyone happy. You positively bring good luck with you. I have always said so, and now would you like to have a proof?"

"Yes, indeed I should. It would be worth while to know how much there is in me without my having any knowledge of it."

"Well," said he, grasping my wrist, "look down there!"

He pointed to a hillock at a couple of gunshots from the castle.

"Do you see there a rock half-buried in the snow, with a ragged bush by its side?"

"Quite well."

"Do you see anything near?"

"No."

"Well, there is a reason for that. You have driven away the Black Plague! Every year at the second attack there she was holding her feet between her hands. By night she lighted a fire; she warmed herself and boiled roots. She bore a curse with her. This morning the very first thing which I did was to get up here. I climbed up the beacon tower; I looked well all round; the old hag was nowhere to be seen. I shaded my eyes with my hand. I looked up and down, right and left, and everywhere; not a sign of the creature anywhere. She had scented you evidently."

And the good fellow, in a fit of enthusiasm, shook me warmly by the hand, crying with unchecked emotion —

"Ah, Fritz, how glad I am that I brought you here! The witch *will* be sold, eh?"

Well, I confess I felt a little ashamed that I had been all my life such a very well-deserving young man without knowing anything of the circumstance myself.

"So, Sperver," I said, "the count has spent a good night?"

"A very good one."

"Then I am very well pleased. Let us go down."

We again traversed the high parapet, and I was now better able to examine this way of access, the ramparts of which arose from a prodigious depth; and they were extended along the sharp narrow ridge of the rock down to the very bottom of the valley. It was a long flight of jagged precipitous steps descending from the wolf's den, or rather eagle's nest, down to the deep valley below.

Gazing down I felt giddy, and recoiling in alarm to the middle of the platform, I hastily descended down the path which led to the main building.

We had already traversed several great corridors when a great open door stood before us. I looked in, and descried, at the top of a double ladder, the little gnome Knapwurst, whose strange appearance had struck me the night before.

The hall itself attracted my attention by its imposing aspect. It was the receptacle of the archives of the house of Nideck, a high, dark, dusty apartment, with long Gothic windows, reaching from the angle of the ceiling to within a couple of yards from the floor.

There were collected along spacious shelves, by the care of the old abbots, not only all the documents, title-deeds, and family genealogies of the house of Nideck, establishing their rights and their alliances, and connections with all the great historic families of Germany, but besides these there were all the chronicles of the Black Forest, the collected works of the old Minnesinger, and great folio volumes from the presses of Gutenberg and Faust, entitled to equal veneration on account of their remarkable history and of the enduring solidity of their binding. The deep shadows of the groined vaults, their arches divided by massive ribs, and descending partly down the cold grey walls, reminded one of the gloomy cloisters of the Middle Ages. And amidst these characteristic surroundings sat an ugly dwarf on the top of his ladder, with a red-edged volume upon his bony knees, his head half-buried in a rough fur cap, small grey eyes, wide misshapen mouth, humps on back and shoulders, a most uninviting object, the familiar spirit — the rat, as Sperver would have it — of this last refuge of all the learning belonging to the princely race of Nideck.

But a truly historical importance belonged to this chamber in the long series of family portraits, filling almost entirely one side of the ancient library. All were there, men and women; from Hugh the Wolf to Yeri-Hans, the present owner; from the first rough daub of barbarous times to the perfect work of the best modern painters.

My attention was naturally drawn in that direction.

Hugh I., a bald-headed figure, seemed to glare upon you like a wolf stealing upon you round the corner of a wood. His grey bloodshot eyes, his red beard, and his large hairy ears gave him a fearful and ferocious aspect.

Next to him, like the lamb next to the wolf, was the portrait of a lady of youthful years, with gentle blue eyes, hands crossed on the breast over a book of devotions, and tresses of fair long silky hair encircling her sweet countenance with a glorious golden aureola. This picture struck me by its wonderful resemblance to Odile of Nideck.

I have never seen anything more lovely and more charming than this old painting on wood, which was stiff enough indeed in its outline, but delightfully refreshing and ingenuous.

I had examined this picture attentively for some minutes when another female portrait, hanging at its side, drew my attention reluctantly away. Here was a woman of the true Visigoth type, with a wide low forehead, yellowish eyes, prominent cheekbones, red hair, and a nose hooked like an eagle's beak.

That woman must have been an excellent match for Hugh, thought I, and I began to consider the costume, which answered perfectly to the energy displayed in the head, for the right hand rested upon a sword, and an iron breastplate inclosed the figure.

I should have some difficulty in expressing the thoughts which passed through my mind in the examination of these three portraits. My eye passed from the one to the other with singular curiosity.

Sperver, standing at the library door, had aroused the attention of Knapwurst with a sharp whistle, which made that worthy send a glance in his direction, though it did not succeed in fetching him down from his elevation.

"Is it me that you are whistling to like a dog?" said the dwarf.

"I am, you vermin! It is an honour you don't deserve."

"Just listen to me, Sperver," replied the little man with sublime scorn; "you cannot spit so high as my shoe!" which he contemptuously held out.

"Suppose I were to come up?"

"If you come up a single step I'll squash you flat with this volume!"

Gideon laughed, and replied —

"Don't get angry, friend; I don't mean to do you any harm; on the contrary, I greatly respect you for your learning; but what I want to know is what you are doing here so early in the morning, by lamplight? You look as if you had spent the night here."

"So I have; I have been reading all night."

"Are not the days long enough for you to read in?"

"No; I am following out an important inquiry, and I don't mean to sleep until I am satisfied."

"Indeed; and what may this very important question be?"

"I have to ascertain under what circumstances Ludwig of Nideck discovered my ancestor, Otto the Dwarf, in the forests of Thuringia. You know, Sperver, that my ancestor Otto was only a cubit high — that is, a foot and a half. He delighted the world with his wisdom, and made an honourable figure at the coronation of Duke Rudolphe. Count Ludwig had him inclosed in a cold roast peacock, served up in all his plumage. It was at that time one of the greatest delicacies, served up garnished all round with suckling pigs, gilded and silvered. During the banquet Otto kept spreading the peacock's tail, and all the lords, courtiers, and ladies of high birth were astonished and delighted at this wonderful piece of mechanism. At last he came out, sword in hand, and shouted with a loud voice — 'Long live Duke Rudolphe!' and the cry was repeated with acclamations by the whole table. Bernard Herzog makes mention of this event, but he has neglected to inform us where this dwarf came from, whether he was of lofty lineage or of base extraction, which latter, however, is very improbable, for the lower sort of people have not so much sense as that."

I was astounded at so much pride in so diminutive a being, yet my curiosity prevented me from showing too much of my feelings, for he alone could supply me with information upon the portraits that accompanied that of Hugh Lupus.

"Monsieur Knapwurst," I began very respectfully, "would you oblige me by enlightening me upon certain historic doubts?"

"Speak, sir, without any constraint; on the subject of family history and chronicles I am entirely at your service. Other matters don't interest me."

"I desire to learn some particulars respecting the two portraits on each side of the founder of this race."

"Aha!" cried Knapwurst with a glow of satisfaction lighting
up his hideous features; "you mean Hedwige and Huldine, the two
wives of Hugh Lupus."

And laying down his volume he descended from his ladder to
speak more at his ease. His eyes glistened, and the delight of gratified vanity beamed from them as he displayed his vast erudition.

When he had arrived at my side he bowed to me with ceremo-
nious gravity. Sperver stood behind us, very well satisfied that I
was admiring the dwarf of Nideck. In spite of the ill luck which, in
his opinion, accompanied the little monster's appearance, he
respected and boasted of his superior knowledge.

"Sir," said Knapwurst, pointing with his yellow hand to the
portraits, "Hugh of Nideck, the first of his illustrious race, married, in 832, Hedwige of Lutzelbourg, who brought to him in
dowry the counties of Giromani and Haut Barr, the castles of
Geroldseck, Teufelshorn, and others. Hugh Lupus had no issue by
his first wife, who died young, in the year of our Lord 837. Then
Hugh, having become lord and owner of the dowry, refused to give
it up, and there were terrible battles between himself and his
brothers-in-law. But his second wife, Huldine, whom you see
there in a steel breastplate, aided him by her sage counsel. It is
unknown whence or of what family she came, but for all that she
saved Hugh's life, who had been made prisoner by Frantz of
Lutzelbourg. He was to have been hanged that very day, and a
gibbet had already been set up on the ramparts, when Huldine, at
the head of her husband's vassals, whom she had armed and
inspired with her own courage, bravely broke in, released Hugh,
and hung Frantz in his place. Hugh had married his wife in 842,
and had three children by her."

"So," I resumed pensively, "the first of these wives was called
Hedwige, and the descendants of Nideck are not related to her?"

"Not at all."

"Are you quite sure?"

"I can show you our genealogical tree; Hedwige had no children; Huldine, the second wife, had three."

"That is surprising to me."

"Why so?"

"I thought I traced a resemblance."

"Oho! Resemblance! Rubbish!" cried Knapwurst with a discordant laugh. "See — look at this wooden snuffbox; in it you see a

portrait of my great-grandfather, Hanswurst. His nose is as long and as pointed as an extinguisher, and his jaws like nutcrackers. How does that affect his being the grandfather of me — of a man with finely-formed features and an agreeable mouth?"

"Oh no! — of course not."

"Well, so it is with the Nidecks. They may some of them be like Hedwige, but for all that Huldine is the head of their ancestry. See the genealogical tree. Now, sir, are you satisfied?"

Then we separated — Knapwurst and I — excellent friends.

CHAPTER V.

"Nevertheless," thought I, "there is the likeness. It is not chance. What is chance? There is no such thing; it is nonsense to talk of chance. It must be something higher!"

I was following my friend Sperver, deep in thought, who had now resumed his walk down the corridor. The portrait of Hedwige, in all its artless simplicity, mingled in my mind with the face of Odile.

Suddenly Gideon stopped, and, raising my eyes, I saw that we were standing before the count's door.

"Come in, Fritz," he said, "and I will give the dogs a feed. When the master's away the servants neglect their duty; I will come for you by-and-by."

I entered, more desirous of seeing the young lady than the count her father; I was blaming myself for my remissness, but there is no controlling one's interest and affections. I was much surprised to see in the half-light of the alcove the reclining figure of the count leaning upon his elbow and observing me with profound attention. I was so little prepared for this examination that I stood rather dispossessed of self-command.

"Come nearer, monsieur le docteur," he said in a weak but firm voice, holding out his hand. "My faithful Sperver has often mentioned your name to me; and I was anxious to make your acquaintance."

"Let us hope, my lord, that it will be continued under more favourable circumstances. A little patience, and we shall avert this attack."

"I think not," he replied. "I feel my time drawing near."

"You are mistaken, my lord."

"No; Nature grants us, as a last favour, to have a presentiment of our approaching end."

"How often I have seen such presentiments falsified!" I said with a smile.

He fixed his eyes searchingly upon me, as is usual with patients expressing anxiety about their prospects. It is a difficult moment for the doctor. The moral strength of his patient depends upon the expression of the firmness of his convictions; the eye of the sufferer penetrates into the innermost soul of his consciousness; if he believes that he can discover any hint or shade of doubt, his fate is sealed; depression sets in; the secret springs that maintain the elasticity of the spirit give way, and the disorder has it all its own way.

I stood my examination firmly and successfully, and the count seemed to regain confidence; he again pressed my hand, and resigned himself calmly and confidently to my treatment.

Not until then did I perceive Mademoiselle Odile and an old lady, no doubt her governess, seated by her bedside at the other end of the alcove.

They silently saluted me, and suddenly the picture in the library reappeared before me.

"It is she," I said, "Hugh's first wife. There is the fair and noble brow, there are the long lashes, and that sad, unfathomable smile. Oh, how much past telling lies in a woman's smile! Seek not, then, for unmixed joy and pleasure! Her smile serves but to veil untold sorrows, anxiety for the future, even heartrending cares. The maid, the wife, the mother, smile and smile, even when the heart is breaking and the abyss is opening. O woman! This is thy part in the mortal struggle of human life!"

I was pursuing these reflections when the lord of Nideck began to speak —

"If my dear child Odile would but consult my wishes I believe my health would return."

I looked towards the young countess; she fixed her eyes on the floor, and seemed to be praying silently.

"Yes," the sick man went on, "I should then return to life; the prospect of seeing myself surrounded by a young family, and of pressing grandchildren to my heart, and beholding the succession to my house, would revive me."

At the mild and gentle tone of entreaty in which this was said I felt deeply moved with compassion; but the young lady made no reply.

In a minute or two the count, who kept his watchful eyes upon her, went on —

"Odile, you refuse to make your father a happy man? I only ask for a faint hope. I fix no time. I won't limit your choice. We will go to court. There you will have a hundred opportunities of marrying with distinction and with honour. Who would not be proud to win my daughter's hand? You shall be perfectly free to decide for yourself."

He paused.

There is nothing more painful to a stranger than these family quarrels. There are such contending interests, so many private motives, at work, that mere modesty should make it our duty to place ourselves out of hearing of such discussions. I felt pained, and would gladly have retired. But the circumstances of the case forbade this.

"My dear father," said Odile, as if to evade any further discussion, "you will get better. Heaven will not take you from those who love you. If you but knew the fervour with which I pray for you!"

"That is not an answer," said the count drily. "What objection can you make to my proposal? Is it not fair and natural? Am I to be deprived of the consolations vouchsafed to the neediest and most wretched? You know I have acted towards you openly and frankly."

"You have, my father."

"Then give me your reason for your refusal."

"My resolution is formed — I have consecrated myself to God."

So much firmness in so frail a being made me tremble. She stood like the sculptured Madonna in Hugh's tower, calm and immovable, however weak in appearance.

The eyes of the count kindled with an ominous fire. I tried to make the young countess understand by signs how gladly I would hear her give the least hope, and calm his rising passion; but she seemed not to see me.

"So," he cried in a smothered tone, as if he were strangling — "so you will look on and see your father perish? A word would restore him to life, and you refuse to speak that one word?"

"Life is not in the hand of man, for it is God's gift; my word can be of no avail."

"Those are nothing but pious maxims," answered the count scornfully, "to release you from your plain duty. But has not God said, 'Honour thy father and thy mother?'"

"I do honour you," she replied gently. "But it is my duty not to marry."

I could hear the grinding and gnashing of the man's teeth. He lay apparently calm, but presently turned abruptly and cried —

"Leave me; the sight of you is offensive to me!"

And addressing me as I stood by agitated with conflicting

feelings —

"Doctor," he cried with a savage grin, "have you any violent malignant poison about you to give me — something that will destroy me like a thunderbolt? It would be a mercy to poison me like a dog, rather than let me suffer as I am doing."

His features writhed convulsively, his colour became livid.

Odile rose and advanced to the door.

"Stay!" he howled furiously — "stay till I have cursed you!"

So far I had stood by without speaking, not venturing to interfere between Father and Daughter, but now I could refrain no longer.

"Monseigneur," I cried, "for the sake of your own health, for the sake of mere justice and fairness, do calm yourself; your life is at stake."

"What matters my life? what matters the future? Is there a knife here to put an end to me? Let me die!"

His excitement rose every minute. I seemed to dread lest in some frenzied moment he should spring from the bed and destroy his child's life. But she, calm though deadly pale, knelt at the door, which was standing open, and outside I could see Sperver, whose features betrayed the deepest anxiety. He drew near without noise, and bending towards Odile —

"Oh, mademoiselle!" he whispered — "mademoiselle, the count is such a worthy, good man. If you would but just say only, 'Perhaps — by-and-by — we will see.'"

She made no reply, and did not change her attitude.

At this moment I persuaded the Lord of Nideck to take a few drops of Laudanum; he sank back with a sigh, and soon his panting and irregular breathing became more measured under the influence of a deep and heavy slumber.

Odile arose, and her aged friend, who had not opened her lips, went out with her. Sperver and I watched their slowly retreating figures. There was a calm grandeur in the step of the young countess which seemed to express a consciousness of duty fulfilled.

When she had disappeared down the long corridor Gideon turned towards me.

"Well, Fritz," he said gravely, "what is your opinion?"

I bent my head down without answering. This girl's incredible firmness astonished and bewildered me.

CHAPTER VI.

Sperver's indignation was mounting.

"There's the happiness and felicity of the rich! What is the good of being master of Nideck, with castles, forests, lakes, and all the best parts of the Black Forest, when an innocent looking damsel comes and says to you in her sweet soft voice, 'Is that your will? Well, it is not mine. Do you say I must? Well, I say no, I won't.' Is it not awful? Would it not be better to be a woodcutter's son and live quietly upon the wages of your day's work? Come on, Fritz; let us be off. I am suffocating here; I want to get into the open air."

And the good fellow, seizing my arm, dragged me down the corridor.

It was now about nine. The sky had been fair when we got up, but now the clouds had again covered the dreary Earth, the north wind was raising the snow in ghostly eddies against the window-panes, and I could scarcely distinguish the summits of the neigh-bouring mountains.

We were going down the stairs which led into the hall, when, at a turn in the corridor, we found ourselves face to face with Tobias Offenloch, the worthy major-domo, in a great state of pal-pitation.

"Halloo!" he cried, closing our way with his stick right across the passage; "where are you off to in such a hurry? What about our breakfast?"

"Breakfast! Which breakfast do you mean?" asked Sperver.

"What do you mean by pretending to forget what breakfast? Are not you and I to breakfast this very morning with Doctor Fritz?"

"Aha! So we are! I had forgotten all about it."

And Offenloch burst into a great laugh which divided his jolly face from ear to ear.

"Ha, ha! This is rather beyond a joke. And I was afraid of being too late! Come, let us be moving. Kasper is upstairs waiting. I ordered him to lay the breakfast in your room; I thought we should be more comfortable there. Good-bye for the present, doctor."

"Are you not coming up with us?" asked Sperver.

"No, I am going to tell the countess that the Baron de Zimmer-Bluderich begs the honour to thank her in person before he leaves the castle."

"The Baron de Zimmer?"

"Yes, that stranger who came yesterday in the middle of the night."

"Well, you must make haste."

"Yes, I shall not be long. Before you have done uncorking the bottles I shall be with you again."

And he hobbled away as fast as he could.

The mention of breakfast had given a different turn to Sperver's thoughts.

"Exactly so," he observed, turning back; "the best way to drown all your cares is to drink a draught of good wine. I am very glad we are going to breakfast in my room. Under those great high vaults in the fencing-school, sitting round a small table, you feel just like mice nibbling a nut in a corner of a big church. Here we are, Fritz. Just listen to the wind whistling through the arrow-slits. In half an hour there will be a storm."

He pushed the door open; and Kasper, who was only drumming with his fingers upon the windowpanes, seemed very glad to see us. That little man had flaxen hair and a snub nose. Sperver had made him his factotum; it was he who took to pieces and cleaned his guns, mended the riding-horses' harness, fed the dogs in his absence, and superintended in the kitchen the preparation of his favourite dishes. On grand occasions he was outrider. He now stood with a napkin over his arm, and was gravely uncorking the long-necked bottle of Rhenish.

"Kasper," said his master, as soon as he had surveyed this satisfactory state of things — "Kasper, I was very well pleased with you yesterday; everything was excellent; the roast kid, the chicken, and the fish. I like fair play, and when a man has done his duty I like to tell him so. Today I am quite as well satisfied. The boar's head looks excellent with its white-wine sauce; so does the crayfish soup. Isn't it your opinion too, Fritz?"

I assented.

"Well," said Sperver, "since it is so, you shall have the honour of filling our glasses. I mean to raise you step by step, for you are a very deserving fellow."

Kasper looked down bashfully and blushed; he seemed to enjoy his master's praises.

We took our places, and I was wondering at this quondam poacher, who in years gone by was content to cook his own potatoes in his cottage, now assuming all the airs of a great seigneur. Had he been born Lord of Nideck he could not have put on a more noble and dignified attitude at table. A single glance brought Kasper to his side, made him bring such and such a bottle, or bring the dish he required.

We were just going to attack the boar's head when Master Tobias appeared in person, followed by no less a personage than the Baron of Zimmer-Bluderich, attended by his groom.

We rose from our seats. The young baron advanced to meet us with head uncovered. It was a noble-looking head, pale and haughty, with a surrounding of fine dark hair. He stopped before Sperver.

"Monsieur," said he in that pure Saxon accent which no other dialect can approach, "I am come to ask you for information as to this locality. Madame la Comtesse de Nideck tells me that no one knows these mountains so well as yourself."

"That is quite true, monseigneur, and I am quite at your service."

"Circumstances of great urgency oblige me to start in the midst of the storm," replied the baron, pointing to the window-panes thickly covered with flakes of snow. "I must reach Wald Horn, six leagues from this place!"

"That will be a hard matter, my lord, for all the roads are blocked up with snow."

"I am aware of that, but necessity obliges."

"You must have a guide, then. I will go, if you will allow me, to Sébalt Kraft, the head huntsman at Nideck. He knows the mountains almost as well as I do."

"I am much obliged to you for your kind offers, and I am very grateful, but still I cannot accept them. Your instructions will be quite sufficient."

Sperver bowed, then advancing to a window, he opened it wide. A furious blast of wind rushed in, driving the whirling snow as far as the corridor, and slammed the door with a crash.

I remained by my chair, leaning on its back. Kasper slunk into a corner. Sperver and the baron, with his groom, stood at the open window.

"Gentlemen," said Sperver with a loud voice to make himself heard above the howling winds, and with arm extended, "you see the country mapped out before you. If the weather was fair I would take you up into the tower, and then we could see the whole of the Black Forest at our feet, but it is no use now. Here you can see the peak of the Altenberg. Farther on behind that white ridge you may see the Wald Horn, beaten by a furious storm. You must make straight for the Wald Horn. From the summit of the rock, which seems formed like a mitre, and is called Roche Fendue, you will see three peaks, the Behrenkopp, the Geierstein, and the Trielfels. It is by this last one at the right that you must proceed. There is a torrent across the valley of the Rhéthal, but it must be frozen now. In any case, if you can get no farther, you will find on your left, on following the bank, a cavern halfway up the hill, called Roche Creuse. You can spend the night there, and tomorrow very likely, if the wind falls, you will see the Wald Horn before you. If you are lucky enough to meet with a charcoal-burner, he might, perhaps, show you where there is a ford over the stream; but I doubt whether one will be found anywhere on such a day as this. There are none from our neighbourhood. Only be careful to go right round the base of the Behrenkopp, for you could not get down the other side. It is a precipice."

During these observations I was watching Sperver, whose clear, energetic tones indicated the different points in the road with the greatest precision, and I watched, too, the young baron, who was listening with the closest attention. No obstacle seemed to alarm him. The old groom seemed not less bent upon the enterprise.

Just as they were leaving the window a momentary light broke through the grey snow-clouds — just one of those moments when the eddying wind lays hold of the falling clouds of snow and flings them back again like floating garments of white. Then for a moment there was a glimpse of the distance. The three peaks stood out behind the Altenberg. The description which Sperver had given of invisible objects became visible for a few moments; then the air again was veiled in ghostly clouds of flying snow.

"Thank you," said the baron. "Now I have seen the point I am to make for; and, thanks to your explanations, I hope to reach it."

Sperver bowed without answering. The young man and his servant, having saluted us, retired slowly and gravely.

Gideon shut the window, and addressing Master Tobias and me, said —

"The deuce must be in the man to start off in such horrible weather as this. I could hardly turn out a wolf on such a day as this. However, it is their business, not mine. I seem to remember that young man's face, and his servant's too. Now let us drink! Maître Tobie, your health!"

I had gone to the window, and as the Baron Zimmer and his groom mounted on horseback in the middle of the courtyard, in spite of the snow which was filling the air, I saw at the left in a turret, pierced with long Gothic windows, the pale countenance of Odile directed long and anxiously towards the young man.

"Halloo, Fritz! What are you doing?"

"I am only looking at those strangers' horses."

"Oh, the Wallachians! I saw them this morning in the stable. They are splendid animals."

The horsemen galloped away at full speed, and the curtain in the turret-window dropped.

CHAPTER VII.

Several uneventful days followed. My life at Nideck was becoming dull and monotonous. Every morning there was the doleful bugle-call of the huntsman, whose occupation was gone; then came a visit to the count; after that breakfast, with Sperver's interminable speculations upon the Black Plague, the incessant gossiping and chattering of Marie Lagoutte, Maître Tobias, and all that pack of idle servants, who had nothing to do but eat and drink, smoke, and go to sleep. The only man who had any kind of individual existence was Knapwurst, who sat buried up to the tip of his red nose in old chronicles all the day long, careless of the cold so long as there was anything left to find out in his curious researches.

My weariness of all this may easily be imagined. Ten times had Sperver taken me over the stables and the kennels; the dogs were beginning to know me. I knew by heart all the coarse pleasantries of the major-domo over his bottles and Marie Lagoutte's invariable replies. Sébalt's melancholy was infecting me; I would gladly have blown a little on his horn to tell the mountains of my *ennui*, and my eyes were incessantly directed towards Fribourg.

Still the disorder of Yeri-Hans, lord of Nideck, was taking its usual course, and this gave my only occupation any serious interest. All the particulars which Sperver had made me acquainted with appeared clearly before me; sometimes the count, waking up with a start, would half rise, and supported on his elbow, with neck outstretched and haggard eyes, would mutter, "She is coming, she is coming!"

Then Gideon would shake his head and ascend the signal-tower, but neither right nor left could the Black Plague be discovered.

After long reflection upon this strange malady I had come to the conclusion that the sufferer was insane. The strange influence that the old hag exercised over him, his alternate phases of madness and lucidity, all confirmed me in this view.

Medical men who have given especial attention to the subject of mental aberrations are well aware that periodical madness is of not unfrequent occurrence. In some cases the illness appears several times in the year, in others at only particular seasons of the year. I know at Fribourg an old lady who for thirty years past has regularly presented herself at the door of the asylum. At her own request they place her in confinement; then the unhappy woman every night passes through the terrible scenes of the French Revolution, of which she was a witness in her youth. She trembles in the hands of the executioner; she fancies herself drenched with the blood of the victims; she weeps and cries aloud incessantly. In the course of a few weeks the mind returns to its wonted seat, and she is restored to liberty with the full expectation that she will return again in a year.

"The Count of Nideck is suffering from a similar attack," I said; "unknown chains unite his fate with that of the Black Plague. Who can tell?" thought I; "that woman once was young, perhaps beautiful!"

And my imagination, once launched, carried me into the interesting regions of romance; but I was careful to tell no one what I thought. If I had opened out those conjectures to Sperver he would never have forgiven me for imagining that there could have been any intimacy between his master and the Black Plague; and as for Mademoiselle Odile, I dared not suggest insanity to her.

The poor young lady was evidently most unhappy. Her refusal to marry had so embittered the count against her that he could scarcely endure to have her in his presence. He bitterly reproached her with her ingratitude and disobedience, and expatiated upon the cruelty of ungrateful children. Sometimes even violent curses followed his daughter's visits. Things at last were so bad that I thought myself obliged to interfere. I therefore waited one evening on the countess in the antechamber and entreated her to relinquish her personal attendance upon her father. But here arose, contrary to all expectations, quite an unforeseen obstacle. In spite of all my entreaties she steadily insisted on watching by her father and nursing him as she had done hitherto.

"It is my duty," she repeated, "and no arguments will shake my purpose," she said firmly.

"Madam," I replied as a last effort, "the medical profession, too, has its duties, and an honourable man must fulfil them even to harshness and cruelty; your presence is killing your father."

I shall remember all my life the sudden change in the expression of the face of Odile.

My solemn words of warning seemed to cause the blood to flow back to the heart; her face became white as marble, and her large blue eyes, fixed steadily upon mine, seemed to read into the most secret recesses of my soul.

"Is that possible, sir?" she stammered; "upon your honour, do you declare this? Tell me truly!"

"Yes, madam, upon my honour."

There was a long and painful silence, only broken at last by these words in a low voice:

"Let God's will be done!"

And with downcast eyes she withdrew.

The day after this scene, about eight in the morning, I was pacing up and down in Hugh Lupus's tower, thinking of the count's illness, of which I could not foretell the issue — and I was thinking too of my patients at Fribourg, whom I might lose by too prolonged an absence — when three discreet taps upon my door turned my thoughts into another channel.

"Come in!"

The door opened, and Marie Lagoutte stood within, dropping me a low curtsey.

This old dame's visit put me out, and I was going to beg her to postpone her visit, when something mysterious in her countenance caught my attention. She had thrown over her shoulders a red-and-green shawl; she was biting her lips, with her head down, and as soon as she had closed the door she opened it again, and peeped out, to make sure that no one had followed her.

"What does she want with me?" I thought; "what is the meaning of all these precautions?"

And I was quite puzzled.

"Monsieur le Docteur," said the worthy lady, advancing towards me, "I beg your pardon for disturbing you so early in the morning, but I have a very serious thing to tell you."

"Pray tell me all about it, then."

"It is the count."

"Indeed!"

"Yes, sir; you know that I sat up with him last night."

"I know. Pray sit down."

She sat before me in a great armchair, and I could not help noticing the energetic character of her head, which on the evening of my arrival at the castle had only seemed to me grotesque.

"Doctor," she resumed after a short pause and with her dark eyes upon me, "you know I am not timid or easily frightened. I have seen so many dreadful things in the course of my life that I am astonished at nothing now. When you have seen Marengo, Austerlitz, and Moscow, there is nothing left that can put you out."

"I am sure of that, ma'am."

"I don't want to boast; that is not my reason for telling you this; but it is to show you that I am not an escaped lunatic, and that you may believe me when I tell you what I say I have seen."

This was becoming interesting.

"Well," the good woman resumed, "last night, between nine and ten, just as I was going to bed, Offenloch came in and said to me, 'Marie, you will have to sit up with the count tonight.' At first I felt surprised. 'What! Is not mademoiselle going to sit up?' 'No, mademoiselle is poorly, and you will have to take her place.' Poor girl, she is ill; I knew that would be the end of it, I told her so a hundred times; but it is always so. Young people won't believe those who are older; and then, it is her Father. So I took my knitting, said good night to Tobias, and went into monseigneur's room. Sperver was there waiting for me, and went to bed; so there I was, all alone."

Here the good woman stopped a moment, indulged in a pinch of snuff, and tried to arrange her thoughts. I listened with eager attention for what was coming.

"About half-past ten," she went on, "I was sitting near the bed, and from time to time drew the curtain to see what the count was doing; he made no movement; he was sleeping as quietly as a child. It was all right until eleven o'clock, then I began to feel tired. An old woman, sir, cannot help herself — she must drop off to sleep in spite of everything. I did not think anything was going to happen, and I said to myself, 'He is sure to sleep till daylight.' About twelve the wind went down; the big windows had been rattling, but now they were quiet. I got up to see if anything was stirring outside. It was all as black as ink; so I came back to my armchair. I took another look at the patient; I saw that he had not stirred an inch, and I took up my knitting; but in a few minutes more I began nodding, nodding, and I dropped right off to sleep. I could not help it, the armchair was so soft and the room was so warm, who could have helped it? I had been asleep an hour, I suppose, when a sharp current of wind woke me up. I opened my eyes, and what do you think I saw? The tall middle window was wide open, the curtains were drawn, and there in the opening stood the count in his white night-dress, right on the windowsill."

"The count?"

"Yes."

"Nay, it is impossible; he cannot move!"

"So I thought too; but that is just how I saw him. He was standing with a torch in his hand; the night was so dark and the air so still that the flame stood up quite straight."

I gazed upon Marie Anne with astonishment.

"First of all," she said, after a moment's silence, "to see that long, thin man standing there with his bare legs, I can assure you it had such an effect upon me! I wanted to scream; but then I thought, 'Perhaps he is walking in his sleep; if I shout he will wake up, he will jump down, and then —' So I did not say a word, but I stared and stared till I saw him lift up his torch in the air over his head, then he lowered it, then up again and down again, and he did this three times, just like a man making signals; then he threw it down upon the ramparts, shut the window, drew the curtains, passed before me without speaking, and got into bed muttering some words I could not make out."

"Are you sure you saw all that, ma'am?"

"Quite sure."

"Well, it is strange."

"I know it is; but it is true. Ah! It did astonish me at first, and then when I saw him get into bed again and cross his hands over his breast just as if nothing had happened, I said to myself, 'Marie Anne, you have had a bad dream; it cannot be true;' and so I went to the window, and there I saw the torch still burning; it had fallen into a bush near the third gate, and there it was shining just like a spark of fire. There was no denying it."

Marie Lagoutte looked at me a few moments without speaking.

"You may be sure, doctor, that after that I had no more sleep; I sat watching and ready for anything. Every moment I fancied I could hear something behind the armchair. I was not afraid — it was not that — but I was uneasy and restless. When morning came, very early I ran and woke Offenloch and sent him to the count. Passing down the corridor I noticed that there was no torch in the first ring, and I came down and found it near the narrow path to the Schwartzwald; there it is!"

And the good woman took from under her apron the end of a torch, which she threw upon the table.

I was confounded.

How had that man, whom I had seen the night before feeble and exhausted, been able to rise, walk, lift up and close down that heavy window? What was the meaning of that signal by night? I seemed to myself to witness this strange, mysterious scene, and my thoughts went off at once to the Black Plague. When I aroused myself from this contemplation of my own thoughts, I saw Marie Lagoutte rising and preparing to go.

"You have done quite right," I said as I took her to the door, "to tell me of these things, and I am much obliged to you. Have you told anyone else of this adventure?"

"No one, sir; such things are only to be told to the priest and the doctor."

"Come, I see you are a very wise, sensible woman."

These words were exchanged at the door of my tower. At this moment Sperver appeared at the end of the gallery, followed by his friend Sébalt.

"Fritz!" he shouted, "I have got news to tell you."

"Oh, come!" thought I, "more news! This is a strange condition of things."

Marie Lagoutte had disappeared, and the huntsman and his friend entered the tower.

CHAPTER VIII.

On the countenance of Sperver was an expression of suppressed wrath, on that of his companion bitter irony. This worthy sportsman, whose woeful physiognomy had struck me on my first arrival at Nideck, was as thin and dry as a lath. His hunting-jacket was girded tightly about him by his belt, from which hung a hunting-knife with a horn handle; long leathern gaiters came above his knees; the horn went over his shoulder from right to left, the wide-expanded opening under his arm; on his head a wide-brimmed hat, with a heron's plume in the buckle. His profile, coming to a point in a reddish tuft, looked not unlike a goat's.

"Yes," cried Sperver, "I have got strange things to tell you."

He threw himself in a chair, seizing his head between his clenched hands, while dismal Sébalt calmly drew his horn over his head and laid it on the table.

"Now, Sébalt," cried Gideon, "speak out."

"The witch is hanging about the castle."

This piece of intelligence would have failed to interest me before seeing Marie Lagoutte, but now it struck more forcibly. There certainly was some mysterious connection between the lord of Nideck and that old woman. I knew nothing of the nature of this connection, and I felt that, at whatever cost, I must know it.

"Just wait a moment, friends," said I to Sperver and his comrade. "I want to know, first of all, where does this Black Pest come from?"

Sperver stared at me with astonishment.

"Come from? Who can tell that?"

"Very well, you can't. But when does she come within sight of Nideck?"

"As I told you, ten days before Christmas, at the same time every year."

"And how long does she stay?"

"A fortnight or three weeks."

"Is she ever seen before? Not even on her way? Nor after?"

"No."

"Then we shall have to catch her, seize upon her," I cried. "This is contrary to nature. We must find out where she comes from, what she wants here, what she is."

"Lay hold of her!" exclaimed Sperver; "seize her! Do you mean it?" and he shook his head. "Fritz, your advice is good enough in its way, but it is easier said than done. I could very easily send a bullet after her, almost at any time; but the count won't consent to that measure; and as for catching in any other way than by powder and shot, why, you had better go first and catch a squirrel by the tail! Listen to Sébalt's story, and you shall judge for yourself."

The master of the hounds, sitting on the table with his long legs crossed, fixed his eyes mournfully upon me, and began his tale.

"This morning, as I was coming down from the Altenberg, I followed the hollow road to Nideck. The snow filled it up entirely. I was going on my way, thinking of nothing particular, when I noticed a foot-track; it was deep down, and went across the road. The person had come down the bank and gone up on the other side. It was not a soft hare's foot, which hardly leaves an impression, it was not forked like a wild boar's track, it was not like a cloven hoof, such as the wolf's — it was a deep hole. I stopped and stooped down, and cleared away the loose snow that fell round, and came upon the very track of the Black Pest!"

"Are you sure it was that?"

"Of course I am. I know the old woman by her foot better than by her figure, for I always go, sir, with my eyes on the ground. I know everybody by their tracks; and as for this one, a child might know it."

"What, then, distinguishes this foot so particularly?"

"It is so small that you could cover it with your hand; it is finely shaped, the heel is rather long, the outline clean, the great toe lies close to the other toes, and they are all as fine as if they were in a lady's slipper. It is a lovely foot. Twenty years ago I should have fallen in love with a foot like that. Whenever I come across it, it has such an effect upon me! No one would believe that such a foot could belong to the Black Plague."

And the poor fellow, joining his hands together, contemplated the stone floor with doleful eyes.

"Well, Sébalt, what next?" asked Sperver impatiently.

"Ah, yes, to be sure! Well, I recognised that track and started off in pursuit. I was hoping to catch the creature in her lair, but I will tell you the way she took me. I climbed up the bank by the roadside, only two gunshots from Nideck. I go along the hill, keeping the track on my right; it led along the side of the wood in the Rhéthal. All at once it jumps over the ditch into the wood. I stuck to it, but, happening to look a little to my left, I saw another track which had, been following the Black Plague. I stopped short: was it Sperver's? or Kasper Trumpfs? or whose? I came to it, and you may fancy how astounded I was when I saw that it was nobody from our place! I know every foot in the Schwartzwald from Fribourg to Nideck. That foot was like none of ours. It must have come from a distance. The boot — for it was a kind of well-made, soft gentleman's boot, with spurs, which leave a little print behind them — the boot was not round at the toes, but square. The sole was thin, and bent with every step, and it had no nails in it. The walk was rapid, and the short steps were like those of a young man of twenty to five-and-twenty. I noticed the stitches in the side leather at once, and I think I never saw finer."

"Who can this be?" Sperver exclaimed.

Sébalt raised his shoulders and extended his hands, but said nothing.

"Who can have any object in following the old woman?" I asked Sperver.

"No one on Earth can tell," was the reply.

And so we sat a few minutes meditating over what we had heard.

At last he went on again with his narrative:

"I kept following the track; it went up the next ridge through the pine-forest. When it doubled round the Koche Fendue I said to myself, 'Ah, you accursed plague! If there was much game of your sort there would not be much sport; it would be preferable to work like a nigger!' So we all three arrive — the two tracks and I — at the top of the Schnéeberg. There the wind had been blowing hard; the snow was knee-deep — but no matter! I must get on! I got to the edge of the torrent of the Steinbach, and there I lost the track. I halted, and I saw that, after trying up and down in several directions, the gentleman's boots had gone down the Tiefenbach. That was a bad sign. I looked along the other side of the torrent, but there was no appearance of a track there — none at all! The old hag had paddled up and down the stream to throw anyone off the scent who should try to follow her. Where was I to go to? — right, or left, or straight on? Not knowing, I came back to Nideck."

"You haven't told us about her breakfast," said Sperver.

"No, I was forgetting. At the foot of Roche Fendue I saw there had been a fire; there was a black place; I laid my hand upon it, thinking it might be warm, which would have proved that the Black Plague had not gone far; but it was as cold as ice. Close by I saw a wire trap in the bushes. It seems the creature knows how to snare game. A hare had been caught in it; the print of its body was still plain, lying flat in the snow. The witch had lighted the fire to cook it; she had had a good breakfast, I'll be bound."

At this Sperver cried indignantly —

"Just fancy that old witch living on meat while so many honest folks in our villages have nothing better than potatoes to eat! That's what upsets me, Fritz! Ah! If I had but —"

But his thoughts remained untold; he turned deadly pale, and all three of us, in a moment, stood rigid and motionless, staring with horror at each other's ghastly countenances.

A yell — the howling cry of the wolf in the long, cold days of winter — the cry which none can imagine who has not heard the most fearful and harrowing of all bestial sounds — that fearful cry was echoing through the castle not far from us! It rose up the spiral staircase, it filled the massive building as if the hungry, savage beast was at our door!

Travellers speak of the deep roar of the lion troubling the silence of the night amidst the rocky deserts of Africa; but while the tropical regions, sultry and baked, resound with the vibrations of the mighty voice of the savage monarch of the desert, making the air tremble with the distant thunder of his awful cry, the vast snowy deserts of the North too have their characteristic cry — a strange, lamentable yell that seems to suit the character of the dreary winter scene. That voice of the Northern desert is the howl of the wolf!

The instant after this awful sound had broken upon the silence followed another formidable body of discordant sounds — the baying and yelling of sixty hounds — answering from the ramparts of Nideck. The whole pack gave voice at the same moment — the deep bay of the bloodhound, the sharp cry of the pointer, the plaintive yelpings of the spaniels, and the melancholy howl of the mastiffs, all mingling in confusion with the rattling of dog-chains, the shaking of the kennels under the struggles of the hounds to get loose; and, dominating over all, the long, dismal, prolonged note of the wolf's monotonous howl; his was the leading part in this horrible canine concert!

Sperver sprang from his seat and ran out upon the platform to see if a wolf had dropped into the moat. But no — the howling came from neither. Then turning to us he cried —

"Fritz! Sébalt! — come, come quickly!"

We flew down the steps four at a time and rushed into the fencing-school. Here we heard the cry of the wolf alone, prolonged beneath the echoing arches the distant barking and yelling of the pack became almost inaudible in the distance; the dogs were hoarse with rage and excitement, their chains were getting entangled together. Perhaps they were strangling each other.

Sperver drew the keen blade of his hunting-knife. Sébalt did the same; they preceded me down the gallery.

Then the fearful sounds became our guide to the sick man's room. Sperver spoke no more; he hurried forward. Sébalt stretched his long legs. I felt a shuddering horror creep through my whole frame — a horrible presentiment of something shocking and abominable came over us.

As we approached the apartments of the count we met the whole household afoot — the gamekeepers, the huntsmen, the kennel-keepers, the scullions were all mingled and jostling each other, asking —

"What is the matter? Where are those cries coming from?"

Without stopping we ran into the passage which led into the count's bedroom, where we met poor Marie Lagoutte, who alone had had the courage to penetrate thither before us. She was holding in her arms the young countess, who had fainted, her head falling back, her hair flowing down behind her; she was carrying her away as fast as she could.

We passed her so rapidly that we scarcely had time to witness this sad sight. But it has since returned to my memory, and the pale face of Odile lying on the ample shoulders of the good servant still makes a vivid impression upon my memory, resembling the poor lamb presenting its throat to the knife without a complaint, dying with fear before the stroke falls.

At last we had reached the count's chamber.

The howling came from behind his door.

We stole fearful glances at one another without attempting to account for the hideous noise, or explaining the presence of such a wild guest in the house. Indeed, we had no time; our ideas were in dire and utter confusion.

Sperver hastily pushed the door open, and, knife in hand,

was darting into the room; but he stood arrested on the threshold motionless as a stone.

Never have I seen such a picture of horror as he displayed standing rooted there, with his eyes starting from his head, and his mouth wide open and gasping for breath.

I gazed over his shoulder, and the sight that met my eyes made the blood run chill as snow in my veins.

The lord of Nideck, crouching on all fours upon his bed, with his arms bending forward, his head carried low, his eyes glaring with fierce fires, was uttering loud, protracted howlings!

He was the wolf!

That low receding forehead, that sharp-pointed face, that foxy-looking beard, bristling off both cheeks; the long meagre figure, the sinewy limbs, the face, the cry. The attitude, declared the presence of the wild beast half-hidden, half-revealed under a human mask!

At times he would stop for a second and listen attentively with head awry, and then the crimson hangings would tremble with the quivering of his limbs, like foliage shaken by the wind; then the melancholy wail would open afresh.

Sperver, Sébalt, and I stood nailed to the floor; we held our breath, petrified with fear.

Suddenly the count stopped. As a wild beast scents the wind, he lifted his head and listened again.

There, there, far away, down among the thick fir forests, whitened with dense patches of snow, a cry was heard in reply — weak at first; then the sound rose and swelled in a long protracted howl, drowning the feebler efforts of the hounds: it was the she-wolf answering the wolf!

Sperver, turning round awe-stricken, his countenance pale as ashes, pointed to the mountain, and murmured low —

"Listen — there's the witch!"

And the count still crouching motionless, but with his head now raised in the attitude of attention, his neck outstretched, his eyes burning, seemed to understand the meaning of that distant voice, lost amidst the passes and peaks of the Schwartzwald, and a kind of fearful joy gleamed in his savage features.

At this moment, Sperver, unable or unwilling to restrain himself any longer, cried in a voice broken with emotion —

"Count of Nideck — what are you doing?"

The count fell back thunderstruck. We rushed into the room to his help. It was time. The third attack had commenced, and it was terrible to witness!

CHAPTER IX.

The lord of Nideck was in a dying state.

What can science do in presence of the great mortal strife between Death and Life? At the supreme hour, when the invisible wrestlers are writhed together body to body and limb to limb, panting, each in turn overthrowing and overthrown, what avails the healing art? One can but watch, and tremble, and listen!

At times the struggle seems suspended — a truce has sounded; Life has retired into her hold. She is resting; she is collecting the courage of despair. But the relentless enemy beats at the gates; he bursts in; then Life springs to the rescue, and again grapples with her adversary. The strife is renewed with fresh fuel added to the fire of mortal energy as the fatal issue draws closer and nearer.

And the exhausted patient, himself the field of battle, weltering in the cold sweat of death, the eye set and the arm powerless, can do nothing for himself. His breathing, sometimes short, broken, and distressing, sometimes long, deep, laboured, and heavy, indicates the varying phases of this dreadful struggle.

The bystanders watch each other's faces, and they think, "The day will come when we in our turns shall be the field of the same strife, and victorious Death will bear us away into the grave, his den, as the spider carries away the fly." But the true life, the only life, the soul, spreading her immortal wings, will speed her flight to another world, with the exulting cry, "I have fought the good fight. I have finished my course. I have kept the faith!" And Death, disappointed of its prey, will look up at the emancipated being, unable to follow, and holding in its clutches only a cold and decaying corpse, soon to be a handful of dust. "O death, where is thy sting? O grave, where is thy victory?" O best and only consolation, the hope and belief in the final triumph of justice, the certainty of immortal life through Jesus Christ the Saviour! Cruel indeed is he who would rob man of the chief brightness and glory of life!

Towards midnight the Count of Nideck seemed almost gone; the agony of death was at hand; the broken, weakened pulse indicated the sinking of the vital powers; then, it might return to a more active state; but there seemed no hope.

My only duty left was to stay and see this unhappy man die.

I was exhausted with fatigue and anxiety; whatever art could do I had tried.

I told Sperver to sit up, and close his master's eyes in death.

The poor faithful fellow was in the utmost distress; he reproached himself with his involuntary cry — "Count of Nideck — what are you doing?" and tore his hair in bitter repentance.

I went away alone to Hugh Lupus's tower, having had scarcely any time to take food, but I did not feel the want of it.

There was a bright fire on the hearth; I threw myself dressed upon the bed, and sleep soon came to relieve my weight of apprehension — that heavy sleep broken by the consciousness that you may any minute be awoke by tears and lamentations.

I was sleeping thus, with my face turned towards the fire, and as it often happens, the flame fitfully rising, and falling threw a fluttering, flickering light like those of ruddy flapping wings against the walls, and wearied still more my dropping eyelids.

Lost in a dreamy slumber, I was half opening my eyes to see the cause of these alternate lights and shadows, but the strangest sight surprised me.

Close by the hearth, hardly revealed by the feeble light of a few dying embers, I recognised with dismay the dark profile of the Black Plague!

She sat upon a low stool, and was evidently warming herself.

At first I thought myself deceived by my senses, which would have been natural enough after the exciting scenes of the last few days; I raised myself upon my elbow, gazing with my eyes starting with fear and horror.

It was she indeed! I lay horrified, for there she sat calm and immovable, with her hands clasped over her skinny knees, just as I had seen her in the snow, with her long scraggy neck out-stretched, her hooked nose, her compressed lips.

How had the Black Pest got here? How had she found her way into this high tower crowning the dangerous precipices? Everything that Sperver had told me of this mysterious being seemed to be coming true! And now the unaccountable behaviour of Lieverlé, growling so fiercely against the wall, seemed clear as the daylight. I huddled myself close up into the alcove, hardly daring to breathe, and staring upon this motionless profile just as a mouse out of its hole fixes its paralysed stare upon the cat that is watching for it.

The old woman stirred no more than the rock-hewn pillars on each side of the hearthstone, and her lips were mumbling inarticulate sounds.

My heart was palpitating, my fears increased momentarily during the long silence, made more startling by the motionless supernatural figure that sat there before me.

This had lasted a quarter of an hour when, the fire catching a splinter of fir-wood, a flash of light broke out, the shaving twisted and flamed, and a few rays of light flared to the end of the room.

That luminous jet was sufficient to show me that the creature was clothed in an old dress of rich purple silk as stiff as cardboard, with a violet pattern; there was a massive bracelet upon her left wrist, and a gold arrow stuck through her thick grey hair twisted over the back of her head. It was like an apparition out of the ages past.

Still the Plague could have had no hostile intentions towards me, or she might easily have taken advantage of my sleep to have put them in execution.

That thought was beginning to give me some confidence, when suddenly she rose from her seat and with slow steps approached my bed, holding in her hand a torch which she had just lighted. I then observed that her eyes were fixed and haggard.

I made an effort to rise and cry aloud, but not a muscle of my body would obey my wishes, not a breath came to my lips; and the old woman, bending over me between the curtains, fixed her stony stare upon me with a strange unearthly smile. I wanted to call for help, I wanted to drive her from me, but her petrifying stare seemed to fascinate and paralyse me, just as that of the serpent fixes the little bird motionless before it.

During this speechless contemplation minutes seemed like hours. What was she about to do? I was ready for any event.

Suddenly she turned her head, went round upon her heel, listened, strode across the room, and opened the door.

At last I recovered a little courage; an effort of the will brought me to my feet as if I were acted on by a spring; I darted after her footsteps; she with one hand was holding her torch on high, and with the other kept the door open.

I was about to seize her by the hair, when at the end of the long gallery, under the Gothic archway of the castle leading to the ramparts, I saw — a tall figure.

It was the Count of Nideck!

The Count of Nideck, whom I had thought a dying man, clad in a huge wolfskin thrown with its upper jaw projecting grimly over his eyes like a visor, the formidable claws hanging over each shoulder, and the tail dragging behind him along the flags.

He wore stout heavy shoes, a silver clasp gathered the wolfskin round his neck, and his whole aspect, but for the ice-cold deathly expression of his face, proclaimed the man born for command — the master!

In the presence of such an imposing personage my ideas became vague and confused. Flight was no longer possible, yet I had the presence of mind to throw myself into the embrasure of the window.

The count entered my room with his eyes fixed on the old woman and his features unrelaxed. They spoke to one another in hoarse whispers, so low that I could not distinguish a word. But there was no mistaking their gestures. The woman was pointing to the bed.

They approached the fireplace on tiptoe. There in the dark shadow of the recess at its side the Black Plague, with a horrible smile, unrolled a large bag.

As soon as the count saw the bag he made a bound towards the bed and kneeled upon it with one knee; there was a shaking of the curtains, his body disappeared beneath their folds, and I could only see one leg still resting on the floor, and the wolf's tail undulating irregularly from side to side.

They seemed to be acting a murder in ghastly pantomime. No real scene, however frightful, could have agitated me more than this mute representation of some horrible deed.

Then the old woman ran to his assistance, carrying the bag with her. Again the curtains shook and the shadows crossed the walls; but the most horrible of all was that I fancied I saw a pool of blood creeping across the floor and slowly reaching the hearth. But it was only the snow that had clung to the count's boots, and was melting in the heat.

I was still gazing upon this dark stream, feeling my dry tongue cleave to the roof of my mouth, when there was a great movement; the old woman and the count were stuffing the sheets of the bed into the sack, they were thrusting and stamping them in with just the same haste as a dog scratching at a hole, then the lord of Nideck flung this unshapely bundle over his shoulder and made for the door; a sheet was dragging behind him, and the old woman followed him torch in hand. They went across the court.

My knees were almost giving way under me; they knocked together for fear. I prayed for strength.

In a couple of minutes I was on their footsteps, dragged forward by a sudden irresistible impulse.

I crossed the court at a run, and was just going to enter the door of the tower when I perceived a deep but narrow pit at my feet, down which went a winding staircase, and there far below I could see the torch describing a spiral course around the stone rail like a little star; at last it was lost in the distance.

Now I also descended the first steps of this newly-discovered staircase, directing my course after this distant light; suddenly it vanished. The old woman and the count had reached the bottom of the precipice. Supported by the stone rail I continued my descent, safe to be able to mount again if I found my further progress stopped.

Soon I came to the last step; I looked around me, and discovered on my left hand a narrow streak of moonlight shining under a low door, through the nettles and brambles; I kicked a way through these obstacles, clearing the snow away with my feet, and then found that I was at the very foot of the keep — Hugh's donjon tower.

Who would have supposed that such a hole would have led up into the castle? Who had shown it to the old woman? I did not stay to satisfy myself on these points.

The vast plain lay spread before me bathed in a light almost equal to that of day. On the right lay extended wide the dark line of the Black Forest with its craggy rocks, its gullies, its passes stretching away as far as the sight could reach.

The night air was keen and sharp, but perfectly calm, and I felt myself awakened to the highest degree, almost as if my senses were volatilised by the still and ice-cold air.

My first examination of the horizon was for the figures of the count and his strange companion. I soon distinguished their tall dark forms standing out sharply against the star-spangled purple heavens. I nearly overtook them at the bottom of the ravine.

The count was moving with deliberate steps, the imaginary winding-sheet dragging slowly after him. There was an automatic precision in the movements of both.

I kept six or eight yards behind them down the hollow road to the Altenberg, now in the shade, now in the full light, for the moon was shining with astonishing brilliancy. A few clouds floated idly across the zenith, seeming to want to clasp her in their long arms, but she ever eluded their grasp, and her rays, keen as a blade of steel, cut me to the marrow of my bones.

I could have wished to turn back, but some invisible power impelled me onwards to follow this funeral procession in pantomime. Even to this day I fancy still I can see the rough mountain path through the Black Forest, I can hear the crisp snow crackling under foot, and the dead leaves rustling in the light north wind; I can see myself following those two silent beings, but I cannot understand what mysterious power drew me in their footsteps.

At last we reach the forest, and advance amongst the tall bare-branched, beeches; the dark shadows of their higher boughs intersect the lower branches, and fall broken upon the snow-encumbered road. Sometimes I fancy I can hear steps behind me; I turn sharply round, but can see no one.

We had just reached the long rocky ridge that forms the crest of the Altenberg; behind it flows the torrent of the Schnéeberg, but in winter no current is visible; scarcely does a mere thread of its blue waters trickle under the thick crust of ice. Here the deep solitude is broken by no murmuring brooks, no warblings of birds, no thunder of the waterfall. In the vast unbroken solitudes the awful silence is terrible.

The Count of Nideck and the old woman found a gap in the face of the rock, up which they mounted straight with marvellous celerity, whilst I had to pull myself up by the help of the bushes.

Hardly had they reached the ridge of the crags, which came almost to a point, when I was within three yards of them, and I beheld beyond a dreadful precipice of which I could not see the bottom. At the left hung in the air like a vast sheet the fall of the Schnéeberg, a mass of ice. That resemblance to an immense wave taking the precipice at one bound, bearing trees on its breast, fringed with the bushes, and winding out the long ivy sprays, which exhibit in their delicate tracery the form of the rigid glassy billow; that mere semblance of movement amidst the stillness and immovableness of death, and the presence of those two speechless creatures pursuing their ghastly work with automatic precision, added to the terror with which I already trembled.

Nature herself seemed to shrink with horror.

The count had laid down his burden; the old woman and he took it up together, swung it for a moment over the edge of the precipice, then the long shroud floated over the abyss, and the imaginary murderers in silence bent forward to see it fall.

That long white sheet floating in the air is still present before my eyes. It descends, it falls like a wild swan shot in the clouds, spreading its wide wings, the long neck thrown back, whirling down to Earth to die.

The white burden disappeared in the dark depths of the precipice.

At last the cloud which I had long seen threatening to cover the moon's bright disc veiled her in its steel-blue folds, and her rays ceased to shine.

The old woman, holding the count by the hand and dragging him forward with hurried steps, came for a moment into view.

The cloud had overshadowed the moon, and I could not move out of their way without danger of falling over the precipice.

After a few minutes, during which I lay as close as I could, there was a rift in the cloud. I looked out again. I stood alone on the point of the peak with the snow up to my knees.

Full of horror and apprehension, I descended from my perilous position, and ran to the castle in as much consternation as if I had been guilty of some great crime.

As for the lord of Nideck and his companion, I lost sight of them.

CHAPTER X.

I wandered around the castle of Nideck unable to find the exit from which I had commenced my melancholy journey.

So much anxiety and uneasiness were beginning to tell upon my mind; I staggered on, wondering if I was not mad, unable to believe in what I had seen, and yet alarmed at the clearness of my own perceptions.

My mind in confusion passed in review that strange man waving his torch overhead in the darkness, howling like a wolf, coldly and accurately going through all the details of an imaginary murder without the omission of one ghastly detail or circumstance, then escaping and committing to the furious torrent the secret of his crime; these things all harassed my mind, hurried confusedly past my eyes, and made me feel as if I were labouring under a nightmare.

Lost in the snow, I ran to and fro panting and alarmed, and unable to judge which way to direct my steps.

As day drew near the cold became sharper; I shivered, I execrated Sperver for having brought me from Fribourg to bear a part in this hideous adventure.

At last, exhausted, my beard a mass of ice, my ears nearly frostbitten, I discovered the gate and rang the bell with all my might.

It was then about four in the morning. Knapwurst made me wait a terribly long time. His little lodge, cut in the rock, remained silent; I thought the little humpbacked wretch would never have done dressing; for of course I supposed he would be in bed and asleep.

I rang again.

This time his grotesque figure appeared abruptly, and he cried to me from the door in a fury —

"Who are you?"

"I? — Doctor Fritz."

"Oh, that alters the case," and he went back into his lodge for a lantern, crossed the outer court where the snow came up to his middle, and staring at me through the grating, he exclaimed —

"I beg your pardon, Doctor Fritz; I thought you would be asleep up there in Hugh Lupus's tower. Were *you* ringing? Now that explains why Sperver came to me about midnight to ask if anybody had gone out. I said no, which was quite true, for I never saw you going out."

"But pray, Monsieur Knapwurst, do for pity's sake let me in, and I will tell you all about that by-and-by."

"Come, come, sir, a little patience."

And the hunchback, with the slowest deliberation, undid the padlock and slipped the bars, whilst my teeth were chattering, and I stood shivering from head to foot.

"You are very cold, doctor," said the diminutive man, "and you cannot get into the castle. Sperver has fastened the inside door, I don't know why; he does not usually do so; the outer gate is enough. Come in here and get warm. You won't find my little hole very inviting, though. It is nothing but a sty, but when a man is as cold as you are he is not apt to be particular."

Without replying to his chatter I followed him in as quickly as I could.

We went into the hut, and in spite of my complete state of numbness, I could not help admiring the state of picturesque disorder in which I found the place. The slate roof leaning against the rock, and resting by its other side on a wall not more than six feet high, showed the smoky, blackened rafters from end to end.

The whole edifice consisted of but one apartment, furnished with a very uninviting bed, which the dwarf did not often take the trouble to make, and two small windows with hexagonal panes, weather-stained with the rainbow tints of mother-of-pearl. A large square table filled up the middle, and it would be difficult to account for that massive oak slab being got in unless by supposing it to have been there before the hut was built.

On shelves against the wall were rolls of parchment, and old books great and small. Wide open on the table lay a fine black-letter volume, with illuminations, bound in vellum, clasped and cornered with silver, apparently a collection of old chronicles. Besides there was nothing but two leathern armchairs, bearing on them the unmistakable impression of the misshapen figure of this learned gentleman.

I need not stay to do more than mention the pens, the jar of tobacco, five or six pipes lying here and there, and in a corner a small cast-iron stove, with its low, open door wide open, and throwing out now and then a volley of bright sparks; and to complete the picture, the cat arching her back, and spitting threateningly at me with her armed paw uplifted.

All this scene was tinted with that deep rich amber light in which the old Flemish painters delighted, and of which they alone possessed the secret, and never left it to the generations after them.

"So you went out last night, doctor?" inquired my host, after we had both installed ourselves, and while I had my hands in a warm place upon the stove.

"Yes, pretty early," I answered. "I had to look after a patient."

This brief explanation seemed to satisfy the little hunchback, and he lighted his blackened boxwood pipe, which was hanging over his chin.

"You don't smoke, doctor?"

"I beg your pardon, I do."

"Well, fill any one of these pipes. I was here," he said, spreading his yellow hand over the open volume. "I was reading the chronicles of Hertzog when you came."

"Ah, that accounts for the time I had to wait! Of course you stayed to finish the chapter?" I said, smiling.

He owned it, grinning, and we both laughed together.

"But if I had known it was you," he said, "I should have finished the chapter another time."

There was a short silence, during which I was observing the very peculiar physiognomy of this misshapen being — those long deep wrinkles that moated in his wide mouth, his small eyes with the crow's feet at the outer corners, that contorted nose, bulbous at its end, and especially that huge double-storied forehead of his. The whole figure reminded me not a little of the received pictures of Socrates, and while warming myself and listening to the crackling of the fire, I went off into contemplations on the very diversified fortunes of mankind.

"Here is this dwarf," I thought, "an ill-shaped, stunted caricature, banished into a corner of Nideck, and living just like the cricket that chirps beneath the hearthstone. Here is this little Knapwurst, who in the midst of excitement, grand hunts, gallant trains of horsemen coming and going, the barking of the hounds, the trampling of the horses, and the shouts of the hunters, is living quietly all alone, buried in his books, and thinking of nothing but the times long gone by, whilst joy or sorrow, songs or tears, fill the world around him, while spring and summer, autumn and winter, come and look in through his dim windows, by turns brightening, warming, and benumbing the face of nature outside. Whilst men in the outer world are subject to the gentle influences of love, or the sterner impulses of ambition or avarice, hoping, coveting, longing, and desiring, he neither hopes, nor desires, nor covets anything. As long as he is smoking his pipe, with his eyes feasting on a musty parchment, he lives in the enjoyment of dreams, and he goes into raptures over things long, long ago gone by, or which have never existed at all; it is all one to him. 'Hertzog says so and so, somebody else tells the tale a different way,' and he is perfectly happy! His leathery face gets more and more deeply wrinkled, his broken angular back bends into sharper angles and corners, his pointed elbows dig beds for themselves in the oak table, his skinny fingers bury themselves in his cheeks, his piggish grey eyes get redder over manuscripts, Latin, Greek, or mediaeval. He falls into raptures, he smacks his lips, he licks his chops like a cat over a dainty dish, and then he throws himself upon that dirty litter, with his knees up to his chin, and he thinks he has had a delightful day! Oh, Providence of God, is a man's duty best done, are his responsibilities best discharged, at the top or at the bottom of the scale of human life?"

But the snow was melting away from my legs, the balmy warmth of the stove was shedding a pleasant influence over my feelings, and I felt myself reviving in this mixed atmosphere of tobacco-smoke and burning pine-wood.

Knapwurst gravely laid his pipe on the table, and reverently spreading his hand upon the folio, said in a voice that seemed to issue from the bottom of his consciousness; or, if you like it better, from the bottom of a twenty-gallon cask —

"Doctor Fritz, here is the law and the prophets!"

"How so? what do you mean?"

"Parchment — old parchment — that is what I love! These old yellow, rusty, worm-eaten leaves are all that is left to us of the past, from the days of Charlemagne until this day. The oldest families disappear, the old parchments remain. Where would be the glory of the Hohenstauffens, the Leiningens, the Nidecks, and of so many other families of renown? Where would be the fame of their titles, their deeds of arms, their magnificent armour, their expeditions to the Holy Land, their alliances, their claims to remote antiquity, their conquests once complete, now long ago annulled? Where would be all those grand claims to historic fame without these parchments? Nowhere at all. Those high and mighty barons, those great dukes and princes, would be as if they had never been — they and everything that related to them far and near. Their strong castles, their palaces, their fortresses fall and moulder away into masses of ruin, vague remembrancers! Of all that greatness one monument alone remains — the chronicles, the songs of bards and minnesingers. Parchment alone remains!"

He sat silent for a moment, and then pursued his reflections.

"And in those distant times, while knights and squires rode out to war, and fought and conquered or fought and fell over the possession of a nook in a forest, or a title, or a smaller matter still, with what scorn and contempt did they not look down upon the wretched little scribbler, the man of mere letters and jargon, half-clothed in untanned hides, his only weapon an inkhorn at his belt, his pennon the feather of a goosequill! How they laughed at him, calling him an atom or a flea, good for nothing! 'He does nothing, he cannot even collect our taxes, or look after our estates, whilst we bold riders, armed to the teeth, sword in hand and lance on thigh, we fight, and we are the finest fellows in the land!' So they said when they saw the poor devil dragging himself on foot after their horses' heels, shivering in winter and sweating in summer, rusting and decaying in old age. Well, what has happened? That flea, that vermin, has kept them in the memory of men longer than their castles stood, long after their arms and their armour had rusted in the ground. I love those old parchments. I respect and revere them. Like ivy, they clothe the ruins and keep the ancient walls from crumbling into dust and perishing in oblivion!"

Having thus delivered himself, a solemn expression stole over his features, and his own eloquence made the tears of moved affection to steal down his furrowed cheeks.

The poor hunchback evidently loved those who had borne with and protected his unwarlike but clever ancestors. And after all he spoke truly, and there was profound good sense in his words.

I was surprised, and said, "Monsieur Knapwurst, do you know Latin?"

"Yes, sir," he answered, but without conceit, "both Latin and Greek. I taught myself. Old grammars were quite enough; there were some old books of the count's, thrown by as rubbish; they fell into my hands, and I devoured them. A little while after the count, hearing me drop a Latin quotation, was quite astonished, and said, 'When did you learn Latin, Knapwurst?' 'I taught myself, monseigneur.' He asked me a few questions, to which I gave pretty good answers. 'Parbleu!' he cried, 'Knapwurst knows more than I do; he shall keep my records.' So he gave me the keys of the archives; that was thirty years ago. Since that time I have read every word. Sometimes, when the count sees me mounted upon my ladder, he says, 'What are you doing now, Knapwurst?' 'I am reading the family archives, monseigneur.' 'Aha! Is that what you enjoy?' 'Yes, very much.' 'Come, come, I am glad to hear it, Knapwurst; but for you, who would know anything about the glory of the house of Nideck?' And off he goes laughing. I do just as I please."

"So he is a very good master, is he?"

"Oh, Doctor Fritz, he is the kindest-hearted master! He is so frank and so pleasant!" cried the dwarf, with hands clasped. "He has but one fault."

"And what may that be?"

"He has no ambition."

"How do you prove that?"

"Why, he might have been anything he pleased. Think of a Nideck, one of the very noblest families in Germany! He had but to ask to be made a minister or a field-marshal. Well! He desired nothing of the sort. When he was no longer a young man he retired from political life. Except that he was in the campaign in France at the head of a regiment he raised at his own expense, he has always lived far away from noise and battle; plain and simple, and almost unknown, he seemed to think of nothing but his hunting."

These details were deeply interesting to me. The conversation was of its own accord taking just the turn I wished it to take, and I resolved to get my advantage out of it.

"So the count has never had any exciting deeds in hand?"

"None, Doctor Fritz, none whatever; and that is the pity. A noble excitement is the glory of great families. It is a misfortune for a noble race when a member of it is devoid of ambition; he allows his family to sink below its level. I could give you many examples. That which would be very fortunate in a trader's family is the greatest misfortune in a nobleman's."

I was astonished; for all my theories upon the count's past life were falling to the Earth.

"Still, Monsieur Knapwurst, the lord of Nideck has had great sorrows, had he not?"

"Such as what?"

"The loss of his wife."

"Yes, you are right there; his wife was an angel; he married her for love. She was a Zaân, one of the oldest and best nobility of

Alsace, but a family ruined by the Revolution. The Countess Odile was the delight of her husband. She died of a decline which carried her off after five years' illness. Every plan was tried to save her life. They travelled in Italy together but she returned worse than she went, and died a few weeks after their return. The count was almost broken-hearted, and for two years he shut himself up and would see no one. He neglected his hounds and his horses. Time at last calmed his grief, but there is always a remainder of grief," said the hunchback, pointing with his finger to his heart; "you understand very well, there is still a bleeding wound. Old wounds you know, make themselves felt in change of weather — and old sorrows too — in spring when the flowers bloom again, and in autumn when the dead leaves cover the soil. But the count would not marry again; all his love is given to his daughter."

"So the marriage was a happy one throughout?"

"Happy! Why it was a blessing for everybody."

I said no more. It was plain that the count had not committed, and could not have committed, a crime. I was obliged to yield to evidence. But, then, what was the meaning of that scene at night, that strange connection with the Black Pest, that fearful acting, that remorse in a dream, which impelled the guilty to betray their past atrocities?

I lost myself in vain conjectures.

Knapwurst relighted his pipe, and handed me one, which I accepted.

By that time the icy numbness which had laid hold of me had nearly passed away, and I was enjoying that pleasant sense of relief which follows great fatigue when by the chimney-corner in a comfortable easychair, veiled in wreaths of tobacco-smoke, you yield to the luxury of repose, and listen idly to the duet between the chirping of a cricket on the hearth and the hissing of the burning log.

So we sat for a quarter of an hour.

At last I ventured to remark —

"But sometimes the count gets angry with his daughter?"

Knapwurst started, and fixing a sinister, almost a fierce and hostile eye upon me, answered —

"I know, I know!"

I watched him narrowly, thinking I might learn something now in support of my theory, but he simply added ironically —

"The towers of Nideck are high, and slander flies too low to reach their elevation!"

"No doubt; but still it is a fact, is it not?"

"Oh yes, so it is; but after all it is only a craze, an effect of his complaint. As soon as the crisis is past all his love for mademoiselle comes back. I assure you, sir, that a lover of twenty could not be more devoted, more affectionate, than he is. That young girl is his pride and his joy. A dozen times have I seen him riding away to get a dress, or flowers, or what not, for her. He went off alone, and brought back the articles in triumph, blowing his horn. He would have entrusted so delicate a commission to no one, not even to Sperver, whom he is so fond of. Mademoiselle never dares express a wish in his hearing lest he should start off and fulfil it at once. The lord of Nideck is the worthiest master, the tenderest father, and the kindest and most upright of men. Those poachers who are for ever infesting our woods, the old Count Ludwig would have strung them up without mercy; our count winks at them; he even turns them into gamekeepers. Look at Sperver! Why, if Count Ludwig was alive, Sperver's bones would long ago have been rattling in chains; instead of which he is head huntsman at the castle."

All my theories were now in a state of disorganisation. I laid my head between my hands and thought a long while.

Knapwurst, supposing that I was asleep, had turned to his folio again.

The grey dawn was now peeping in, and the lamp turning pale. Indistinct voices were audible in the castle.

Suddenly there was a noise of hurried steps outside. I saw someone pass before the window, the door opened abruptly, and Gideon appeared at the threshold.

CHAPTER XI.

Sperver's pale face and glowing eyes announced that events were on their way. Yet he was calm, and did not seem surprised at my presence in Knapwurst's room.

"Fritz," he said briefly, "I am come to fetch you." I rose without answering and followed him. Scarcely were we out of the hut when he took me by the arm and drew me on to the castle.

"Mademoiselle Odile wants to see you," he whispered.

"What! Is she ill?"

"No, she is much better, but something or other that is strange is going on. This morning about one o'clock, thinking that the count was nearly breathing his last, I went to wake the countess; with my hand on the bell my heart failed me. 'Why should I break her heart?' I said to myself, 'She will learn her misfortune only too soon; and then to wake her up in the middle of the night, weak and frail as she is, after such shocks, might kill her at a stroke.' I took a few minutes to consider, and then I resolved I would take it all on myself. I returned to the count's room. I looked in — not a soul was there! Impossible! The man was in the last agonies of death. I ran into the corridor like a madman. No one was there! Into the long gallery — no one! Then I lost my presence of mind, and rushing again into the young countess's room, I rang again. This time she appeared, crying out — 'Is my father dead?' 'No.' 'Has he disappeared?' 'Yes, madam. I had gone out for a minute — when I came in again —' 'And Doctor Fritz, where is he?' 'In Hugh Lupus's tower.' 'In *that* tower?' She started. She threw a dressing-gown around her, took her lamp, and went out. I stayed behind. A quarter of an hour after she came back, her feet covered with snow, and so pale and so cold! She set her lamp upon the chimney-piece, and looking at me fixedly, said — 'Was it you who put the doctor into that tower?' 'Yes, madam.' 'Unhappy man! You will never know the extent of the harm you have done.' I was about to answer, but she interrupted me — 'No more; go and fasten every door and lie down. I will sit up. Tomorrow morning you will find Doctor Fritz at Knapwurst's, and bring him to me. Make no noise, and mind, you have seen nothing and know nothing!'"

"Is that all, Sperver?" I asked.

He nodded gravely.

"And about the count?"

"He is in again. He is better."

We had got to the antechamber. Gideon knocked at the door gently, then he opened it, announcing — "Doctor Fritz."

I took a pace forward, and stood in the presence of Odile. Sperver had retired, closing the door.

A strange impression crossed my mind at the sight of the young countess standing pale and still, leaning upon the back of an armchair, her eyes of feverish brightness, and robed in a long dress of rich black velvet. But she stood calm and firm.

"Doctor," she said, motioning me to a chair, "pray sit down; I have a very serious matter to speak to you about."

I obeyed in silence.

In her turn she sat down and seemed to be collecting her thoughts.

"Providence or an evil destiny, I know not which, has made you witness of a mystery in which lies involved the honour of my family."

So she knew it all!

I sat confounded and astonished.

"Madam, believe me, it was but by chance —"

"It is useless," she interrupted; "I know it all, and it is frightful!"

Then, in a heartrending appealing voice, she cried —

"My father is not a guilty man!"

I shuddered, and with hands outstretched cried —

"Madam, I know it; I know that the life of your father has been one of the noblest and loveliest."

Odile had half-risen from her seat, as if to protest, by anticipation, against any supposition that might be injurious to her father. Hearing me myself taking up his defence, she sank back again, and covering her face with her hands, the tears began to flow.

"God bless you, sir!" she exclaimed. "I should have died with the very thought that a breath of suspicion was harboured against him."

"Ah! Madam, who could possibly attach any reality to the action of a somnambulist?"

"That is quite true, sir; I had had that thought myself, but appearances — pardon me — yet I feared — still I knew Doctor Fritz was a man of honour."

"Pray, madam, be calm."

"No," she cried, "let me weep on. It is such a relief; for ten years I have suffered in secret. Oh, how I suffered! That secret, so long shut up in my breast, was killing me. I should soon have died, like my dear mother. God has had pity upon me, and has sent you, and made you share it with me. Let me tell you all, sir, do let me!"

She could speak no more. Sobs and tears broke her voice. So it always is with proud and lofty natures. After having conquered grief, and imprisoned it, buried, and, as it were, crushed down in the secret depths of the mind, they seem happy, or, at any rate, indifferent to the eyes of the uninformed around, and the eye of the most watchful observer might be mistaken; but let a sudden shock break the seal, an unexpected rending of a portion of the veil, then, as with the crash of a thunderstorm, the tower in which the sufferer hid his sorrow falls in ruins to the ground. The conquered foe rises more fierce than before his defeat and captivity; he shakes with fury the prison doors, the frame trembles with long shudderings, sobs and sighs heave the breast, the tears, too long contained within bounds, overflow their swollen banks, bounding and rushing as if after the heavy rain of a thunderstorm.

Such was Odile.

At length she lifted her beautiful head; she wiped her tear-stained cheeks, and with her arm on the elbow of her chair, her cheek resting on her hand, and her eyes tenderly fixed on a picture on the wall, she resumed in slow and melancholy tones:

"When I go back into the past, sir, when I return to my first impressions, my mother's is the picture before me. She was a tall, pale, and silent woman. She was still young at the period to which I am referring. She was scarcely thirty, and yet you would have thought her fifty. Her brow was silvered round with hair white as snow; her thin, hollow cheeks, her sharp, clear profile — her lips ever closed together with an expression of pain — gave to her features a strange character in which pride and pain seemed to contend for the mastery. There was nothing left of the elasticity of youth in that aged woman of thirty — nothing but her tall, upright figure, her brilliant eyes, and her voice, which was always as gentle and as sweet as a dream of childhood. She often walked up and down for hours in this very room, with her head hanging down, and I, an unthinking child, ran happily along by her side, never aware that my mother was sad, never understanding the meaning of the deep melancholy revealed by those furrows that traversed her fair brow. I knew nothing of the past, to me the present was joy and happiness, and oh! The future! — The dark, miserable future! — There was none! My only future was tomorrow's play!"

Odile smiled bitterly and went on:

"Sometimes I would happen, in my noisy play, to disturb my mother in her silent walk; then she would stop, look down, and, seeing me at her feet, would slowly bend, kiss me with an absent smile, and then again resume her interrupted walk and her sad gait. Since then, sir, whenever I have desired to search back in my memory for remembrances of my early days that tall, pale woman has risen before me, the image of melancholy. There she is," pointing to a picture on the wall — "there she is! — not such as illness made her as my father supposes, but that fatal and terrible secret. See!"

I turned round, and as my eye dwelt upon the portrait the lady pointed to, I shuddered.

It was a long, pale, thin face, cold and rigid as death, and only luridly lighted up by two dark, deepset eyes, fixed, burning, and of a terrible intensity.

There was a moment's silence.

"How much that woman must have suffered!" I said to myself

with a pain striking at my heart.

"I know not how my mother made that terrible discovery," added Odile, "but she became aware of the mysterious attraction of the Black Pest and their meetings in Hugh Lupus's tower; she knew it all — all! She never suspected my father — ah no! — but she perished away by slow degrees under this consuming influence! And I myself am dying."

I bowed my head into my hands and wept in silence.

"One night," she went on, "one night — I was only ten — and my mother, with the remains of her superhuman energy, for she was near her end that night, came to me when I lay asleep. It was in winter; a stony cold hand caught me by the wrist. I looked up. Before me stood a tall woman; in one hand she held a flaming torch, with the other she held me by the arm. Her robe was sprinkled with snow. There was a convulsive movement in all her limbs and her eyes were fired with a gloomy light through the long locks of white hair which hung in disorder round her face. It was my mother; and she said, 'Odile, my child, get up and dress! You must know it all!' Then taking me to Hugh Lupus's tower she showed me the open subterranean passage. 'Your father will come out that way,' she said, pointing to the tower; 'he will come out with the she-wolf; don't be frightened, he won't see you.' And presently my father, bearing his funereal burden, came out with the old woman. My mother took me in her arms and followed; she showed me the dismal scene on the Altenberg of which you know. 'Look, my child,' she said; 'you must for I — am going to die soon. You will have to keep that secret. You alone are to sit up with your father,' she said impressively — 'you alone. The honour of your family depends upon you!' And so we returned. A fortnight after my mother died, leaving me her will to accomplish and her example to follow. I have scrupulously obeyed her injunctions as a sacred command, but oh, at what a sacrifice! You have seen it all. I have been obliged to disobey my father and to rend his heart. If I had married I should have brought a stranger into the house and betrayed the secret of our race. I resisted. No one in this castle knows of the somnambulism of my father, and but for yesterday's crisis, which broke down my strength completely and prevented me from sitting up with my father, I should still have been its sole depositary. God has decreed otherwise, and has placed the honour and reputation of my family in your keeping. I might demand of you, sir, a solemn promise never to reveal what you have seen tonight. I should have a right to do so."

"Madam," I said, rising, "I am ready."

"No, sir," she replied with much dignity, "I will not put such an affront upon you. Oaths fail to bind base men, and honour alone is a sufficient guarantee for the upright. You will keep that secret, sir, I know you will keep it, because it is your duty to do so. But I expect more than this of you, much more, and this is why I consider myself obliged to tell you all!"

She rose slowly from her seat.

"Doctor Fritz," she resumed in a voice which made every nerve within me quiver with deep emotion, "my strength is unequal to my burden; I bend beneath it. I need a helper, a friend. Will you be that friend?"

"Madam," I replied, rising from my seat, "I gratefully accept your offer of friendship. I cannot tell you how proud I am of your confidence; but still, allow me to unite with it one condition."

"Pray speak, sir."

"I mean that I will accept that title of friend with all the duties and obligations which it shall impose upon me."

"What duties do you mean?"

"There is a mystery overhanging your family; that mystery must be discovered and solved at any cost. That Black Pest must be apprehended. We must find out where she comes from, what she is, and what she wants!"

"Oh, but that is impossible!" she said with a movement of despair.

"Who can tell that, madam? Perhaps Divine Providence may have had a design connected with me in sending Sperver to fetch me here."

"You are right, sir. God never acts without consummate wisdom. Do whatever you think right. I give my approval in advance."

I raised to my lips the hand which she tremblingly placed in mine, and went out full of admiration for this frail and feeble woman, who was, nevertheless, so strong in the time of trial. Is anything grander than duty nobly accomplished?

CHAPTER XII.

An hour after the conversation with Odile, Sperver and I were riding hard, and leaving Nideck rapidly behind us.

The huntsman, bending forward over his horse's neck, encouraged him with voice and action.

He rode so fast that his tall Mecklemburger, her mane flying, tail outstretched, and legs extended wide, seemed almost motionless, so swiftly did she cleave the air. As for my little Ardenne pony, I think he was running right away with his rider. Lieverlé accompanied us, flying alongside of us like an arrow from the bow. A whirlwind seemed to sweep us in our headlong way.

The towers of Nideck were far away, and Sperver was keeping ahead as usual when I shouted —

"Halloo, comrade, pull up! Halt! Before we go any farther let us know what we are about."

He faced round.

"Only just tell me, Fritz, is it right or is it left?"

"No; that won't do. It is of the first importance that you should know the object of our journey. In short, we are going to catch the hag."

A flush of pleasure brightened up the long sallow face of the old poacher, and his eyes sparkled.

"Ha, ha!" he cried, "I knew we should come to that at last!"

And he slipped his rifle round from his shoulder into his hand.

This significant action roused me.

"Wait, Sperver; we are not going to kill the Black Pest, but to take her alive!"

"Alive?"

"No doubt, and it will spare you a good deal of remorse perhaps if I declare to you that the life of this old woman is bound up with that of your master. The ball that hits her hits your lord."

Sperver gazed at me in astonishment.

"Is this really true, Fritz?"

"Positively true."

There was a long silence; our mounts, Fox and Rappel, tossed their heads at each other as if in the act of saluting one another, scraping up the snow with their hoofs in congratulation upon so pleasant an expedition. Lieverlé opened wide his red mouth, gaping with impatience, extending and bending his long meagre body like a snake, and Sperver sat motionless, his hand still upon his gun.

"Well, let us try and catch her alive. We will put on gloves if we have to touch her, but it is not so easy as you think, Fritz."

And pointing out with extended hand the panorama of mountains which lay unrolled about us like a vast amphitheatre, he added —

"Look! There's the Altenberg, the Schnéeberg, the Oxenhorn, the Rhéthal, the Behrenkopf, and if we only got up a little higher we should see fifty more mountaintops far away, right into the Palatinate. There are rocks and ravines, passes and valleys, torrents and waterfalls, forests, and more mountains; here beeches, there firs, then oaks, and the old woman has got all that for her camping-ground. She tramps everywhere, and lives in a hole wherever she pleases. She has a sure foot, a keen eye, and can scent you a couple of miles off. How are you going to catch her, then?"

"If it was an easy matter where would be the merit? I should not then have chosen you to take a part in it."

"That is all very fine, Fritz. If we only had one end of her trail, who knows but with courage and perseverance —"

"As for her trail, don't trouble about that; that's my business."

"Yours?"

"Yes, mine."

"What do you know about following up a trail?"

"Why should not I?"

"Oh, if you are so sure of it, and you know more about it than I do, of course march on, and I'll follow!"

It was easy to see that the old hunter was vexed that I should presume to trespass upon his special province; therefore, only laughing inwardly, I required no repetition of the request to lead on, and I turned sharply to the left, sure of coming across the old woman's trail, who, after having left the count at the postern gate, must have crossed the plain to reach the mountain. Sperver rode behind me now, whistling rather contemptuously, and I could hear him now and then grumbling —

"What is the use of looking for the track of the she-wolf in the plain? Of course she went along the forest side just as usual. But it seems she has altered her habits, and now walks about with her hands in her pockets, like a respectable Fribourg tradesman out for a walk."

I turned a deaf ear to his hints, but in a moment I heard him utter an exclamation of surprise; then, fixing a keen eye upon me, he said —

"Fritz, you know more than you choose to tell."

"How so, Gideon?"

"The track that I should have been a week finding, you have got it at once. Come, that's not all right!"

"Where do you see it, then?"

"Oh, don't pretend to be looking at your feet."

And pointing out to me at some distance a scarcely perceptible white streak in the snow —

"There she is!"

Immediately he galloped up to it; I followed in a couple of minutes; we had dismounted, and were examining the track of the Black Pest.

"I should like to know," cried Sperver, "how that track came here?"

"Don't let that trouble you," I replied.

"You are right, Fritz; don't mind what I say; sometimes I do speak rather at random. What we want now is to know where that track will lead us to."

And now the huntsman knelt on the ground.

I was all ears; he was closely examining.

"It is a fresh track," he pronounced, "last night's. It is a strange thing, Fritz, during the count's last attack that old witch was hanging about the castle."

Then examining with greater care —

"She passed here between three and four o'clock this morning."

"How can you tell that?"

"It is quite a fresh track; there is sleet all round it. Last night, about twelve, I came out to shut the doors; there was sleet falling then, there is none upon the footsteps, therefore she has passed since."

"That is true enough, Sperver, but it may have been made much later; for instance, at eight or nine."

"No, look, there is frost upon it! The fog that freezes on the snow only comes at daybreak. The creature passed here after the sleet and before the fog — that is, about three or four this morning."

I was astonished at Sperver's exactitude.

He rose from his knee, clapping his hands together to get rid of the snow, and looking at me thoughtfully, as if speaking to himself, said —

"It is twelve, is it not, Fritz?"

"A quarter to twelve."

"Very well; then the old woman has got seven hours' start of us. We must follow upon her trail step by step; on horseback we can do it in half the time, and, if she is still going, about seven or eight tonight we have got her, Fritz. Now then, we're off."

And we started afresh upon the track. It led us straight to the mountains.

Galloping away, Sperver said —

"If good luck only would have it that she had rested an hour or two in a hole in a rock, we might be up with her before the daylight is gone."

"Let us hope so, Gideon."

"Oh, don't think of it. The old she-wolf is always moving; she never tires; she tramps along all the hollows in the Black Forest. We must not flatter ourselves with vain hopes. If, perhaps, she has stopped on her journey, so much the better for us; and if she still keeps going, we won't let that discourage us. Come on at a gallop."

It is a very strange feeling to be hunting down a fellow-creature; for, after all, that unhappy woman was of our own kind and nature; endowed like ourselves with an immortal soul to be saved, she felt, and thought, and reflected like ourselves. It is true that a strange perversion of human nature had brought her near to the nature of the wolf, and that some great mystery overshadowed her being. No doubt a wandering life had obliterated the moral sense in her, and even almost effaced the human character; but still nothing in the world can give one man a right to exercise over another the dominion of the man over the brute.

And yet a burning ardour hurried us on in pursuit; my blood was at fever heat; I was determined to stand at no obstacle in laying hold of this extraordinary being. A wolf-hunt or a boar-hunt would not have excited me near so much.

The snow was flying in our rear; sometimes splinters of ice, bitten off by the horseshoes, like shavings of iron from machinery, whizzed past our ears.

Sperver, sometimes with his nose in the air and his red moustache floating in the wind, sometimes with his grey eyes intently following the track, reminded me of those famous Cossacks that I had seen pass through Germany when I was a boy; and his tall, lanky horse, muscular and full-maned, its body as slender as a greyhound's, completed the illusion.

Lieverlé, in a high state of enthusiasm and excitement, took bounds sometimes as high as our horses' backs, and I could not but tremble at the thought that when we came up at last with the Pest he might tear her in pieces before we could prevent him.

But the old woman gave us all the trouble she could; on every hill she doubled, at every hillock there was a false track.

"After all, it is easy here," cried Sperver, "to what it will be in the wood. We shall have to keep our eyes open there! Do you see the accursed beast? Here she has confused the track! There she has been amusing herself sweeping the trail, and then from that height which is exposed to the wind she has slipped down to the stream, and has crept along through the cresses to get to the underwood. But for those two footsteps she would have sold us completely."

We had just reached the edge of a pine-forest. In woods of this description the snow never reaches the ground except in the open spaces between the trees, the dense foliage intercepting it in its fall. This was a difficult part of our enterprise. Sperver dismounted to see our way better, and placed me on his left so as not to be hindered by my shadow.

Here were large spaces covered with dead leaves and the needles and cones of the fir-trees, which retain no footprint. It was, therefore, only in the open patches where the snow had fallen on the ground that Sperver found the track again.

It took us an hour to get through this thicket. The old poacher bit his moustache with excitement and vexation, and his long nose visibly bent into a hook. When I was only opening my mouth to speak, he would impatiently say —

"Don't speak — it bothers me!"

At last we descended a valley to the left and Gideon pointing to the track of the she-wolf outside the edge of the brushwood, triumphantly remarked —

"There is no feint in this sortie, for once. We may follow this track confidently."

"Why so?"

"Because the Pest has a habit every time she doubles of going three paces to the right; then she retraces her steps four, five, or six in the other direction, and jumps away into a clear place. But when she thinks she has sufficiently disguised her trail she breaks out without troubling herself to make any feints. There now! What did I say? Now she is burrowing beneath the brushwood like a wild boar, and it won't be so difficult to follow her up."

"Well, let us put the track between us and smoke a pipe."

We halted, and the honest fellow, whose countenance was beginning to brighten up, looking up at me with enthusiasm, cried —

"Fritz, if we have luck this will be one of the finest days in my life. If we catch the old hag I will strap her across my horse behind me like a bundle of old rags. There is only one thing troubles me."

"And what is that?"

"That I forgot my bugle. I should have liked to have sounded the return on getting near the castle! Ha, ha, ha!"

He lighted his stump of a pipe and we galloped off again.

The track of the she-wolf now passed on to the heights of the forest by so steep an ascent that several times we had to dismount and lead our horses by the bridle.

"There she is, turning to the right," said Sperver. "In this direction the mountains are craggy; perhaps one of us will have to lead both horses while the other climbs to look after the trail. But don't you think the light is going?"

The landscape now was assuming an aspect of grandeur and magnificence. Vast grey rocks, sparkling with long icicles, raised here and there their sharp peaks like breakers amidst a snowy sea.

There is nothing more sadly impressive than the aspect of winter in a mountainous region. The jagged crests of the precipices, the deep, dark ravines, the woods sparkling with boar-frost like diamonds, all form a picture of desertion, desolation, and unspeakable melancholy. The silence is so profound that you hear a dead leaf rustling on the snow, or the needle of the fir dropping to the ground. Such a silence is oppressive as the tomb; it urges on the mind the idea of man's nothingness in the vastness of creation.

How frail a being is man! Two winters together, without a summer between, would sweep him off the Earth!

At times we felt it a necessity to be saying something if only to show that we were keeping up our spirits.

"Ah, we are getting on! How fearfully cold! Lieverlé, what is the matter? what have you found now?"

Unfortunately Fox and Rappel were beginning to tire; they sank deeper in the snow and no longer neighed joyfully.

And added to this the endless mazes of the Black Forest wearied us too. The old woman affected this solitary region greatly; here she had trotted round a deserted charcoal-burner's hut; farther on she had torn out the roots that projected from a moss-grown rock; there she had sat at the foot of a tree, and that very recently — not more than two hours since, for the track was quite fresh — and our hope and our ardour rose together. But the daylight was slowly fading away!

Very strangely, ever since our departure from Nideck we had met neither wood-cutters, nor charcoal-burners, nor timber-carriers. At this season the silence and solitude of the Black Forest is as deep as that of the North-American steppes.

At five o'clock it was almost dark. Sperver halted and said —

"Fritz, my lad, we have started a couple of hours too late. The she-wolf has had too long a start. In ten minutes it will be as dark as a dungeon. The best way would be to reach Roche Creuse, which is twenty minutes' ride from here, light a good fire, and eat our provisions and empty our flasks. When the moon is up we will follow the trail again, and unless the old hag is the foul fiend himself, ten to one we shall find her dead and stiff with cold against the foot of a tree, for nothing can live after such a tremendous tramp in weather like this. Sébalt is the best walker in the Black Forest, and he would not have stood it. Come, Fritz, what is your opinion?"

"I am not so mad as to think differently. Besides, I am perishing with hunger!"

"Well, let us start again."

He took the lead and passed into a close and narrow glen between two precipitous faces of rock. The fir-trees met over our heads; under our feet ran a mere thread of the stream, and from time to time some ray from above was dimly reflected in the depths below and glinted with a dull leaden light.

The darkness was now such that I thought it prudent to drop my bridle on Rappel's neck. The steps of our horses on the slippery gravel awoke strange discordant sounds like the screaming of monkeys at play. The echoes from rock to rock caught up and repeated every sound, and in the distance a tiny space of deep blue widened as we advanced; it was the issue from the glen.

"Fritz," said Sperver, "we are in the bed of the Tunkelbach. This is the wildest spot in the Black Forest. The end is a pit called La Marmite du Grand Gueulard, the muckle-mouthed giant's kettle. In the spring, when the snow is melting, the Tunkelbach hurls all its waters into it, a depth of two hundred feet. There is an awful uproar; the waters dash down and then splash up again and fall in spray on all the hills around. Sometimes it even fills the Roche Creuse, but just now it must be as dry as a powder-flask."

Whilst I was listening to Gideon's explanations I was at the same time meditating upon this dark and fearful glen, and I reflected that the instinct which attracts the brutes into such retreats as these, far from the light of Heaven, away from everything bright and cheerful, must partake of the nature of remorse. Those animals which love the open sunshine — the goat aloft upon a high conspicuous peak, the horse flying across the wide plain, the dog capering round his master, the bird bathed in sunlight — all breathe joy and happiness; they bask, and sing, and rejoice in dancing and delight. The kid nibbling the tender grass under the shade of the great trees is as poetic an object as the shelter that it loves; the fierce boar is as rough as the tangled brakes through which he loves to run his huge bristly back; the eagle is as proud and lofty as the sky-piercing crags on which he perches as his home; the lion is as majestic as the arching vaults of the caves where he makes his den; but the wolf, the fox, and the ferret seek the darkness that conforms to their ugly deeds; fear and remorse dog their steps.

I was still dreamily pursuing these thoughts, and I was beginning to feel the keen air moving upon my face, for we were approaching the outlet of the gorge, when all at once a red light struck the rock a hundred feet above us, purpling the dark green of the fir-trees and lighting up the wreaths of snow.

"Ha!" cried Sperver, "we have got her at last!"

My heart leaped; we stood, closely pressed, the one against the other.

The dog growled low and deep.

"Cannot she escape?" I asked in a whisper.

"No; she is caught like a rat in a trap. There is no way out of La Marmite du Grand Gueulard but this, and everywhere all round the rocks are two hundred feet high. Now, vile hag, I hold you!"

He alighted in the ice-cold stream, handing me his bridle. I caught in the silence the click of the lock of his gun, and that slight noise threw me into a tremor of apprehension.

"Sperver, what are you about?"

"Don't be alarmed; it is only to frighten her."

"Very well, then, but no blood. Remember what I told you — the ball which strikes the Pest slays the count!"

"Don't trouble yourself," was the answer.

He went away without further parley. I could hear the splash of his feet in the water; then I saw his tall figure emerge at the opening of the dark glen, black against a purple background. He stood five minutes motionless. Attentive, bending forward, I looked and listened, still moving onward. As he returned I was but a few yards from him.

"Hark!" he whispered mysteriously. "Look there!"

At the end of the hollow, scooped out perpendicularly like a quarry in the mountain side, I saw a bright fire unrolling its golden spires beneath the vault of a cave, and before the fire sat a man with his hands clasped about his knees, whom I recognised by his dress as the Baron de Zimmer-Bluderich.

He sat motionless, his forehead resting between his hands. Behind him lay a dark gaunt form extended on the ground. Farther on, his horse, half lost in the shade, reared his neck, gazed on us with eyes fixed, ears erect, and nostrils distended.

I stood rooted to the ground.

How did the Baron de Zimmer happen to be in that lonely wilderness at such a time? What did he want here? Had he lost his way?

The most contradictory conjectures were passing in confusion through my excited brain, and I could not tell what conclusion to arrive at, when the baron's horse began to neigh, and the master raised his head.

"Well, Donner, what is the matter now?" said he.

Then he, too, directed his gaze our way, straining his eyes through the darkness.

That pale face, with its strongly-marked features, thin lips, and thick black eyebrows meeting together, and forming a deep hollow on the brow in the form of a long vertical wrinkle, would have struck me with admiration at any other time; while now an inexplicable anxiety laid hold of me, and I was filled with vague apprehensions.

Suddenly the young man exclaimed —

"Who goes there?"

"I, monseigneur," answered Sperver, coming forward — "Sperver, chief huntsman to the lord of Nideck."

A flash shot from the baron's quick eye; not a muscle of his countenance quailed. He rose to his feet, gathering his pelisse over his shoulders. I drew towards me the horses and the dog, and this animal suddenly began howling fearfully.

Is not every one, more or less, subject to superstitious fears? At these dismal sounds I trembled, and a cold shudder crept through my whole body.

Sperver and the baron stood at a distance of fifty yards from each other; the first immovable in the midst of the deep glen, his gun unslung from his shoulder, the other erect upon the level platform outside of the cave, carrying his head high, fixing on us a haughty eye and a proud look of superiority.

"What do you want here?" he asked aggressively.

"We are looking for a woman," replied the old poacher — "a woman who comes every year prowling about Nideck, and our orders are to take her."

"Has she stolen anything?"

"No."

"Has she committed murder?"

"No, monseigneur."

"Then what do you want with her? What right have you to pursue her?"

"And you — what right have you over her?" answered Sperver with an ironical smile. "See, there she is. I can see her at the bottom of the cave. What right have you to meddle with our affairs? Don't you know that we are here in the domains of Nideck, and that we administer justice and execute our own decrees?"

The young man changed colour, and said coldly —

"I have no account to render to you."

"Beware," replied Sperver. "I am come with proposals of peace and conciliation. I am here on behalf of the lord Yeri-Hans. I am in the execution of my duty, and you are putting yourself in the wrong."

"Your duty!" cried the young man bitterly. "If you talk about your duty you will oblige me to do mine!"

"Well, do it!" cried the huntsman, whose features were becoming disturbed with anger.

"No," replied the baron, "I am not responsible to you, and you shall not come here!"

"That's what we shall soon see!" said Sperver, drawing nearer to the cave.

The young man drew his hunting-knife. Perceiving this menacing action, I was about to dart between them, but happily the hound which I was holding by his collar slipped from me with a violent shock and threw me on the ground. I thought the baron would be lost, but at that instant a wild shriek rose from the dark bottom of the cavern, and as I rose to my feet I saw the old woman standing erect before the fire, her tattered garments hanging loosely about her, her grey and tangled locks floating wildly in the wind; she flung her bony arms in the air and uttered prolonged piercing howls like the cry of agony of the hungry wolf in the long cold nights of winter when famine is gnawing his entrails.

Never in my life have I seen a more fearful apparition. Sperver, motionless, his eyes riveted on the fearful object before him, and his mouth open with astonishment, stood as if rooted to the earth. But the powerful dog, surprised himself at this unexpected sight, stood still for a moment; then with a bend of his bristling back in preparation for a mighty leap, he made a rush with a deep, impatient growl which made me tremble. The platform before the cave was about eight or nine feet from the level where we stood, or he would have reached it at a single bound. I can yet hear him clearing a way through the snowy brambles, the baron flinging himself before the woman with a piercing cry, "My mother!" then the dog taking another spring, and Sperver, quick as lightning, raising his gun, and bringing down the poor animal dead at the young man's feet.

This was but the work of a second. The gulf had been illuminated with a momentary flash, and the wild echoes were vibrating with the explosion from rock to rock, till it died in the far distance. Then silence again settled on the gloomy scene, as darkness after the lightning.

When the smoke of the explosion had cleared away I saw Lieverlé lying outstretched at the foot of the rock, and the woman fainting in the arms of the young man. Sperver, pale with concentrated rage and excitement, and eyeing the young baron darkly, dropped the butt of his gun to the ground, his features discomposed, and his eyes half-hid in his gloomy frown.

"Seigneur de Bluderich," he cried, with his hand extended, "I have killed my best friend to save the life of that unhappy woman, your mother! Thank God that her life is bound up with that of the Count of Nideck! Take her away! Take her hence, and never let her return here again; if you do I cannot answer for what old Sperver may be driven to do!"

Then, with a glance at the poor dog —

"Oh! Lieverlé, Lieverlé!" he cried, "was it to end thus? Come, Fritz, let us go. I cannot stay here. I might do something that I should have to repent of!"

And, laying hold of Fox by the mane, he was going to throw himself into the saddle, but suddenly his feelings of distress overcame all restraint, and bowing his head upon his horse's neck, he burst into sobs and tears, and wept like a child.

CHAPTER XIII.

Sperver had gone, bearing the body of poor Lieverlé in his cloak. I had declined to follow; my sense of duty kept me by this unhappy woman, and I could not leave her without violence to my own feelings.

Besides, I must confess I was curious to see a little more closely this strange mysterious being, and therefore as soon as Sperver had disappeared in the darkness of the glen I began to climb up to reach the cavern.

There I beheld a strange sight.

Extended upon a large cloak of white fur lay the aged woman in a long and ragged robe of purple, her fingers clutching her breast, a golden arrow through her grey hair.

Never shall I forget the figure of this strange woman; her vulturelike features distorted with the last agonies of death, her eyes set, her gasping mouth, were fearful to look upon. Such might have been the terrible Queen Frédégonde.

The baron, on his knees at her side, was trying to restore her to animation; but I saw at a glance that the wretched creature was dying, and it was not without a profound sense of pity that I took her by the arm.

"Leave madame alone — don't touch her," cried the young man with irritation.

"I am a surgeon, monseigneur."

He looked in silence at me for a moment, then rising, said —

"Pardon me, sir; pray forgive my hasty language."

He trembled with excitement, scarcely yet subdued, and presently he went on —

"What is your opinion, sir?"

"It is over — she is dead!"

Then, without speaking another word, he sat upon a large stone, with his forehead resting upon his hand and his elbow on his knee, his eyes motionless, as still as a statue.

I sat near the fire, watching the flames rising to the vaulted roof of the cave, and casting lurid reflections upon the rigid features of the corpse.

We had sat there an hour as motionless as statues, each deep in thought, when, suddenly lifting his head, the baron said —

"Sir, all this utterly confounds me. Here is my mother — for twenty-six years I thought I knew her — and now an abyss of horrible mysteries opens before me. You are a doctor; tell me, did you ever know anything so dreadful?"

"Monseigneur," I replied, "the Count of Nideck is afflicted with a complaint strikingly similar to that from which your mother appears to have suffered. If you feel enough confidence in me to communicate to me the facts which you have yourself observed, I will gladly tell you what I know myself; for perhaps this exchange of our experiences might supply me with the means to save my patient."

"Willingly, sir," he replied, and without any further prelude he informed me that the Baroness de Bluderich, a member of one of the noblest families in Saxony, took, every year towards autumn, a journey into Italy, with no attendant besides an old manservant, who possessed her entire confidence; that that man, being at the point of death, had desired a private interview with the son of his old master, and that at that last hour, prompted, no doubt, by the pangs of remorse, he had told the young man that his mother's visit to Italy was only a pretence to enable her to make, you observed, a certain excursion into the Black Forest, the object of which was unknown to himself, but which must have had something fearful in its character, since the baroness returned always in a state of physical prostration, ragged, half dead, and that weeks of rest alone could restore her after the hideous labours of those few days.

This was the purport of the old servant's disclosures to the young baron, who believed that in so doing he was only fulfilling his duty.

The son, anxious at any sacrifice to know the truth of this account, had, that very year, ascertained it, first by following his mother to Baden, and then by penetrating on her track into the gorges of the Black Forest. The footsteps which Sébalt had tracked in the woods were his.

When the baron had thus imparted his knowledge to me, I thought I ought not to conceal from him the mysterious influence which the appearance of the old woman in the neighbourhood of the castle exercised over the count, nor the other circumstances of this unaccountable series of events.

We were both amazed at the extraordinary coincidence between the facts narrated, the mysterious attraction which these beings unconsciously exercised the one over the other, the tragic drama which they performed in union, the familiarity which the old woman had shown with the castle, and its most secret passages, without any previous examination of them; the costume which she had discovered in which to carry out this secret act, and which could only have been rummaged out of some mysterious retreat revealed to her by the strange instinct of insanity. Finally, we were agreed that there are unknown, unfathomed depths in our being, and that the mystery of death is not the only secret which God has veiled from our eyes, although it may seem to us the most important.

But the darkness of night was beginning to yield to the pale tints of early dawn. A bat was sounding the departure of the hours of darkness with a singular note resembling the gurgling of liquid from a narrow bottleneck. A neighing of horses was heard far up the defile; then, with the first rays of dawn, we distinguished a sledge driven by the baron's servant; its bottom was littered with straw; on this the body was laid.

I mounted my horse, who seemed not sorry to use his limbs again, which had been numbed by standing upon ice and snow the whole night through. I rode after the sledge to the exit from the defile, when, after a grave salutation — the usual token of courtesy between the nobility and the people — they drove off in the direction of Hirschland and I rode towards the towers of Nideck.

At nine I was in the presence of Mademoiselle Odile, to whom I gave a faithful narrative of all that had taken place.

Then repairing to the count's apartments, I found him in a very satisfactory state of improvement. He felt very weak, as was to be expected after the terrible shocks of such crises as he had gone through, but had returned to the full possession of his clear faculties, and the fever had left him the evening before. There was, therefore, every prospect of a speedy cure.

A few days later, seeing the old lord in a state of convalescence, I expressed a desire to return to Fribourg, but he entreated me so earnestly to stay altogether at Nideck, and offered me terms so honourable and advantageous, that I felt myself unable to refuse compliance with his wishes.

I shall long remember the first boar-hunt in which I had the honour to join with the count, and especially the magnificent return home in a torchlight procession after having sat in the saddle for twelve hours together.

I had just had supper, and was going up into Hugh Lupus's tower completely knocked up, when, passing Sperver's room, whose door was half open, shouts and cries of joy reached my ears. I stopped, when the most jovial spectacle burst upon me. Around the massive oaken table beamed twenty square rosy faces, bright and ruddy with health and fun.

The hob and nobbing of the glasses gave out an incessant tinkling and clattering. There was sitting Sperver with his bossy forehead, his moustaches bedewed with Rhenish wine, his eyes sparkling, and his grey hair rather disordered; at his right was Marie Lagoutte, on his left Knapwurst. He was raising aloft the ancient silver-gilt and chased goblet dimmed with age, and on his manly chest glittered the silver plate of his shoulder-belt, for, according to his custom on a hunting day, he was still wearing the uniform of his office.

The colour of Marie Lagoutte's cheeks, rather redder even than usual, told of an evening of jollity, and her broad cap-frills seemed as if they were wanting to fly all abroad; she sat laughing, now with one, then with another.

Knapwurst, squatting in his armchair, with his head on a level with Sperver's elbow, looked like a big pumpkin. Then came Tobias Offenloch, so red that you would have thought he had bathed his face in the red wine, leaning back with his wig upon the chair-back and his wooden leg extended under the table. Farther on loomed the melancholy long face of Sébalt, who was peeping with a sickly smile into the bottom of his wine-glass.

Besides these worthies there were present the waiting-people, men and women servants, comprising all that little community which springs up around the board of the great people of the land and belongs to them as the ivy, and the moss, and the wild convolvulus belong to the monarch of the forests.

Upon the groaning board lay a vast ham, displaying its concentric circles of pink and white. Then among the gaily-patterned plates and dishes came the long-necked bottles containing the produce of the vineyards that border the broad and flowing Rhine — long German pipes with little silver chains, and long shining blades of steel.

The light of the lamp shed over the whole scene its amber-coloured hue and left in the shade the old grey and time-stained walls, where hung in ample numbers the brazen convolutions of the hunting-horns and bugles.

What an original picture! The vaulted roof was ringing with the joyous shouts of laughter.

Sperver, as I have already told, was lifting high the full bumper and singing the song of Black Hatto, the Burgrave,

"I am king on these mountains of mine,"

while the rosy dew of Affénthal hung trembling from his long moustaches. As soon as he caught sight of me he stopped, and holding out his hand —

"Fritz," said he, "we only wanted you. It is a long time since I felt so comfortable as I do tonight. You are welcome, old boy!"

As I gazed upon him with surprise — for since the death of Lieverlé I had never seen him smile — he added more seriously —

"We are celebrating the return of monseigneur to his health, and Knapwurst is telling us stories."

All the guests turned my way, and I was saluted with kindly welcomes on all sides.

I was dragged in by Sébalt, seated near Marie Lagoutte, and found a large glass of Bohemian wine in my hand before I could quite understand the meaning of it all.

The old hall was echoing with merry peals of laughter, and Sperver, throwing his arm round my neck, holding his cup high, and with an attempt at gravity which showed plainly that the wine was up in his head, he shouted —

"Here is my son! He and I — I and he — until death! Here's the health of Doctor Fritz!"

Knapwurst, standing as high as he was able upon the seat of his armchair, not unlike a turnip half divided in two, leaned towards me and held me out his glass. Marie Lagoutte shook out the long streamers of her cap, and Sébalt, upright before his chair, as gaunt and lean as the shade of the wild jäger amongst the heather, repeated, "Your health, Doctor Fritz!" whilst the flakes of silvery foam ran down his cup and floated gently down upon the stone-flagged floor.

Then there was a moment's silence. Every guest drank. Then, with a single clash, every glass was set vigorously down upon the table.

"Bravo!" cried Sperver.

Then turning to me —

"Fritz, we have already drunk to the health of the count and of Mademoiselle Odile; you will do the same."

Twice had I to drain the cup before the vigilant eyes of the whole table. Then I too began to look grave. Could it have been drunken gravity? A luminous radiance seemed shed on every object; faces stood out brightly from the darkness, and looked more nearly upon me; in truth, there were youthful faces and aged, pretty and ugly, but all alike beamed upon me kindly, and lovingly, and tenderly; but it was the youngest, at the other end of the table, whose bright eyes attracted me, and we exchanged long and wistful glances, full of affection and sympathy!

Sperver kept on humming and laughing. Suddenly putting his hand upon the dwarf's misshapen back, he cried —

"Silence! Here is Knapwurst, our historian and chronicler! He is preparing to speak. This hump holds all the history of the house of Nideck from the beginning of time!"

The little hunchback, not at all indignant at so ambiguous a compliment, directed his benevolent eyes upon the face of the huntsman, and replied —

"You, Sperver, you are one of the *reiters* whose story I have been telling you. You have the arm, and the courage, and the whiskers of a *reiter* of old! If that window opened wide, and a *reiter* was to hold out his hand at the end of his long arm to you, what would you say to him?"

"I would say, 'You are welcome, comrade; sit down and drink. You will find the wine just as good and the girls just as pretty as they were in the days of old Hugh Lupus.' Look!"

And he pointed with his glass at the jolly young faces that brightened the farther end of the table.

Certainly the damsels of Nideck were lovely. Some were

blushing with pleasure to hear their own praises; others half-veiled their rosy cheeks with their long drooping eyelashes, while one or two seemed rather to prefer to display their, sweet blue eyes by raising them to the smoky ceiling. I wondered at my own insensibility that I had never before noticed these fair roses blooming in the towers of the ancient manor.

"Silence!" cried Sperver for the second time. "Our friend Knapwurst is going to tell us again the legend he related to us just now."

"Won't you have another instead?" asked the hunchback.

"No. I like this best."

"I know better ones than that."

"Knapwurst," insisted the huntsman, raising his finger impressively, "I have reasons for wishing to hear the same again and no other. Cut it shorter if you like. There is a great deal in it. Now, Fritz, listen!"

The dwarf, rather under the influence of the sparkling wine he had taken, rested his elbows on the table, and with his cheeks clutched in his bony fingers, and his eyes starting from his head with his concentrated efforts to speak with becoming seriousness, he cried as if he were publishing a proclamation —

"Bernard Hertzog relates that the burgrave Hugh, surnamed Lupus, or the Wolf, when he was old, used to wear a cowl, which was a kind of knitted cap that covered in the crest of the knight's helmet when engaged in fighting. When the helmet tired him he would take it off and put on the knitted cowl, and its long cape fell around his shoulders.

"Up to his eighty-second year Hugh still wore his armour, though he could hardly breathe in it.

"Then he sent for Otto of Burlach, his chaplain, his eldest son Hugh, his second son Berthold, and his daughter the red-haired Bertha, wife of a Saxon chief named Bluderich, and said to them —

"'Your mother the she-wolf has bequeathed you her claws; her blood flows, mingled with mine, in your veins. In you the wolf's blood will flow from generation to generation; it shall weep and howl among the snows of the Black Forest. Some will say, 'Hark! The wind howls!' others, 'No, it is the owl hooting!' But not so; it is your blood, mine and the blood of the she-wolf who drove me to murder Hedwige, my wife before God and the Church. She died under my bloody hands! Cursed be the she-wolf! For it is written, 'I will visit the sins of the fathers upon the children. The crime of the father shall be visited upon the children until justice shall have been satisfied!'

"Then old Hugh the Wolf died.

"From that dreary day the north wind has howled across the wilds, and the owl has hooted in the dark, and travellers by night know not that it is the blood of the she-wolf weeping for the day of vengeance that will come, whose blood will be renewed from generation to generation — so says Hertzog — until the day when the first wife of Hugh, Hedwige the Fair, shall reappear at Nideck under the form of an angel to comfort and to forgive!"

Then Sperver, rising from his seat, took a lamp and demanded of Knapwurst the keys of the library, and beckoned to me to follow him.

We rapidly traversed the long dark gallery, then the armoury, and soon the archive-chamber appeared at the end of the great corridor.

All noises had died away in the distance. The place seemed quite deserted.

Once or twice I turned round, and could then see with a creeping feeling of dread our two long fantastic shadows in ghostly fashion writhing in strange distortions upon the high tapestry.

Sperver quickly opened the old oak door, and with torch uplifted, his hair all bristling in disorder, and excited features, walked in the first. Standing before the portrait of Hedwige, whose likeness to the young countess had struck me at our first visit to the library, he addressed me in these solemn words:

"Here is she who was to return to comfort and pity me! She has returned! At this moment she is downstairs with the old count. Look well, Fritz; do you recognise her? Is it not Odile?"

Then turning to the picture of Hugh's second wife —

"There," he said, "is Huldine, the she-wolf. For a thousand years she has wept in the deep gorges amongst the pine forests of the Schwartzwald; she was the cause of the death of poor Lieverlé; but henceforward the lords of Nideck may rest securely, for justice is done, and the good angel of this lordly house has returned!"

MYRTLE

CHAPTER I.

Just at the end of the village of Dosenheim, in Alsace, about fifty yards from the gravelly road that leads into the wood, is a pretty cottage surrounded with an orchard, the flat roof loaded with boulder-stones, the gable-end looking down the valley.

Flights of pigeons wheel around it, hens are scratching and picking up what they can under the fences, the cock takes his stand majestically on the low garden wall, and sounds the *réveillée*, or the retreat, for the echoes of Falberg to repeat; an out-side staircase, with its wooden banisters, the linen of the little household hanging over it, leads to the first story, and a vine climbs up the front, and spreads its leafy branches from side to side.

If you will only go up these steps you will see at the end of the narrow entry the kitchen, with its dresser and its pewter plates and dishes, its soup-tureens puffing out like balloons; open the door to the right and you are in the parlour with its dark oak fur-niture, a ceiling crossed by brown smoke-stained rafters, and its old Nuremberg clock click-clacking monotonously.

Here sits a woman of five-and-thirty, spinning and dreaming, her waist encircled with a long black taffety bodice, and her head covered with a velvet headdress, with long ribbons.

A man in broad-skirted velveteen coat, with breeches of the same, and with a fine open brow, looking calm and thoughtful, is dandling on his knee a fine stout boy, whistling the call to "boot and saddle."

There lies the quiet village at the end of the valley, framed, as you sit, in the little cottage window; the river is leaping over the mill-dam and crossing the winding street; the old houses, with their deep and gloomy eaves, their barns, their gabled windows, their nets drying in the sun; the young girls, kneeling by the river-side on the stones, washing linen; the cattle lazily lounging down to drink, and gravely lowing amidst the willows; the young herds-men cracking their whips; the mountain summit, jagged like a saw by the pointed fir-tree tops — all these rural objects lie reflected in the flowing blue stream, only broken by the fleets of ducks sailing down or the occasional passage of an old tree rooted up on the mountainside.

Looking quietly on these things, you are impressed with a

sense of the ease and comfort of which they speak, and you are moved with gratitude to the Giver of all good.

Well, my dear friends and neighbours, such was the cottage of the Brémers in 1820, such were Brémer himself, his wife Catherine, and their son, little Fritz.

To my own mind they come back exactly as I have described them to you.

Christian Brémer had served in the chasseurs of the Imperial Guard. After 1815 he had married Catherine, his old sweetheart, grown a little older, but quite fresh and fair, and full of grace. With his own little property, his house, and his four or five acres of vineyard, and Catherine's added to it, Brémer had become one of the most substantial bourgeois of Dosenheim; he might have been mayor, or adjoint, or municipal councillor, but these honours had no attractions for him; and what pleased him best was, after work was over, to take down his old gun, whistle for Friedland, and take him a turn in the woods.

Now it fell out one day that this worthy man, coming home after a day's shooting, brought in his bag a little gipsy girl two or three years old, as lively as a squirrel, and as brown as a hazelnut. He had found her in the bundle of an unhappy gipsy woman who had died of fatigue or hunger, or both, at the foot of a tree.

You may well imagine what an outcry Catherine raised against this new uninvited member of her family. But as Brémer was master in his own house, he simply announced to his wife that the child should be christened by the name of Susanna Frederica Myrtle, and that she should be brought up with little Fritz.

As a matter of course, all the women in the place, old and young, came to pass their observations upon the little gipsy, whose serious and thoughtful expression of countenance surprised them.

"This is not a child like others," said they; "she is a heathen — quite a heathen! You may see by her eyes that she understands every word! She is listening now! Mind what I say, Maître Christian! Gipsies have claws at the ends of their fingers. If you will rear young ferrets and weasels you must not expect your poultry to be safe. They will have the run of all the farm-yard!"

"Go and mind your own business!" shouted Brémer. "I have seen Russians and Spaniards, I have seen Italians, and Germans, and Jews; some were brown, and some were black, some white, and others red; some had long noses, and others had turned-down noses, but I found good fellows amongst them all."

"Very likely," said the ladies, "but those people lived in houses, and gipsies live in the open air."

He vouchsafed no reply to this argument, but with all possible politeness he put them out by the shoulders.

"Go away," he cried; "I don't want your advice. It is time to air the rooms, and then I have to go and attend to the stables."

But, after all, the rejected counsels were not so bad, as the event unhappily showed a dozen or fourteen years afterwards.

Fritz was always delighted to feed the cattle, and take the horses to the pond, and follow his father and learn to plough and sow, to reap and mow, to tie up the sheaves and bring them home. But Myrtle had no wish to milk the cows, churn the butter, shell peas, or peel potatoes.

When the maidens of Dosenheim, going out to wash clothes in the morning at the river, called her the *heathen*, she mirrored herself complacently in the fountain, and when she had admired her own long dark tresses, her violet lips, her white teeth, her necklace of red berries, she would smile and murmur to herself—

"Ah! They only call me a heathen because I am prettier than they are," and she would dip the tip of her little foot in the fountain and laugh.

But Catherine could not approve of such conduct, and said—

"Myrtle is not the least good to us. She won't do a single thing that is useful. It is no use for me to preach, and advise, and scold, she does everything the wrong way. The other day, when we were stowing away apples in the closet, she took bites out of the best to see if they were ripe! She has no pleasure but in gobbling up the best of everything."

Brémer himself could not help admitting that there was a very heathenish spirit in her when he heard his wife crying from morning till night, "Myrtle, Myrtle! Where are you now? Ah, naughty, bad girl! She has run away into the woods again to gather blackberries." But still he laughed to himself, and pitied poor Catherine, whom he compared to a hen with a brood of ducklings.

Every year after harvest-time Fritz and Myrtle spent whole days far away from the farm, pasturing the cattle, singing, and whistling, and baking potatoes under the ashes, and coming down the rocky hill in the evening blowing the shepherd's horn.

These were some of Myrtle's happiest days. Seated before the burning hemp-stalks, with her pretty brown face between her hands, she lost herself in endless reveries.

The long strings of wild ducks and geese which traverse,

about the end of autumn, the boundless heavens spread from the mountains on the east to the western hills, seemed to have a depressing effect upon her mind. She used to follow them with longing eyes, straining them as if to overtake the wild birds in the immeasurable distance; and suddenly she would rise, spread out her arms, and cry —

"I must go! I must go! I can't stay!"

Then she would weep with her head bowed down, and Fritz, seeing her in tears, would cry too, asking —

"Why do you cry, Myrtle? Has anybody hurt you? Is it any of the boys in the village? — Kasper, Wilhelm, Heinrich? Only tell me, and I will knock him down at once! Do tell!"

"No; it is not that."

"Well, why are you crying?"

"I don't know."

"Do you want to run as far as the Falberg?"

"No; that is not far enough."

"Where do you want to go?"

"Down there! Down there! Ever so far! Where the birds are going."

This made Fritz open his eyes and his mouth very wide.

One day in September, when they were idling along by the woods, about noon, the heat was so great and the air so still that the smoke of their little fire, instead of rising straight into the air, fell like water and crept among the briars. The grasshopper had ceased its dull monotonous chirp, not the buzzing of a fly was to be heard, nor the warbling of a bird. The oxen and the cows, with sleepy eyes half-closed, their knees bent under them, were resting together under a spreading oak in the meadow, now and then lowing in a slow, protracted way as if in idle protest against such hot weather.

Fritz had begun by plaiting the strands of his whip, but he soon lay down in the long grass with his hat over his eyes, and Friedland came to lie near him, gaping from ear to ear.

Myrtle alone suffered no inconvenience from the overwhelming heat; sitting on the ground near the fire, with her arms wreathed around her knees, full in the sun, her large dark eyes slowly surveyed the dark arches formed by the branches of the forest.

Time passed on slowly. The distant village clock had struck twelve, then one, and two, and the young gipsy never stirred. In the woods and jagged mountaintops, the crags, the forests, descending into the valleys, she heard some mysterious call. They spoke to her in a language not unknown to her.

"Yes," she said to herself, "yes; I have seen all that before — long ago — a long time ago."

Then with a quick, sharp glance at Fritz, who was in a deep sleep, she rose to her feet and began to fly. Her light footsteps scarcely bent the grass beneath her; she ran on and on, up the hill; Friedland turned his head round with a careless glance, then stretched out once more his languid limbs, and composed himself to sleep.

Myrtle disappeared in the midst of the brambles which border the common wood. At one bound she cleared the muddy ditch where a single frog was croaking amongst the rushes, and twenty minutes after she reached the top of the Roche Creuse, whence you may have a wide prospect of Alsace and the blue summits of the Vosges.

Then she turned to see if anybody was following her. She could still distinguish Fritz asleep in the green meadow with his hat over his eyes, and Friedland and the sleeping cattle under their tree.

Farther on she could see the village, the river, the roof of the farmhouse, with its flights of pigeons eddying round; the long, crooked street and red-petticoated women walking leisurely up and down; the little ivy-covered church where the good *curé* Niclausse had baptised her into the Christian faith and afterwards confirmed her.

And when she had sufficiently contemplated these objects, turning her face the other way towards the mountain, she was filled with delight to mark how the densely-crowded firs covered the hillsides, up to their highest ridge, close as the grass of the fields.

At the sight of all this grandeur the young gipsy felt her heart beating and expanding with unknown delight, and again running on she darted through a rift between the rocks, lined with mosses and ferns, to reach the beaten track through the woods.

Her whole soul — that wild, untrained soul of hers — was rushing with her and impelling her onwards, kindling her countenance with a new ardour. With her hands she clung to the ivy, with her naked feet she clung to the projections and the crevices to push on her way.

Soon she was on the other slope, running, tripping, leaping, sometimes stopping short to gaze upon surrounding objects — a large tree, a ravine, a lonely sheet of water, or a pond full of flowers and sweet-smelling water-plants.

Although she could not remember ever having seen those copses, those clearings, those heaths, at every turn in the path she would say to herself, "There, I knew it was so! I knew that tree would be there! I was sure of that rock! And there's the waterfall just below!" Although a thousand strange remembrances passed with momentary flashes, like sudden visions, through her mind, she could not understand it all and could explain nothing. She had not yet been able to say to herself, "What Fritz and the rest of them want to make them happy is the village, and the meadow, and the farmhouse, and the fruit-trees, and the orchard, and the milk-cows, and the laying hens; plenty in the cellar, plenty in the granary, and a nice warm fire on the hearth in winter. But what have I to do with all these things? Wasn't I born a heathen, quite a heathen? I was born in the woods, just as the squirrel was born in an oak, just as a hawk was hatched on the crag and the thrush in the fir-tree!"

It is true she had never thought of these things, but she was guided by instinct; and this mysterious force drew her unconsciously about sunset to the bare heaths of the Kohle Platz, where the gangs of gipsies that wander between Alsace and Lorraine are accustomed to stay the night, and hang up their kettles among the dry heath.

Here Myrtle sat down at the foot of an old oak-tree, tired, footsore, and ragged; and here she long sat motionless, gazing into vacant space, listening to the rustling of the wind amongst the tall fir-trees, happy, and feeling herself quite alone in the wide solitude.

Night came. The stars broke out by thousands in the purple depths of the autumn sky. The moon rose and silvered with soft light the white stems of the birch-trees, which hung in graceful groups along the mountain sides.

The young gipsy was beginning to yield to sleep when cries in the distance roused her into an impulse to fly.

Hark! She knows the voices! They are those of Brémer, Fritz, and all the people of the farm searching for her!

Then, without a moment's hesitation, Myrtle flew, light as a roe, farther into the forest, stopping only at long intervals to listen attentively and anxiously.

The cries died away in the distance, and soon the only sound she could hear was the loud beating of her own heart, and she went on her way at a less rapid pace.

Very late, when the moon's rays became less brilliant, unable to stand out against her fatigue any longer, she sank down on the heath and fell fast asleep.

She was four leagues from Dosenheim, near the source of the Zinzel. Brémer was not likely to come so far to look for her.

CHAPTER II.

It was broad daylight when Myrtle awoke amidst the deep solitudes of the Schlossberg, beneath an old fir-tree overgrown with moss and lichen. A thrush was whistling overhead; another was answering in the distance far down the valley. The morning breeze was fanning the rustling foliage; but the air, already warm, was loaded with the sweet perfumes of the ground-ivy, the honeysuckle, the woodruff, and the sweetbriars.

The young gipsy opened her eyes with astonishment remembering, with surprise and delight, that the voice of Catherine would no more trouble her, calling, "Myrtle! Myrtle! Where are you, you idle child?" she smiled, and listened to what gave her pleasure, the note of the thrush singing among the trees.

Near at hand a spring was bubbling out of a cleft; the girl had but to look round to see the living stream running, sparkling and clear, amidst the long grass. From the rock high overhead hung an arbutus loaded with its gorgeous freight of scarlet berries.

Though Myrtle was thirsty she felt too idle to move amongst all this beauty and all this harmony, and she dropped her pretty brown face, smiling and admiring the daylight through her long dark lashes.

"This is how I am always going to be," she said. "How can I help it? I am an idle girl. I was made so."

Dreaming in this lazy way, the picture rose up in her mind of the farm-yard with the proud cock strutting among his hens, and then she remembered the eggs, how they used to find them in the straw in some corner of the barn.

"If I had a couple of hardboiled eggs," she thought, "just like those Fritz had yesterday in his bag, with a crust of bread and a little salt, I should like it very well. But what signifies? When you can't get eggs you have blackberries and whinberries."

A scent of whinberries made her little nostrils dilate with expectation.

"There are some here," she said; "I can smell them."

She was right. The wood was full of them.

In another minute, not hearing the thrush, she raised herself on her elbow and noticed the bird picking at the arbutus-berries.

Then she went to the brook and took a little clear water in her hollow hand, and observed that there was plenty of watercress.

Then she remembered what she had never taken the trouble to think of before, some words of the *curé*, Niclausse about the birds of the air that God provided for, and the lilies of the field that were more beautiful than the glory of Solomon, and she remembered the lesson about not being anxious for food and clothing, and thought that that would just suit her, for she did not think of any of the teaching of the same great Teacher about industry, and frugality, and living honestly, and so she came to the satisfying conclusion that the true heathens were Catherine and all her people, who were so foolish and wicked as to plough, and sow, and reap, while she was the good Christian, because she was as idle as the day was long.

She was still dwelling on these satisfactory deductions when there was a sudden rustling among the dead leaves and a noise of footsteps.

She was going to run away when a gipsy lad of eighteen or twenty appeared before her — a tall, lithe, dark fellow with thick woolly hair, shining black eyes, and thick parted lips.

His eyes glittered as he cried —

"Almâni!"

"Almâni!" replied Myrtle, moved with much interest.

"Ha, ha!" cried the lad, "what gang do you go with?"

"I don't know — I am looking for it."

And without any concealment she told him how Brémer had found her and brought her up, and how she had escaped yesterday from his house.

The young gipsy grinned, and showed a long double row of white teeth.

"I am going to Hazlach," he cried. "Tomorrow there's a *fête* there; our band will all be there — Pfiffer Karl, Melchior, Blue-Titmouse, Fritz the clarionet, Coucou-Peter, and Magpie. The women are going fortune-telling, and we play the music. If you like, you may go with me."

"I will," said Myrtle, looking down.

Then he kissed her, laid his bag upon her back, and grasping his stick in both his hands, he cried —

"Now you are my wife! You will carry the bag for me, and I will keep you. Forward!"

And now Myrtle, lazy as she had always been at the farm, started off with all possible willingness.

He followed her, singing, and tumbling over on his hands and feet to express his joy!

From that day Myrtle has never been heard of.

Fritz almost died of grief when he found that she did not return; but a few years later he found comfort in marrying Gredel Dich, the miller's daughter, a fine, stout, active girl, who made him an excellent wife; and Catherine, his mother, was quite pleased, for Gredel Dich was quite an heiress!

Only Brémer could not be comforted; he was as fond of Myrtle as if she had been his own child, and he drooped visibly from day to day.

One winter's day when he had got up, and was looking out of the window, he saw a ragged but pretty gipsy girl passing through the village covered with snow, and with a heavy bag upon her shoulders, and sat down again with a deep sigh.

"What is the matter, Brémer?" asked his wife.

There was no answer. She came close. His eyes were closing. There he lay dead.

UNCLE CHRISTIAN'S INHERITANCE

When my excellent uncle Christian Hâas, burgomaster of Lauterbach, died, I had a good situation as maître de chapelle, or precentor, under the Grand Duke Yeri Peter, with a salary of fifteen hundred florins, notwithstanding which I was a poor man still.

Uncle Christian knew exactly how I was situated, and yet had never sent me a kreutzer. So when I learned that he had left me owner of two hundred acres of rich land in orchards and vineyards, a good bit of woodland, and his large house at Lauterbach, I could not help shedding tears of gratitude.

"My dear uncle," I cried, "now I can appreciate the depth of your wisdom, and I thank you most sincerely for your judicious illiberality. Where would now the money be, supposing you had sent me anything? In the hands of the Philistines, no doubt; whereas by your prudent delays you have saved the country, like another Fabius Cunctator —

"*'Qui cunctando restituit rem —* '

"I honour your memory, Uncle Christian! I do indeed!"

Having delivered myself of these deep feelings, and many more which I cannot enter into now, I got on horseback and rode off to Lauterbach.

Strange, is it not, how the Spirit of Avarice, hitherto quite a stranger to me, came to make my acquaintance?

"Caspar!" he whispered, "now you are a rich man! Hitherto vain shadows have filled your mind. A man must be a fool to follow glory. There is nothing solid but acres, and buildings, and crown-pieces, put out in safe mortgages. Fling aside all your vain delusions! Enlarge your boundaries, round off your estate, heap up money, and then you will be honoured and respected! You will be a burgomaster as your uncle was before you, and the country folks, when they see you coming a mile off, will pull off their hats, and say — 'Here is Monsieur Caspar Hâas, the richest man and the biggest *herr* in the country.'"

These notions kept passing and repassing in my mind like the figures in a magic-lantern, with grave and measured step. The whole thing seemed to me perfectly reasonable.

It was the middle of July. The lark was warbling in the sky. The crops were waving in the plain, the gentle breezes carried on them the soft cry of the quail and the partridge amongst the standing wheat; the foliage was glancing in the sunshine, and the Lauter ran its course beneath the willows; but what was all that to me, the great burgomaster? I puffed up my cheeks and rounded off my figure in anticipation of the portly appearance I was to present, and repeated to myself those delightful observations —

"This is Monsieur Caspar Hâas; he is a very rich man! He is the first *herr* in the country! Get on, Blitz!"

And the nag trotted forward.

I was anxious to try on my uncle's three-cornered hat and scarlet waistcoat. "If they fit me," I said, "what is the use of buying?"

About four in the afternoon the village of Lauterbach appeared at the end of the valley, and very proud I felt as I surveyed the tall and handsome house of the late Christian Hâas, my future abode, the centre of my property, real and speculative. I admired its situation by the long dusty road, its vast roof of grey shingle, the sheds and barns covering with their broad expanse the wagons, the carts, and the crops; behind, the poultry-yard, then the little garden, the orchard, the vineyards up the hill, the green meadows farther off.

I chuckled with delight over all these comforts and luxuries.

As I went down the principal street the old women with nose and chin nearly meeting at the extremity, the bare-pated children with ragged hair, the men in their otterskin caps, and silver-chained pipes in their mouths, all gaze upon me, and respectfully salute me —

"Good day, Monsieur Caspar! How do you do, Monsieur Hâas?"

And all the small windows were filled with wondering faces. I am at home now; I seem as if I had always been a great landowner at Lauterbach, and a notable. My kapellmeister's life seems a dream, a thing of the past, my enthusiastic fondness for music a youthful folly! How money does modify men's views of things!

And now I draw bridle before the house of the village notary, Monsieur Becker. He has my title-deeds under his care, and is to hand them over to me. I fasten my horse to the ring at the door, I run up the steps, and the ancient scribe, with his bald head very respectfully uncovered, and his long spare figure clad in a green dressing-gown with full skirts, advances alone to receive me.

"Monsieur Caspar Hâas, I have the honour to salute you."

"Your servant, Monsieur Becker."

"Pray walk in, Monsieur Hâas."

"After you, sir, after you."

We cross the vestibule, and I find at the end of a small, neat, and well-aired room a table nicely and comfortably laid, and sitting by it a young maiden rosy and fresh-coloured, the very picture of modesty and propriety.

The venerable notary announced me —

"Monsieur Caspar Hâas!"

I bowed.

"My daughter Lothe!" added the good man.

And whilst I felt in myself a reviving taste for the beautiful, and was admiring Mademoiselle Lothe's pretty little chubby nose, the rosy lips, and the large blue eyes, her dainty little figure, and her dimpled hands, Maître Becker invited me to sit down at the table, informing me that he had been expecting me, and that before entering on matters of business it would be well to take a little refreshment, a glass of Bordeaux, etc., an invitation of which I fully recognised the propriety, and which I accepted very willingly.

And so we sit down. We talk first of the beautiful country. And I form opinions about the old gentleman, and wonder what a notary is likely to make at Lauterbach!

"Mademoiselle, will you take a wing?"

"Monsieur, you are very kind; thank you, I will."

Lothe looks down bashfully. I fill her glass, in which she dips her rosy lips. Papa is in good spirits; he tells me about hunting and fishing.

"Of course Monsieur Hâas will live as we do in the country. We have excellent rabbit-warrens. The rivers abound in trout. The shooting in the forests is let out. People mostly spend their evenings at the inn. Monsieur the inspector of woods and forests is a delightful young man. The *juge-de-paix* is a capital whist-player," and so on, and so on.

I listen, and think all this quiet life must be delightful. Mademoiselle Lothe pleases me a good deal. She does not talk much, but she smiles and looks so agreeable! How loving and amiable she must be!

At last the coffee came, then the kirschwasser. Mademoiselle Lothe retires, and the old lawyer gradually passes to business. He explains to me the nature of my uncle's property, and I listen attentively. There was no part of the will in dispute; there were no legacies, no mortgages. Everything is clear and straightforward. Happy Caspar! Happy man!

Then we went into the office to look over the deeds. The close air of this place of dry, hard business, those long rows of boxes, the files of bills — all these together put weak notions of love out of my head. I sat down in an armchair while Monsieur Becker, collecting his thoughts, puts his horn spectacles in their place upon his long, sharp nose.

"These deeds relate to your meadowland at Eichmatt. There, Monsieur Hâas, you have a hundred acres of excellent land, the finest and best-watered in the commune; two and even three crops a year are got off that land. It brings in four thousand francs a year. Here are the deeds belonging to your vine-growing land at Sonnenthâl, thirty-five acres in all. One year with another you may get from this two hundred hectolitres (4,400 gals.) of light wine, sold on the ground at twelve or fifteen francs the hectolitre. Good years make up for the bad. This, Monsieur Hâas, is your title to the forest of Romelstein, containing fifty or sixty hectares (a hectare is 2½ acres) of excellent timber. This is your property at Hacmatt; this your pastureland at Tiefenthal. This is your farm at Grüneswald, and here is the deed belonging to your house at Lauterbach; it is the largest house in the place, and was built in the sixteenth century."

"Indeed, Monsieur Becker! But is that saying much in its favour?"

"Certainly, certainly. It was built by Jean Burckhardt, Count of Barth, for a hunting-box. Many generations have lived in it since then, but it has never been neglected, and it is now in excellent repair."

I thanked Monsieur Becker for the information he had given me, and having secured all my title-deeds in a large portfolio which he was good enough to lend me, I took my leave, more full than ever of my vast importance!

Arriving before my house, I enjoyed introducing the key into the lock of the door, and bringing down my foot firmly and proudly on the first step.

"This is all mine!" I cried enthusiastically.

I enter the hall — "Mine!" I open the wardrobes — "Mine!" Mine — all that linen piled up to the top! I pace majestically up the broad staircase, repeating like a fool, "This is mine, and that is mine! Here I am, owner of all this! No more uneasiness about the future! Not an anxious thought for the morrow! Now I am going to make a figure in the world! — not on the weak ground of merit — not for anything that fashion can alter. I am a great man because I hold really and effectually that which the world covets.

"Ye poets and artists! What are you in comparison with the rich proprietor who has everything he wants, and who feeds your inspiration with the crumbs that fall from his table? What are you but ornamental portions of his feasts and banquets, just to fill up a weary interval? You are no more than the sparrow that warbles in his hedges, or the statue that figures in his garden-walk. It is by him and for him that you exist. What need has he to envy you the incense of pride and vanity — he who possesses the only solid good this world has to offer?"

At that moment of inflated conceit if the poor Kapellmeister Hâas had appeared before me I might very likely have turned and looked at him over my shoulder and asked, "What fool is that? What business has he with me?"

I threw a window open; evening was closing in. The setting sun gilded my orchards and my vines as far as I could see. On the declivity of the hill a few white patches indicated the cemetery.

I turned round. A great Gothic hall, with rich mouldings decorating the ceiling, pleased my taste exceedingly. This was the Seigneur Burckhardt's hunting-saloon.

An old spinet stood between two windows; I ran my fingers absently over the keys, and the loose strings jingled with the disagreeable squeaking of a toothless old woman trying to sing like a young damsel.

At the end of this long apartment was an arched alcove closed in by deep red curtains, and containing a lofty four-post bedstead with a kind of grand baldacchino covering it in. The sight of this reminded me that I had been six hours on horseback, and undressing with a self-satisfied smirk on my face all the time —

"It is the first time," I said, "that I shall sleep in a bed of my own."

And laying myself comfortably down, with my eyes dreamily wandering over the distant plains on which the shadows of evening were settling down, I felt my eyelids gently yielding to the sweet influence of sleep. Not a leaf was stirring; the village noises ceased one by one, the last golden rays of the sun had disappeared, and I dropped into the unconsciousness of welcome sleep.

Dark night fell on the face of the Earth, and then the moon was rising in all her splendour, when I awoke, I cannot tell why. The wandering scents of summer air reached me through the open window, fragrant with the sweet perfume of the new-mown hay. I gazed with surprise, then I made an effort to rise and open the window, but some obstacle prevented me. To my astonishment, though my head was perfectly free to move in any direction, my body was buried in a deep sleep like a lump of lead. Not a single muscle obeyed my repeated efforts to raise my body; I was conscious of my arms lying extended near me, and my legs being stretched out straight and immovable; but my head was swaying helplessly to and fro. My breathing, deep and regular — the breathing of my body went on all the same, and frightened me dreadfully. My head, exhausted with its vain efforts to obtain obedience from the limbs, fell back in despair, and I said, "What! Is it paralysis?"

My eyes closed. I was reflecting with a feeling of horror upon this strange phenomenon, and my ears were listening intently to the agitated beating of my heart, over whose hurried flow of blood the mind had no power.

"What, what is this?" I thought presently. "Do my own body and limbs refuse to obey my will? Cannot Caspar Hâas, the undisputed lord of so many rich vineyards and fat pastures, move this wretched clod of earth which most certainly belongs to him? Oh, what does it all mean?"

As I was thus wondering and meditating I heard a slight noise. The door of my alcove opened, and a man clothed in some stiff material resembling felt, such as is worn by the monks in the chapel of St. Werburgh at Mayence, with a broad-brimmed hat and feather pushed off from the left ear, his hands buried up to the elbows in gauntlets of strong untanned leather, entered the room. This gentleman's huge jackboots came over the knees, and were folded down again. A heavy chain of gold, with decorations suspended to it, hung from his shoulders. His tanned and angular countenance, his sallow complexion, his hollow eyes, bore an expression of bitterness and melancholy.

This dismal personage traversed the hall with a hard and sounding step as measured as the ticking of a clock, and placing his skinny hand upon the hilt of an immense long rapier, and stamping with his heel on the floor, he uttered in a horribly disagreeable creaking voice resembling the grating of an engine these words, which dropped in a dry mechanical fashion from his ashy lips:

"This is mine — mine — Hans Burckhardt, Count of Barth!"

I felt a creeping sensation coming all over me.

At the same instant the door opposite flew open wide, and the Count of Barth disappeared in the next apartment; and I could hear his hard, dry automatic tread upon the stairs descending the steps, one by one, for a long time; there seemed no end to it, until at last the awful sounds died in the remote distance as if they had descended into the bowels of the Earth.

But as I was still listening, and hearing nothing further, all in a moment the vast hall filled as if by magic with a numerous company; the spinet began to jingle; there was music and singing of love, and pleasure, and wine.

I gazed and saw by the bluish-grey moonlight ladies in the bloom of youth negligently floating over the floor, and chiefly about the old spinet; elegant cavaliers attired, as in the olden time, in innumerable dangling ribbons, and the very perfection of lace collars and ruffles, seated crosslegged upon gold-fringed stools, affectedly inclining sidelong, shaking their perfumed locks, making little bows, studying all kinds of graceful attitudes, and paying their court to the ladies, all so elegantly, and with such an air of gallantry, that it reminded me of the old mezzotint engravings of the graceful school of Lorraine in the sixteenth century.

And the stiff little fingers of an ancient dowager, with a parrot bill, were rattling the keys of the old spinet; bursts of thin laughter set discordant echoes flying, and ended in little squeaks with such a sharp discordant rattle of constrained laughter as made my hair stand on end.

All this silly little world — all this quintessence of fashion and elegance, long out of date, all exhaled the acrid odour of rose-water and essence of mignonette turned into vinegar.

I made new and superhuman exertions to get rid of this disagreeable nightmare, but it was all in vain. But at that instant a lady of the highest fashion cried aloud —

"Lords, you are at home here in all this domain —"

But she was cut short in her compliments; a silence like death fell on the whole assembly. They faded away. I looked, and the whole picture had vanished from my sight.

Then the sound of a trumpet fell on my listening ears. Horses were pawing the ground outside, dogs were barking, while the moon, calm, clear, inviting to meditation, still poured her soft light into my alcove.

The door opened as if by a blast of wind, and fifty huntsmen, followed by a company of young ladies attired as they were two centuries ago, in long trains, defiled with majestic pace out of one chamber into the other. Four serving-men passed amongst them, bearing on their brawny shoulders on a stout litter of oak boughs the bloody carcass of a monstrous wild boar, with dim and faded eye, and with the foam yet lying white on his formidable tusks and grisly jaws.

Then I heard the flourishes of the brazen trumpets redoubled in loudness and energy; but silence fell, and the pomp and dignity, passed away with a sigh like the last moans of a storm in the woods; then — nothing at all — nothing to hear — nothing to see!

As I lay dreaming over this strange vision, and my eyes wandering vaguely over the empty space in the silent darkness, I observed with astonishment the blank space becoming silently occupied by one of the old Protestant families of former days, calm, solemn, and dignified in their bearing and conversation.

There sat the white-haired patriarch with the big Bible upon his knees; the aged mother, tall and pale, spinning the flax grown by themselves, sitting as straight and immovable as her own distaff, her ruff up to her ears, her long waist compressed in a stiff black bodice; then there sat the fat and rosy children, with serious countenances and thoughtful blue eyes, leaning in silence with their elbows on the table; the dog lay stretched by the great hearth apparently listening to the reading; the old clock stood in the corner ticking seconds; farther on in the shadow were girls' faces and young men, talking seriously to them about Jacob and Rachel by way of love-making.

And this good family seemed penetrated with the truth of the sacred story; the old man in broken accents was reading aloud the edifying history of the settlement of the children of Israel in the Land of Canaan —

"This is the Land of Promise — the land promised to Abraham and Isaac and Jacob your fathers — that you may be multiplied in it as the stars of Heaven for multitude, and as the sand which is upon the seashore. And none shall disturb you, for ye are the chosen people."

The moon, which had veiled her light for a few minutes, reappeared, and hearing no more sounds of voices, I looked round, and her clear cold rays fell in the great empty hall. Not a figure, not a shade, was left. The moonlight poured its silver flood upon the floor, and in the distance the forms of a few trees stood out against the dark purple sky.

But now suddenly the high walls appeared lined with books, the old spinet gave way to the *secrétaire* of some man of learning, whose full-bottomed wig was peering above the back of a red-leather armchair. I could hear the quill coursing over the paper. The learned man, buried in thought, never moved; the silence was oppressive.

But fancy my astonishment when, slowly turning, the great scholar faced me, and I recognised the portrait of the famous lawyer Gregorius, marked No. 253 in the portrait-gallery at Darmstadt.

How on Earth had this personage walked out of his grave?

I was asking myself this question when, in a hollow sepulchral voice, he pronounced these words:

"Dominorum, ex jurè Quintio, est jus utendi et abutendi quatenus naturalis ratio patitur."

As this sapient precept dropped oracularly from his lips, a word at a time, his figure faded and turned pale. With the last word he had passed out of existence.

What more shall I tell you, my dear friends? For hours, twenty generations came defiling past me in Hans Burckhardt's ancient mansion — Christians and Jews, nobles and commoners, fools and wise men of high art, and men of mere prose. Every one proclaimed his indefeasible right to the property; every one firmly believed himself sole lord and master of all he surveyed. Alas! Death breathed upon one after another, and they were all carried out, each as his turn came!

I was beginning to be familiar with this strange phantasmagoria. Each time that any of these honest folks turned round and declared to me, "This is mine!" I laughed and said, "Wait a bit, my fine fellow! — you will melt away just like the rest!"

At last I began to feel tired of it, when far away — very far — the cock crowed, announcing the dawn of day. His piercing call began to rouse the sleeper. The leaves rustled with the morning air; a slight shiver shook my frame; I felt my limbs gradually regaining their freedom, and, resting upon my elbow, I gazed with rapture upon the silent wide-spread land. But what I saw presently did not tend to exalt my spirits.

Along the little winding path to the cemetery were moving, in solemn procession, all the ghosts that had visited me in the night. Step by step they approached the decaying moss-grown door of the sacred inclosure; that silent, mournful march of spectres under the dim grey light of early morning was a gaunt and fearful sight.

And as I lay, more dead than alive, with gaping mouth and my face wet with cold perspiration, the head of the dismal line melted and disappeared among the weeping willows.

There were not many spectres, left, and I was beginning to feel a little more composed, when the very last, my uncle Christian himself, turned round to me under the mossy gate and beckoned me to follow! A distant faint ironical voice said —

"Caspar! Caspar! Come! Six feet of this ground belong to you!"

Then he too disappeared.

A streak of crimson and purple stretched across the eastern sky announced the coming day.

I need not tell you that I did not accept my uncle Christian's invitation, though I am quite aware that a similar call will one day arrive from One who must be obeyed. The remembrance of my brief abode at Burckhardt's fort has wonderfully brought down the great opinion I had once formed of my own importance, for the vision of that night taught me that though orchards and meadows may not pass away their owners do, and this fact compels to serious reflection upon the nature of our duties and responsibilities.

I therefore wisely resolved not to risk the loss of manly energy and of the best prizes of life by tarrying at that Capua, but to betake myself, without further loss of time, to the pursuit of music as a science, and I hope to produce next year, at the Royal Theatre of Berlin, an opera which, I hope, will disarm all criticism at once.

I have come to the final conclusion that glory and renown, which speculative people speak of as if they were mere smoke, is, after all, the most enduring good. Life and a noble reputation do not depart together; on the contrary, death confirms well-deserved glory and adds to it a brighter lustre.

Suppose, for instance, that Homer returned to life, no one would dispute with him his claim to be the author of the *Iliad*, and each would vie with the rest to do honour to the father of epic poetry. But if peradventure some rich landowner of that day came back to assert a claim to the fields, the woods, the pastures of which he used to be so proud, ten to one he would be received like a thief and perhaps die a miserable death.

THE BEAR-BAITING

"If any one thing distresses my dear aunt," said Caspar, "more than my fondness for Sébaldus Dick's tavern, it is that there is an artist in the family!

"Dame Catherine would have been glad to see me an advocate, a priest, or a councillor. If I had become a councillor, like Monsieur Andreas Van Berghem; if I had snuffled out long and weary sentences, caressing my lace bands with dainty fingertips, with what esteem and veneration would not that worthy woman have regarded monsieur her nephew! She would have greeted Monsieur le Conseiller Caspar with profound respect; she would have set before me her best preserves, she would have poured out for me, in the midst of her circle of gossips, just a drop of Muscadel of the year XI. with —

"Pray take this, monsieur le conseiller; I have but two bottles left!"

Anything that monsieur my nephew Caspar, conseiller at the court of justice, could do would certainly have been perfectly right and suitable, and quite perfect in its way.

Alas for the vanity of human wishes! The poor woman's ambition was never to be gratified. Her nephew is plain Caspar — Caspar Diderich; he has no title, no wand of office, no big wig — he is just an artist! And Dame Catherine has running in her head the old proverb, "Beggarly as an artist," which distresses her more than she can tell.

At first I used to try to make her understand that a true artist is worthy of great respect, that his works sometimes endure for ages, and are admired by many successive generations, and that, in point of fact, a good artist is quite as good as a councillor. Unhappily, I failed to convince her; she merely shrugged her shoulders, clasped her hands in despair, and vouchsafed no answer.

I would have done anything to convert my aunt Catherine to my views — anything; but I would rather die than sacrifice art and an artist's life, music, painting, and Sébaldus's tavern!

Sébaldus's tavern is delightful. It is the corner house between the narrow Rue des Hallebardes and the little square De la Cigogne. As soon as you are through the archway you find within a spacious square court, with old carved wooden galleries all round it, and a wooden staircase to reach it; everywhere are scattered in disorder small windows of last century with leaden sashes, skylights, and air-holes; old wooden posts are nearly yielding under the weight of a roof that threatens to sink in. The barn, the rows of casks piled up in a corner, the cellar door at the left, a pigeon-cote forming the point of the gable end; then, again, beneath the galleries, other darkened windows in the same style, where you can see swillers and topers in three-cornered hats, distinguished by noses red, purple, or crimson; little women of Hundsruck, in velvet caps with long fluttering ribbons, some grave, some laughing, others queer and grotesque-looking; the hay-loft high up under the roof; stables, pigsties, cowsheds, all in picturesque confusion attract and confound your attention. It is a strange sight!

For fifty years not a hammer has been lifted against this venerable ruin. You would think it was left for the special accommodation of rats! And when the glowing autumn sun, red as fire, showers golden rain upon the decaying walls and timbers; when, as daylight fades into evening, the angular projections stand out more boldly, and the shadows deepen; when all the tavern rings with songs, and shouts, and roars of laughter; when fat Sébaldus, in leathern apron, runs to and from the cellar with the big jug in his hand; when his wife Gredel throws up the kitchen window, and with her long knife, well hacked along the edge, cleans the fish, or cuts the necks of hens, ducks, or geese which struggle and gurgle in their own blood; when pretty Fridoline, with her rosy little mouth and her long fair hair, leans out of her window to tend the honeysuckle, and over her head the neighbour's tabby cat is gently swaying her tail and watching, with her cunning green eyes, the swallow circling in the deepening purple — I do assure you that a man must be utterly devoid of taste for the picturesque not to stop and contemplate in ecstasy and listen to the murmuring sounds, or the louder din, or the falling whispers, and observe with an artist's eye the trembling lights, the flying shadows, and whisper to himself, "Is not this beautiful?"

But you should see Maître Sébaldus's tavern on a great occasion, when all the jovial folks of Bergzabern crowd into the immense public room — some day when a cock-fight is going on, or a dog-fight, or a magic-lantern.

Last autumn, on a Saturday — and it was Michaelmas Day — we were all sitting round the oaken table, between one and two o'clock in the afternoon; old Doctor Melchior, Eisenloffel the blacksmith, and his old wife, old Berbel Rasimus, Johannes the capuchin monk, Borves Fritz the clarionet-player at the Pied de

Boeuf, and half a hundred more, laughing, singing, drinking, playing at *youker*, draining jugs and glasses, eating puddings and *andouilles*.

Mother Gredel was coming and going; the pretty maid-servants, Heinrichen and Lotté, were flying up and down the kitchen stairs like squirrels, and outside, under the broad archway, was the booming, and banging, and jingling of the big drum and the cymbals, while the exciting proclamation was being made: "Ho! Ho! Hi! Great battle to come off! The Asturian bear, Beppo, and Baptist, the Savoyard bear, against all dogs that may come. Boom! Boom! Walk in, ladies! Walk in, gentlemen! Here's the buffalo from Calabria, and the onagra of the desert! Walk in, walk in! Don't be frightened! All walk in!"

And they did come in, in crowds.

Sébaldus, barring the passage with his burly form, as Horatius guarded the bridge in the brave days of old, shouted to all —

"Your five kreutzers, friends and neighbours! Five kreutzers for admittance! Pay, or I'll throttle you!"

It was an awful confusion; people climbed over each other's backs to get in faster, until Bridget Kéra lost a stocking and Anna Seiler half her petticoat.

About two, the bear-leader, a tall, rough-looking fellow, with red ragged hair and beard, and mounting a high sugar-loafed hat, pushed the door ajar, and cried, looking in —

"Just going to begin the fight!"

In an instant all the tables were emptied, many an untasted glass being left upon it. I ran to the hay-loft, climbed up the ladder four steps at a time, and drew it up after me. There, seated all alone upon a bundle of hay, just inside the little skylight, I had a capital view.

What a throng! The old galleries were bending under their weight, the roofs were visibly swaying. I shuddered to think of what might happen. It seemed inevitable that they would all come down together like grapes in the wine-press, heaped up in a sea of heads.

They were hanging in clusters on the wooden pillars; yet higher in the gutters along the roof; yet higher about the pigeon-cote; higher still over the skylights in the roof of the *mairie*; yet higher in the spire of St. Christopher's; and all this multitude were howling and shouting —

"The bears! The bears!"

When I had sufficiently admired and wondered at the immense crowd, looking down I saw in the middle of the court a poor, wretched, depressed-looking donkey, lean and ragged, his sleepy eyes half-closed, his ears hanging down. This dreadful object was to open the sports.

"What fools some people are!" I thought.

Minutes were passing away, the tumult increased, impatience was waxing into anger, when the great red scoundrel, with his immense sugar-loaf hat, advanced carelessly into the middle of the open space, and cried solemnly, with his fist upon his hips —

"The onagra of the desert against any dog in the town!"

There was a silence of astonishment. Daniel, the butcher, with staring eyes and gaping mouth, asks —

"Where is the onagra?"

"There she stands!"

"That! Why, it's an ass!"

"It's an onagra."

"Well, let us see what it is," cried the butcher, laughing.

He whistled his dog to come, and, pointing to the ass, cried —

"Foux, catch him!"

But, strange to say, as soon as the ass saw the dog running to the attack, he turned nimbly round, and launched out with the whole length of his leg — so well aimed a kick that the dog fell back as if struck by lightning, with his jaw fractured!

Loud laughter rang all round, while the poor dog fled with a piteous yell of pain.

The bear-leader smiled at the butcher, and asked —

"Well, what's your opinion? Is my onagra an ass?"

"No," said Daniel, rather ashamed, "it is an onagra."

"All right! All right! Any more dogs coming to fight my desert-born, desert-bred onagra? Come on, the onagra is ready!"

But no one came forward; and the bear-leader shouted in vain in his shrill tones —

"Gentlemen! Ladies! Are you all afraid? afraid of the onagra? The dogs of your town ought to be ashamed of themselves. Come on! Courage, gentlemen! Courage, ladies!"

But no one was inclined to risk his dog's life or limbs against so dangerous an animal, and the cries for the bears were beginning again.

"The bears! The bears! Bring out the bears!"

After waiting a quarter of an hour the fellow saw that his onagra was not likely to get any more customers, so, putting the beast up in the stable, he approached the pigsty, opened it, and drew out by his chain Baptiste, the Savoy bear, an old brute with a brown mangy-looking coat, as sulky and ashamed as a sweep coming down a chimney. For all he was not handsome the shouts of applause rang out, and the fighting dogs themselves, shut into the tavern porch, smelling a wild beast, set up a tragic howl that made your hair stand on end. The miserable bear was led quietly enough to a stake firmly driven in the ground, to which he was chained, all the time slowly surveying the excited crowd with a melancholy eye.

"Poor old traveller!" I cried to myself, "would anybody have told you ten years ago, when grave, terrible, and solitary you were traversing from side to side the high glaciers in Switzerland, in the gloomy glens of the Unterwald, and your deep growls made the old oaks tremble in every leaf — who could have told you that the day would come when, sad and resigned, with an iron collar round your throat, you would be tied to a post and devoured by dogs to amuse a mob at Bergzabern? Alas! *Sic transit gloria mundi!*"

As these meditations were occupying my thoughts, noticing that everybody was bending forward to see, I did like the rest, and I soon saw the possibility of warm work.

A pair of boar-hounds, belonging to old Heinrich, were being led to the other end of the court. Struggling in the chain, these ferocious creatures were foaming with rage. One was of the large Danish breed, white, with large black spots, supple of limb, with muscles like steel springs, jaws opening wide like an alligator's; the other a huge hound from the Tannewald, never disabled in one leg according to law, ribs barely covered, the backbone hard and knotted like a bamboo cane. They did not bark, but they were straining against the chain with all their might, and there stood old Heinrich with his grey broad head flung back, his ruddy moustache bristling, his thin razorbacked nose hooked over his lips, and his long leather-gaitered legs firmly planted against the stones in his strenuous efforts to restrain with both hands the eager appetite of his dogs for the fight, while he opposed to their attempts to bound forward the whole weight of his body.

"Back! Back!" he shouted to the bear-leader, and the ruffian ran back to the shelter of a faggot-stack.

Then every face bending over the galleries grew red and hot with the excitement of the horrid fray, and starting eyes glanced from every nook and corner.

The bear sat on his haunches gathered together ready for action, his huge paws uplifted. I could see how he quivered in his rough skin, and his muzzle seemed to annoy him terribly. All at once the chain was slipped; at a single leap the hounds cleared the intervening space, and their sharp fangs were in a moment fixed in both poor Baptiste's ears, whose heavy paws and long sharp claws hugged each bitter enemy around the neck, slowly digging into their straining bodies till the blood spurted out in streams. But he, too, was bleeding, for his ears were suffering cruel lacerations; the dogs held on, and his tawny eyes were raised to the sky with a pitiable look of appeal. Not a cry, not a sigh or a groan escaped from a single combatant; the three animals formed a group as motionless as if they had been carved in wood.

I could feel the perspiration running down my face.

This went on for five minutes.

At length the Tannenthaler seemed to be relaxing slightly; the bear weighed more heavily on him with his heavy paw, his eye kindling with a gleam of hope; then there was another brief pause. There was a horrid groan, a cracking; the hound's backbone was broken, and he fell back upon the stones, his jaws reeking with blood.

Then Baptiste, with a tremor of delight, threw both paws round the Dane, who had not yet let go his hold, but his teeth were slipping from the torn and bloody ear. Suddenly he shook himself and sprang backward; the bear made a rush at his flying foe, but the chain held him back. The dog fled, red with blood, and only stopped when he had got safe behind his master, who gave him a favourable reception, while casting a glance at his other dog, which lay motionless.

And here Baptiste placed his mighty paw upon the victim of his fury and his valour; carrying his head high, he snuffed the carnage with distended nostrils and panting sides; the veteran warrior was himself again. Frantic applause rose from the galleries to the church spire. The bear seemed to understand. I have never seen a more proud and resolute bearing.

After this fight all the spectators were taking breath; the capuchin friar Johannes, seated upon the banister facing the field of battle, shook his stick, smiling with satisfaction in his long brown beard. People wanted a little relief; pinches of snuff were offered and accepted, and the voice of Doctor Melchior, discussing and explaining the different phases of the conflict, was heard over the noise of many talkers. But he had no time to finish his speech, for in a moment the barn door flew open, and more than five-and-twenty dogs, great and small, the very vagrants and scum of the town, offered up as a sacrifice to do honour to the occasion, wallowed in a heap into the yard, howling and yelling, barking, snapping, and snarling; then, as if second thoughts had rather modified their ideas about valour, they all retreated into a safe corner of the yard, the farthest from the bear, where they contented themselves with angry protests, making short runs at the enemy and quick retreats, making a very sorry pretence of war.

"Oh, those cowardly curs! The miserable little brutes!" cried the valorous occupants in the gallery.

And the much wiser and discreeter dogs looked up in answer, and seemed to say —

"Go yourselves!"

Still the bear was standing well on the defensive when, to the general astonishment, Heinrich reappeared, holding his Danish hound by the chain.

I have since been informed that he had wagered fifty florins with Joseph Kilian, the gamekeeper, that the boar-hound would renew the attack. He advanced slowly, patting the dog with his hand, and saying persuasively —

"Good dog, Blitz! Good dog!"

And the noble animal, in spite of his bleeding wounds, rushed in; then the whole pack of mongrels, curs, puppies, lurchers, and turnspits ran in too in a long string, till poor Baptiste was covered with the vile rabble rout; he did what he could, he rolled over and over as far as his chain would let him, growling and grunting, crushing one, sending another away with a bite, struggling furiously. The brave Dane still showed the greatest intrepidity; he had caught the bear between the ears, and rolled over with him, his forelegs in the air, whilst the rest were biting, some his legs, and some his torn and bleeding ears. There seemed no end to this plague of dogs.

"Enough! Enough!" was the cry in every direction.

Yet still some were not satisfied, and kept crying on the dogs.

Heinrich at that moment darted across the yard like a flash of lightning; he seized his clog by the ear, and pulling it away with all his strength, cried —

"Blitz, Blitz, let go!"

But this was of no use. At last the man succeeded in making him loose his hold by a tremendous cut with his whip across his body, and, dragging the animal away, they both disappeared under the archway.

The mongrels had not waited for this event to give up the battle; four or five only still hung upon Bruin's side; the rest, scared, limping, yelping, were trying to find a way out. Suddenly one of those heroes, a cur belonging to Rasimus, caught sight of the kitchen window, and, fired by a noble enthusiasm for his safety, he crashed through glass and all. All the rest of the yelling crew, struck by the ingenuity of this plan, followed in the same road without a moment's hesitation. Plates and dishes, glasses and bottles, saucepans and kettles were all heard making a fearful clatter, while Mother Gredel rent the air with her piercing cries of "Help, help!"

This was the best joke of the day. Roars of laughter hailed the propitious escape of the dogs, even at the cost of so much good crockery. They laughed till the tears came into their eyes, and rolled down their red faces, and they panted for breath.

In a quarter of an hour there came a lull; then people began to think it was time for the terrible bear from Asturias to make his appearance.

"The Asturian bear! The Spanish bear!" was the cry.

The bear-leader made signs to the people to be quiet, as he had something to say to them. It was impossible! The cries and the uproar redoubled.

"The bear of Asturias! The bear of Asturias!"

Then the fellow muttered a few unintelligible words, unfastened the brown bear, and took it back into its den; then with every appearance of precaution he loosened the door of the pigsty and took the end of a chain which was lying on the ground. A formidable growling was heard inside. The man quickly passed the chain through a ring in the wall and fled, crying —

"Now, you there, let the dogs go!"

Immediately a black bear, low, and almost stunted in its stature, with a low forehead, ears wide apart, eyes red as fire, and glowing with a fierce sullen passion, hurled himself out into the open, and finding the chain fast in the wall, howled furiously. Evidently this was a bear of the most deplorably low moral character! Moreover, he had been roused to madness by the noise of the preceding combats, and his master had good reason for not trusting himself much to him.

"Let go the dogs!" cried the bear-leader, putting his head out of the granary skylight; "let them loose!"

Then he added —

"If you are not satisfied this time it won't be my fault. There will be a battle now!"

At that moment Ludwig Karl's big mastiff and Fischer de Heischland's pair of wolfhounds, with tails low, hair straight and smooth, heads advanced and ears erect, came into the court together.

The heavy-headed mastiff calmly yawned as he stretched his sinewy legs and caved in his long back. But after a long and leisurely yawn he slowly turned round, and catching sight of the bear he stood immovable as if stupefied. The bear, too, fixed his vicious glowing eyes upon him with ears expanded and his huge claws indenting the ground under them.

The wolfhounds drew up as reserves in the rear of the mastiff.

Then such silence fell upon all that excited multitude that a dead leaf might have been heard rustling to the ground; but there followed a deep, low, fierce growl, like a coming thunderstorm, which sent a shudder through the crowd.

Suddenly the mastiff sprang forward, the two others followed, and then for several seconds nothing was seen but a confused mass rolling round the chain, then blood and entrails mingled flowing over the stones, then the bear rising on his haunches hugging the mastiff between his terrible claws, swaying to and fro his heavy head, for a moment and gaping wide with his crimson jaws, for the muzzle was gone; in the struggle it had fallen off!

Then a low but rising cry of fear passed over the crowd in the galleries. No applause now, only a well-grounded alarm! The mastiff was in the agonies of death, with a rattling in his throat; the wolfhounds lay torn and dead on the bloodstained earth; in the stables all round the court long agitated roaring and bellowing betrayed the terror of the cattle, whose kicking and plunging made the walls shake; but the bear never stirred: he seemed to be enjoying the universal alarm.

But lo! In this predicament was heard a slight but unmistakable cracking like timber giving way, then more cracks; the old rotten galleries were beginning to yield under the heavy pressure of the crowd; and there was in this noise, just heard in the midst of the dead silence of suspense, something so dreadful that I, in my place of safety, felt a cold shiver pass over me. Taking a rapid survey of the galleries before me, I saw every face changed in colour, pale with a bluish, ashy paleness; some open-mouthed, others with bristling hair, listening intently, holding their breath. The capuchin friar Johannes seated on the banister had turned from crimson to a greenish hue, and the big red nose of Doctor Melchior had turned from red to sallow the first time for twenty years; the poor little women trembled without stirring from their places, knowing that the least agitation would bring down the whole place.

I could have wished to fly too. I fancied I could see the thick oaken pillars of the gallery bowing to the ground. I cannot tell whether this was illusion or not, but in a moment the principal beam gave a loud crack and became depressed by three inches at the least. Then, my friends, it was horrible to behold — the deep silence of a minute before was succeeded by tumult, cries, screams, and ravings. That mass of human beings heaped up in the galleries, one above another, were some clutching the walls, the pillars, the banisters; others were fighting with fury, and even biting, to get away faster, and from the midst of this frightful confusion arose the plaintive voices of the suffering women. I shudder at the remembrance. Oh, may I never see such a sight as this again!

But, most terrible circumstance of all, the bear was chained close by the staircase that leads up to the galleries!

If I were to live a thousand years never should I forget the horror of Friar Johannes, who had cleared a way for himself with his long staff, and was placing his foot on the last step when he discovered, just before the bottom of the staircase, Beppo seated calmly on his tail, his chain tightened, his eye expressive of joy, ready to snap him up first!

None can tell the muscular power which Maître Johannes was obliged to put forth to stem the force that was driving him in from behind. Convulsively grasping the banister with both hands, his broad shoulders formed a mighty buttress against the pressing flood. Like Atlas, I do believe he would have borne the Earth upon his back to save his precious skin.

In the midst of this confusion and tumult, and when there seemed no way to avert the threatening catastrophe, suddenly the door of the cattle-shed opened violently, and the redoubtable Horni, Maître Sébaldus's magnificent bull, rushed into the arena, his massive dewlap shaking loosely like an apron, his tail extended straight, his mouth and nostrils white with fleecy foam.

It was an inspiration of the master's. He had resolved to risk his bull to save human life. At the same moment the fat, round, rosy face of our landlord appeared through the skylight of the stable, crying to the crowd not to be alarmed, for that he would open the inner door which abuts into the old synagogue, and let out the crowd by the Jews' street, which was done in two or three minutes, to the immense relief and comfort of the public.

But now listen to the end of my story.

Scarcely had the bear caught sight of the bull when he made an ugly rush upon this new adversary with so terrible a shock that the chain burst. The bull retired, facing his foe, to a corner of the court near the pigeon-cote, and there, head well down between his short legs and horns presented, he awaited the shock of war.

The bear made several feints, slipping along by the wall from right to left; but the bull, with his forehead almost touching the ground, followed the enemy's movements with marvellous coolness.

In five minutes the galleries had been cleared; the noise of the crowd taking refuge down the Jews' street was becoming more remote, and this manoeuvring of the two huge brutes seemed as if they were meditating a drawn battle, when suddenly the bull, losing patience, threw himself upon the bear with the whole momentum of his monstrous bulk. The unhappy brute, pressed so closely, took refuge under the woodshed, but the head and horns of his foe pursued him thither, and there no doubt he nailed his adversary to the wall, for although I could only see the bull's hindquarters, I could hear a dreadful shriek, followed by a crunching of bones, and presently a pool of blood was flowing over the pavement.

I could only see the bull's hindquarters and his tail waving aloft like a battle-flag. You would have thought he wanted to bring the walls down by the furious and violent pounding of his hind feet. That silent scene in shadow was fearful. I did not wait to see the end. I came carefully down my ladder, and slipped out of the court like a thief. You may imagine with what pleasure I inhaled the pure open air; and passing through the crowd collected round the door where the bear-leader was tearing his hair in his wild despair, I ran off to my aunt's house.

I was just going round under the arcades when I was stopped by my old drawing-master, Conrad Schmidt.

"Caspar!" he cried, "where are you going in such a hurry?"

"I am going to paint the great bear-fight!" I answered enthusiastically.

"Another tavern scene, I suppose," he remarked with a shrug.

"Why not, Master Conrad? Is not a tavern scene as good as one in the forum?"

I would have said a good deal, but we were standing at his door.

"Good night, Maître Conrad," I cried, pressing his hand. "Don't bear a grudge against me for not going to study in Italy."

"Grudge! No," replied the old master, smiling. "You know that privately I am of your opinion. If I tell you now and then to go to Italy, it is to satisfy Dame Catherine. But follow out your own idea, Caspar. Men who only follow other men's ideas never do any good."

THE SCAPEGOAT

Note
This story, allowing for the exercise of fancy in its construction, is only too faithful a picture of German student life and habits, with its ignorance or disregard of the Christianity taught us in the Gospel, its only half-concealed leaning towards the ancient systems of religion properly known as heathen, and its careless indifference to human life. The translator has ventured to deviate slightly from the original in one or two places in order to avoid giving an unnecessary shock to the susceptibilities of readers trained and educated in principles widely differing from these. — *Transl.*

Doesn't everybody at Tubingen know the lamentable history of the quarrel between the Seigneur Kaspar Evig and the young Jew Elias Hirsch? Kaspar Evig was courting Mademoiselle Eva Salomon, the daughter of the old picture-dealer in the Rue de Jericho. One day he found my friend Elias In the broker's shop, and, on what pretext I know not, he boxed his ears soundly three or four times.

Elias Hirsch, who had begun his medical studies only about five months before, was called upon by a council of the students to challenge the Seigneur Kaspar to fight, a step which he took with the greatest repugnance, for it was quite to be expected that a seigneur should be a perfect swordsman.

For all that Elias put himself well on the defensive, and, watching his opportunity, inserted his finely-pointed sword so neatly between the ribs of the above-mentioned seigneur as considerably to affect his breathing, the consequence of which was that he was dead in ten minutes.

The Rector Diemer, being informed of this transaction by credible witnesses, listened coldly and remarked briefly —

"I understand you, gentlemen. He is dead, is he? Very well, then; bury him."

Elias was carried about in triumph, like another Mattathias; but, far from accepting the proffered glory, he drooped under a profound melancholy.

He lost flesh, he sighed, he groaned; his nose, already a pretty long one, seemed to gain in prominence what it lost in solidity, and often in the evening, as he was passing down the Rue des Trois Fontaines, he might be heard murmuring —

"Kaspar Evig, forgive me; I did not mean to take your life. Oh, unhappy Eva! What have you done? By your thoughtless flirting you made two brave men quarrel, and now the shade of the Seigneur Kaspar pursues me everywhere, even in my sleep. Oh, Eva! Wretched Eva! Why did you behave so?"

So poor Elias moaned in his misery; and he was the more to be pitied because the sons of Israel are not bloodthirsty, and they know it is written in their law, "Whosoever sheddeth man's blood by man shall his blood be shed."

Now one fine day in July, while I was drinking at the Faucon, in walks Elias Hirsch, just as miserable as ever, with hollow cheeks, hair hanging in disorder about his face, and downcast eyes. He laid his hand upon my shoulder, and said —

"Dear Christian, will you do me a pleasure?"

"Of course I will, Elias; only say what."

"Let us go for a walk together in the country; I want to consult you about my grief. You know many things human and divine; perhaps you can point me out a remedy for so much trouble of mind. I can trust in you, Christian, entirely."

As I had already had five or six pints of beer and two or three glasses of schnapps, there was nothing more to detain me, and I consented to go with him. Besides, I felt flattered with his confidence in my wisdom.

So we came through the town, and in twenty minutes we were walking along the little violet-bordered path which winds up to the ancient ruins of Triefels.

Then, feeling alone, passing between hedges balmy with honeysuckle and musical with the song of birds, and slowly climbing up to the lofty pines which crown the Rothalp, Elias breathed more freely; he raised his eyes and cried —

"In all your theological studies, Christian, have you met with a way in which great crimes may be expiated? I know that you have studied this question a good deal. Tell me. Whatever you recommend to put to flight the avenging shade of Kaspar Evig, I will do it."

Hirsch's question made me thoughtful. We walked together, with heads bowed down in thought, in deep silence. He watched me, I could see, out of the corner of his eye, whilst I was endeavouring to collect my thoughts upon this delicate question, but at last I made answer —

"Now, if we were inhabitants of India, Elias, I should tell you to go and bathe in the Ganges, for the waters of that river wash away the pollutions of both body and soul — so, at least, the people of that country think; and they kill, and burn, and steal without fear under the protection of that marvellous river. It is a great comfort for scoundrels! It is a matter of great regret that we have no such river! If we were living in the days of Jason, I should prescribe to you the salt-cakes of Queen Circe, which had the remarkable property of whitening blackened consciences and saving people the trouble of repenting. Finally, if you had the happiness to belong to our holy religion, I would order you to have masses said, and to give up your goods to the Church. But in your state as to locality, time, and belief, I know of only one way to relieve you."

"What is it?" cried Hirsch, already kindling with hope.

We had now reached the Rothalp, and were standing in a lonely place called the Holderloch. It is a deep dark gorge, encircled with gloomy firs; a level rock crowns the abyss, whence fall the dark waters of the Marg with roaring deep and loud.

Our path had brought us there. I sat down upon the mossy turf to breathe the moist air which rises from the gulf, and at that very moment I espied below me a magnificent goat, reaching up to crop the wild cresses that grow on the edge of the cliff.

Let it be remembered that the rocks of the Holderloch rise in the form of successive terraces, each terrace ten feet high perhaps, but not more than a foot wide, and upon these little narrow ledges grow a thousand sweet-smelling plants — thyme and honeysuckle, ivy and convolvulus, and the wild vine, perpetually bedewed with the spray from the falling torrent, and falling over in the loveliest clusters of bloom and foliage.

Now my goat — an animal with a broad brow, garnished with heavy knotted curling horns, with eyes gleaming like a pair of gold buttons, a reddish beard, exhibiting a proud, defiant bearing under those festoons of verdure, and a countenance as bold as that of a prowling satyr — my goat was making a progress upwards towards the very highest of these narrow ledges, and was enjoying a sweet repast of dainty herbs.

"Elias!" I cried, "I feel an inspiration! Just as I was thinking of a scapegoat, there is one! I see it! Look! — behold! There he is! Is not your course plain now? Lay your crime upon that goat, and then forget all about it."

Elias looked at me in stupid ignorance.

"I should like to do that, Christian, but how am I to lay my remorse upon that goat?"

"Nothing can be plainer. What did the Romans do to get rid of their criminals, polluted with every crime? Why they flung them off the Tarpeian rock, to be sure. Well, having laid your imprecations upon that goat, fling him down the Holderloch, and there will be an end of it all."

"But" — replied Elias.

"I know your objections beforehand," I replied. "You are going to say that you see no connection between Kaspar Evig, whose shade follows you, and that goat. But beware! Be careful! Where was the connection between the waters of the Ganges, Circe's salt-cakes, and the scapegoat with the crimes to be expiated? None at all. Well, for all that, the expiation was held to be good; therefore lay your curses and imprecations upon that goat, and throw him over! I order you to do that! I feel it my duty to see this thing done. I can see a connection between that goat and your fault, but I cannot explain it because the light of my vast information dazzles me just now!"

Elias did not move a step. I even thought I detected a smile upon his countenance, which irritated me.

"How!" said I; "here am I pointing out to you an infallible method to get rid of the just punishment of your crime, and you doubt — you hesitate — you even smile!"

"No," said he, "but I am not accustomed to walk on the edges of precipices, and I am afraid I should fall into the Holderloch along with the goat."

"Ah, you are a coward! I can see it all. You have just once displayed a little courage to get exemption for the rest of your days. Well, sir, if you refuse to carry out my advice, I will do it myself."

And I rose.

"Christian! Christian!" cried my friend, "don't trust yourself too far. Your foot is not steady — just now."

"My foot not steady! Do you dare to insinuate that I am drunk because I have just had ten or a dozen glasses of beer and three glasses of schnapps this morning? Away with you! Back! Back, son of Belial!"

And advancing a few feet above the goat, with my head raised and hands extended, I cried solemnly —

"Azazel! Goat destined for misery and expiation, I lay upon your hairy back the remorse of my friend Elias Hirsch, and I send you down to the spirits of darkness!"

Then, passing round the ledge on which we stood, I descended to the next below to catch the goat and throw him over.

A sacred rage and fury seemed to possess me. I took no notice of the abyss. I stepped along the edge of the precipice like a cat.

The goat, perceiving my approach, eyed me suspiciously, and

stepped back a little way.

"Ha!" I cried, "you may flee from me, but you shall not escape from me, accursed beast! I have got you!"

"Oh, Christian, Christian!" Elias kept repeating in a heart-rending voice, "do come back. You are risking your life!"

"Silence, unbeliever!" I cried. "You are unworthy of the great sacrifice which I am making for your happiness! But your friend Christian never draws back. Azazel must perish!"

A little farther on the ledge narrowed and ended in a point.

The goat, having a second time examined me with a curious eye, drew back a little farther, but not without some hesitation.

"Aha!" I exclaimed, "you are beginning to understand what is going to happen. Yes, let me get you into that corner, and your doom is sealed!"

And undoubtedly, when he had got to the spot where the ledge came to an end, Azazel seemed puzzled to know what to do next. I edged up to him closer and closer, full of a noble excitement, and laughing in anticipation at the coming descent and the splash in the torrent below.

I now beheld him at four paces from me, and I was grasping tightly a root of holly that was growing out of a rock to launch out a kick at the devoted beast.

"Look, Elias, see the accursed!" I cried.

When, all in a moment, I felt in my stomach a most awful blow, a butt which would have sent *me* into the Holderloch had I not kept hold of that blessed root of holly. The fact was that that miserable goat, seeing himself driven into a corner, had himself commenced the attack.

Oh, what was my astonishment! Before I knew where I was or what had happened, there was the brute standing up again on his hind legs, and his horns digging into my stomach and my sides with a hollow sound.

What a position to be in! It is impossible to be more astounded than I was at that moment! It was the world upside down. It was a bad dream — a nightmare! The precipice with all its jagged peaks seemed to dance around me, and so did the trees and sky above. At the same moment I heard piercing cries from Elias of "Help! Help!" while Azazel's horns were ploughing up my sides.

Then I lost all presence of mind. The goat with his long beard and his hard, sharp horns pounding me, now in my chest, now in my stomach, and then in my shaking limbs, produced a most diabolical effect upon me. My hold on the root slowly relaxed, and I let go. But happily something kept me from falling, something which I could not understand at first. But it was the shepherd Yeri, of the Holderloch, who from the next platform above had caught me by the coat-collar with his crook.

Thanks to his assistance, instead of falling down into the chasm I lay full length along the ledge, and that awful goat walked over my body to get away about his business.

"Come, take firm hold of my crook," cried the shepherd to Elias; "now I will go down for him. Don't let go!"

"You may rely upon me," answered Elias.

I heard all that as if it were a nightmare. I had almost lost consciousness.

When I opened my eyes I saw standing before me that gigantic shepherd, with his grey eyes sunk underneath his bushy eyebrows, his yellow beard, a sheepskin thrown over his shoulders, and I thought I had awoke in the age of Oedipus, which made me wonder a good deal.

"Well," cried the shepherd, in a harsh guttural, "this will teach you not to curse my goat any more!"

Then I saw Azazel rubbing himself comfortably against his master's colossal legs, and looking slily, and I thought ironically, at me; and then I saw Elias standing behind me, and making the greatest efforts not to laugh.

My scattered senses were beginning to return. I sat myself down with pain and difficulty, for Azazel had bruised me all over, and I felt fearfully stiff and sore.

"Was it you who saved me?" I asked the shepherd.

"Yes, my boy, it was."

"Well, you are a good fellow, and I am much obliged to you. I withdraw the curse I laid upon your goat. Here, take this."

I handed him my purse with sixteen florins in it.

"Thank you, sir," said he, "and now you can begin again if you like on even ground. Down there it was not fair; the goat had all the advantage."

"Thank you very much! But I have had quite enough. Shake hands, old fellow; I'll never forget you. Let us go now."

My comrade and I, arm-in-arm, then descended the hill.

The shepherd, leaning on his crook, watched us till we disappeared. The goat had resumed his walk and his supper on the very edge of the crags. The sky was lovely, the air balmy with a thousand sweet mountain perfumes carried on it with the distant sounds of the shepherd's horn and the booming of the torrent.

We returned to Tubingen with our hearts full.

Since that time my friend Elias has found some comfort for slaying the Seigneur Kaspar, but in an original fashion.

Scarcely had he taken his doctor's degree when he married Mademoiselle Eva Salomon, with the hope of having a numerous family to make up for the loss of that individual who had met with an untimely end at his hand.

Four years ago I was at his wedding as best man, and already there are two fat babies making the pretty little house in Crispin street to rejoice.

This was a promising commencement!

Don't let me be misunderstood. I don't pretend to say that the method I prescribed for making expiation for taking away a life is better than that taught in our holy religion, which, according to the Catholic Church, consists in masses and in giving away your goods to the Church. But I do think it better than the Hindoo practice, and I think the theory of the famous scapegoat is not to be compared with that which is taught us by pure religion.

A NIGHT IN THE WOODS

CHAPTER I.

My worthy uncle, Bernard Hertzog, the historian and anti-quary, surmounted with his grand three-cornered hat and wig, and with a long iron-shod mountain-pole firmly grasped in his hand, was coming down one evening by the Luppersberg, hailing every turn in the landscape with enthusiastic exclamations.

Years had never quenched in him the love of knowledge. At sixty he was still at work upon his *History of Alsacian Antiquities*, and never allowed himself to write a complete account of a ruined and defaced monument, or any relic of former days, until he had examined it a hundred times from every point of view.

"No man," said he, "who has had the happy privilege of being born in the Vosges, between Haut Bar, Nideck, and Geierstein has any business to think of travelling. Where are there nobler forests, older fir and beech trees, more lovely smiling valleys, wilder rocks? Where is the country with richer possessions in memorable story? Here, in olden times, used the high and pow-erful lords of Lutzelstein, Dagsberg, Leiningen, and Fénétrange, to fight clad in mail from head to foot. Here the eldest son of the Church and the rulers of the Holy Roman Empire exchanged blows in the Middle Ages with swords two yards long. What are our wars compared with those terrible battles where warriors fought hand to hand, where they hammered upon each other's skulls with huge battle-axes, and drove the dagger between the bars of the closed visor? Were not those heroic feats of arms? was not that a courage worthy to be chronicled to all posterity? But our young people want to see new things; they are not satisfied with their own native land: they must wander through Germany, make tours in France. Worse still, they abandon science and its noble fields for trade, arts, industry, as if there had not been in the former glorious days much more curious industrial arts and pursuits than in our own day! Witness the Hanseatic League, the maritime enterprise of Venice, Genoa, and the Levant, Flemish manufactures, Florentine art, the triumphs in art of Rome and Antwerp! No! All that is laid aside; people nowadays pride them-selves upon their ignorance of those glorious days; above all, they neglect our dear old Alsace. Now, candidly, Theodore, don't all those tourists remind you of husbands leaving their fair sweet lawful wives to run after ugly coquettes?"

And Bernard Hertzog shook his learned head, his eyes rounded with wonder and excitement, just as if he had been standing before the ruins of Babylon.

His partiality to the usages and customs of old times accounted for his having, for forty years past, worn the full-skirted plush coat, the velvet breeches, the black silk stockings, and the silver shoe-buckles of our grandfathers. He would have thought himself disgraced had he put on trousers; and to cut off his pigtail would have been a profane deed.

So the worthy chronicler was going to Haslach on the 3rd of July, 1835, to examine with his own eyes a little bronze Mercury recently unearthed in the old cloister of the Augustins.

He trotted on with a tolerably elastic stop under a burning sun. Mountains succeeded mountains, valleys sank into other valleys, the footpath went up, then went down again, turned, now to the right, now to the left, until Maître Hertzog began to wonder how it was that he had not caught sight of the village spire an hour ago.

The fact was that after leaving Saverne he had inclined to the right, and was now penetrating into the Dagsberg woods with juvenile energy. At the rate he was going, in five or six hours he would have reached Phramond, eight leagues from his destination. But night was coming on apace, and the path was now becoming fainter, and under the tall trees only an indistinct track appeared.

The approach of night among the mountains is a melancholy sight; the shadows lengthen in the valleys, the sun withdraws, one by one, his rays from the darkening foliage, the silence deepens every minute. You look behind you; the groups and clumps of trees assume colossal proportions; a blackbird at the summit of a tree bids farewell to the parting day, then silence covers all like a funeral pall. You can only hear now the last year's dead leaves crisping under foot, and far, far, away a waterfall filling the valley with its monotonous hum. Bernard Hertzog began to pant a little; his clothes adhered to his skin with the running perspiration. His legs were beginning to give hints of surrendering.

"Confound that foolish Mercury!" he cried. "At this moment I ought to have been quiet at home in my own armchair, and Berbel, according to her praiseworthy custom, ought to be bringing me up upon a tray a cup of smoking hot coffee, while I am winding up my chapter upon the ancient armoury at Nideck. Instead of which, here I am floundering in holes, stumbling everywhere, and suppose I lost my way altogether and then broke my neck! There! — I said so! Was that a tree I knocked against? A hundred thousand bans and maledictions fall upon Mercury and Haas, the architect, who sent for me to look at it! And the scoundrels, too, who dug it up! I'll lay any wager that the boasted Mercury is nothing but some defaced and corroded bit of stone, without either nose or legs — some shapeless deformity like that little Hesus last year at Marienthal. Oh, you architects! You architects! — you are always finding antiquities everywhere. Luckily I had not my spectacles on, or I should have smashed them against that tree; but now I shall be obliged to find a bed somewhere among the bushes. What a road this is! — nothing but ruts, and holes, and pits, and loose rocks and boulders!"

In one of those moments when the good man, getting exhausted, was stopping for breath, he thought he could hear the grating of a saw far down the valley. What was his joy when he became certain that it was that!

"Heaven be praised!" he cried, plucking up his spirits; "now to push on with halting steps. Now I shall get a little rest. What a lesson this will be for me! Providence had compassion upon my rheumatism. What an old fool to go and expose myself to have to lie out in the woods at my time of life, to ruin my health and undermine my constitution! I shall remember this! Never shall I forget this warning!"

In a quarter of an hour the noise of falling water became more distinct; then a faint light broke through the trees. Maître Bernard then found himself at the top of the wood; he observed below the heath a stream running down the winding valley as far as he could see, and just before him the sawmill, with its long dark posts and beams crossing and recrossing in the gloom like a huge spider.

He crossed the high-arched bridge over the rushing dam, and looked through the little window into the woodman's hut.

It was a low, dark shed leaning against a hollow in the rock. At the farther end of the natural cavity was a small pile of smouldering sawdust. In the front the boarded roof, weighted with heavy stones, descended to within three feet of the ground; in a corner at the right, a kind of box, full of dried heather; a few logs of oak, an axe, a massive bench, and other implements of toil, were lost in the shade. A resinous odour of pine-wood impregnated the air, and the ruddy smoke eddied through a fissure in the rock.

Whilst the good man was observing these objects, the woodman, coming out from the mill, saw him, and cried —

"Halloo! — who is that?"

"I beg your pardon; pray pardon me," said my worthy uncle, rather startled. "I am a traveller who has lost his way."

"Hey!" cried the other man; "good guide us! Is not that Maître Bernard, of Saverne? You are very welcome indeed, Maître Bernard. Don't you know me?"

"No, indeed! How should I in this dark night?"

"*Parbleu!* — of course not! But I am Christian; I bring you your contraband snuff every fortnight. But come in, come in! We will soon get a light."

They passed stooping under the little low door, and the woodman, having lighted a pine-torch, stuck it into a split iron rod to serve as a candlestick, and a bright light, clear and white as moonshine, filled the hut, lighting up every corner of it.

Christian, standing in shirtsleeves, his broad chest uncovered, and with a pair of canvas trousers hitched up about his hips, looked a good-natured fellow enough; his tawny beard came down in a point to his waist; his huge bull head was covered with bristling brown hair; his small grey eyes inspired confidence.

"Take a seat, master," he said, rolling a log of wood before the fire. "Are you hungry?"

"Why, you know, my lad, your mountain air does excite one's appetite."

"Very well; you are just in time. I have got some very good potatoes quite at your service."

At the mention of potatoes Uncle Bernard could not help grimacing; he remembered, with the longing of affection, old Berbel's good suppers, and had a difficulty in coming down to the humble realities before him.

Christian seemed to take no notice; he took five or six potatoes out of a sack, and put them into the embers, taking care to cover them entirely; then, sitting down on the hearthstone, he lighted his pipe.

"But just tell me, master, how is it that you are here tonight, at six leagues' distance from Saverne, in the gorge of Nideck?"

"The gorge of Nideck!" cried my uncle Bernard, springing from his seat in great surprise.

"To be sure! You may see the ruins from here, about two gun-shots distant."

Master Bernard looked out, and really did recognise the ruins of Nideck, just as he had described them in the twenty-fourth chapter of his *History of Alsacian Antiquities*, with their high towers crumbling away at the foot, and dominating over the abyss into which the torrent falls.

"But I thought I was near Haslach!" he cried with amazement.

The woodcutter burst out laughing.

"Haslach! — you are two leagues away from it! I see how it is. You went wrong at the old oak-tree. You took the right instead of the left path. When you are in the woods you must look well about you. A few yards wrong at starting come to leagues at the end!"

Bernard Hertzog at this discovery was in consternation.

"Six leagues from Saverne," he murmured, "and all mountains! — and if I have to go two more tomorrow, that will be eight!"

"Oh, don't mind that! I will guide you to the road down the valley. And don't forget. You are very fortunate."

"Fortunate? You are joking with me, Christian."

"Yes, you are lucky. You might have had to spend the night in the woods. There is a thunderstorm coming on from Schnéeberg; if that had overtaken you you might have had some reason to complain, with the rain at your back and thunder and lightning all round. But now you shall sleep in a good bed," pointing to the box in the corner; "you will sleep there like a log, and tomorrow, when the sun is up, we will start; you will be rested, and you will get there in very good time."

"You are very kind, Christian," said Uncle Bernard with tears in his eyes. "Give me a potato, and then I will go to bed. I am more tired than anything else. I am not hungry. One hot potato will be quite enough for me."

"Here is a couple as mealy as chestnuts. Taste that, master; take a small glass of kirschwasser, and then lie down. I have to set to work again. I have got to saw fifteen more planks before I can go to bed."

Christian rose, set the bottle of kirschwasser on the windowsill, and went out. The alternate movement of the saw, which had for a time ceased, now recommenced amidst the rushing of the stream.

Maître Hertzog, astonished as he was to find himself in those remote solitudes between Dagsberg and the ruins of Nideck, sat long meditating what he must do to rejoin his household gods; then, gliding down the stream of his usual meditations, he went over the fabulous, heroic, or barbarous legends and chronicles of the former lords of that land. He went back to the Tribocci, that German nation settled about Strasbourg, remembering Clovis, Chilperic, Theodoric, Dagobert, the furious struggle between Brunehaut, Queen of Austrasia, and Frédégonde, queen of Chilperic of France, and many heroes and heroines besides. All these fierce personages passed in review before his eyes. The vague murmuring of the trees, the inky blackness of the rocks, favoured this strange invocation. All the distinguished personages of his chronicle were there, and the boar, and the wolf, and the bear were among them.

At last, unable to hold out any longer, the good man hung his three-cornered hat upon a peg in the wall and lay down upon the heath. The cricket sang its monotonous song upon the hearth, a few surviving sparks were running hither and thither in the smouldering fire, his eyelids dropped, and he slept a deep, sound sleep.

CHAPTER II.

Maître Bernard Hertzog had slept a couple of hours, and the boiling of the water in the millrace alone competed with the noise of his loud snoring, when suddenly a guttural voice, arising in the midst of the deep silence, cried —

"Dröckteufel! Dröckteufel! Have you forgotten everything?"

The voice was so piercing that Maître Bernard, waking with a sudden start, felt his hair creeping with horror. He raised himself upon his elbow and listened again with eyes starting with astonishment. The hut was as dark as a cellar; he listened, but not a breath, not a sound, came; only far away, far beyond the ruins, a dull, distant roar was heard among the mountains.

Bernard, with neck outstretched, heaved a deep sigh; in a minute he began to stammer out —

"Who is there? What do you want?"

But no answer came.

"It was a dream," he said, falling back upon his heather couch. "I must have been lying upon my back. There is nothing at all in dreams and nightmares — nothing! Nothing!"

But in the midst of the restored silence the same doleful cry was again repeated —

"Dröckteufel! Dröckteufel!"

And as Maître Bernard, fairly beside himself, was preparing for instant flight, but with his face to the wall, and unable to move from his couch, the voice, in a dissonant chant, with pauses and strange accents, went on —

"The Queen Faileube, espoused to our king, Chilperic — Queen Faileube, learning that Septimanie, the governess of the young princes, had conspired against the king's life — Queen Faileube said to the lord, 'My lord, the viper waits until you are asleep to give you a mortal wound. She has conspired with Sinnégisile and Gallomagus against your life! She has poisoned her husband, your faithful Jovius, to live with Dröckteufel. Let your anger come down upon her like lightning, and your vengeance with a bloody sword!' And Chilperic, assembling all his council in the castle of Nideck, said, 'We have cherished a viper; she has plotted our death. Let her be cut into three pieces. Let Dröckteufel, Sinnégisile, and Gallomagus perish with her! Let the ravens rejoice!' And the vassals cried, 'So let it be! The wrath of Chilperic is an abyss into which his enemies fall and perish!' Then Septimanie was brought to be put to the torture and examined; a ring of iron was bound around her temples; it was tightened; her eyes started; her blood-dropping mouth murmured, 'Lord king, I have offended. Dröckteufel, Gallomagus, and Sinnégisile have also conspired!' And the following night a festoon of corpses dangled and swung from the towers of Nideck! The foul birds of prey rejoiced over the rich spoil. Dröckteufel, what would I not have done for thee? I would have had thee King of Austrasia, and thou hast forgotten me!"

The guttural voice sank down, and my uncle Bernard, more dead than alive, breathing a sigh of terror, murmured —

"Oh, I have never done anybody any wrong! I am only a poor old chronicler! Let me not die without absolution, far from the succour of the Church!"

The great wooden box full of heather seemed at every effort to escape to sink deeper and deeper. The poor man thought he was going down into a gulf, when, happily, Christian reappeared, crying —

"Well, Maître Bernard, what did I say? here is the storm."

And now the hut was for an instant full of dazzling light, and my worthy uncle, who was lying facing the door, could see the whole valley lighted up, with its innumerable fir-trees crowded along the slopes down the valley as close as the grass of the fields, its rocks piled up on the banks of the river, which was rolling its sulphurous blue waves over the rounded boulders of the ravine, and the towers of Nideck rising proudly in the air fifteen hundred feet above.

Then the darkness covered all up again. That was the first flash.

But in that instant of time he caught sight of a strange figure crouching at the end of the hut without being able to make out what it really was.

Great drops were beginning to patter on the roof. Christian

lighted a rush, and seeing Maître Bernard with his hands convulsively clutching the edge of his box of heather, and his face covered with beads of cold sweat, he cried —

"Why! Master Bernard! What is the matter with you?"

But, without answering, he merely pointed to the figure huddled up in the corner; it was an old woman, so very advanced in extreme old age, so yellow and wrinkled, with such a hooked nose, fingers so skinny, and lips so lean, that she looked like an old owl with all its feathers gone. There were only a few hairs left on the back of her head; the rest of her skull was as bare of covering as an egg. A threadbare ragged linen gown covered her poor skeleton figure. She was sightless, and the expression of her face was one of constant reverie.

Christian, noticing my uncle's inquiring look, turned his head and said quietly —

"It's old Irmengarde, the old teller of legends. She is waiting to die till the old tower falls into the torrent."

Uncle Bernard, stupefied, looked at the woodman; he did not seem inclined to joke; on the contrary, he looked serious.

"Come, Christian," said the good man, "you mean to have your joke."

"Joke! No indeed, old and feeble as you see her, that old woman knows everything; the spirit of the ruins is in her. She was living when the old lords of the castle lived."

Now my old uncle was very nearly falling backwards at this astounding disclosure.

"But what do you mean?" he cried; "the castle of Nideck has been down these thousand years!"

"What if it was two thousand years?" said the woodman, making the sign of the cross as a new flash lighted up the valley; "what does that prove? The spirit of the ruins lives in her. A hundred and eight years Irmengarde has lived with this spirit in her. Before her it was in old Edith of Haslach; before Edith in some other —"

"Do you believe that?"

"Do I believe it! It is as sure, Master Bernard, as that the sun will be back in three hours' time. Death is night, life is day. After night comes day, then night again, and so on without end. The sun is the soul of the sky, the great spirit that is in us all, and the souls of the saints are like the stars which shine in the night, and which will never cease to return."

Bernard Hertzog replied not another word, but having risen, he began suspiciously to consider the aspect of that aged woman, who sat still in a niche carved out of the rock. He noticed above the niche some rough carving on the stone representing three trees with their branches touching, and forming a sort of crown; lower down were three toads cut in the granite. Three trees are the arms of the Tribocci (*dreien büchen*), three toads are the arms of the Merovingian kings.

What was the surprise of the old chronicler! Covetousness now took the place of alarm.

"Here," thought he, "is the oldest monument of the Frankish race in Gaul. That old woman reminds me of some fallen queen, left here a relic of ages long gone by. But how am I to carry the niche away?"

He began to consider.

Then was heard far away in the woods the trampling of the hoofs of many cattle and deep bellowing. The rain fell faster; the flashes of lightning, like flights of frightened birds in the dark, touched each other by the tips of their wings; one never waited for another to be gone, and the rolling of the thunder became incessant and terrible.

Soon the storm reached the very gorge of Nideck and hung over it closely, and swooped down with implacable fury; the explosions succeeded each other without intermission. It seemed as if the very mountains were falling.

At every fresh crash Uncle Bernard shrank, feeling as if the lightning were coming down his back.

"The first Triboceus who built a hut to cover his head was no fool," thought he. "He was a sensible man, with some experience of atmospheric changes. What would have become of us in this emergency had we not a roof over our heads? We should be greatly to be pitied. The invention of that Triboccus was quite as useful as that of the steam-engine; what a pity his name is not known!"

The worthy man had scarcely concluded his reflections when a young maiden of sixteen, wearing a very wide-brimmed straw hat, her white skirts dripping with rain and her little bare feet covered with sand, advanced to the doorstep, and said —

"The Lord bless you!"

"Amen," answered Christian solemnly.

This young girl was of the purest Scandinavian type, with cheeks of rose pink upon a face of pure whiteness, and long waving tresses, so fair and so silky that the finest wheat straw would hardly bear comparison with it. Her figure was tall and slender, and her blue eyes beamed with inexpressible sweetness.

Maître Bernard stood a few moments in rapt admiration, and

the woodman, kindly addressing the young girl, said —

"I am glad to see you, Fuldrade. Irmengarde is still asleep. What a storm it is! Is it coming to an end yet?"

"Yes, the wind is driving it down to the plain. It will be over before daylight."

Then, without looking at Maître Bernard, she went to sit before the old woman, who now seemed to revive.

"Fuldrade," she murmured, "is the great tower yet standing?"

"Yes."

The aged woman bowed her head, and her lips moved.

After the last thunderclaps the rain fell in torrents. All down the valley was heard an incessant loud beating of falling sheets of rain, and the rushing of the swollen stream, then, at intervals, after a brief cessation of rain, again the heavier dashing of repeated and more violent showers.

Between the heavy showers the tinkling which Uncle Bernard had distinguished in the distance when he awoke gradually became more distinct, and at last arrived under the window of the hut, and almost immediately five long-horned head of beautiful cows, spotted equally with white and black, appeared at the door.

"Why! Here's Waldine!" cried Christian, laughing; "she is looking for you, Fuldrade."

The gentle creature calmly and quietly came straight in, and seemed to examine old Irmengarde.

"Go away!" cried Fuldrade; "go along with the others!"

And the obedient heifer turned back to the cabin door.

But the falling floods seemed to give her matter for reflection, for she stood quietly there, contemplating the deluge, and slowly swinging her beautiful head, lowing in a deep, subdued tone.

The fresh air was now penetrating the hut and bringing with it the sweet perfumes of honeysuckle and wild roses, excited by the freshening rain. All the birds in the woods — redbreasts, thrushes, and blackbirds — formed a concert under the trees; the air was filled with the little love-tales of the happy birds and the fluttering of their eager wings.

Then Maître Bernard, recovering from his reverie, took a few paces outside, raised his eyes, and contemplated the white and fleecy clouds hastily crossing the still troubled sky. On the hill opposite he could see the whole herd of cattle, all lying sheltered beneath the overhanging rocks, some lazily extended, their knees bent beneath them, with sleepy eyes; others, with neck outstretched, lowing solemnly. A few young animals were gazing at the hanging festoons of honeysuckle, and seemed to enjoy the balmy air that wafted from them.

All these diverse forms and attitudes stood clearly out upon the reddish background of the rock; and the immense expanded vault of the cavern, with its setting of oak and pine whose twisted roots appeared where they had pierced through the rock, gave a majestic air of grandeur to the spectacle.

"Well, Maître Bernard," cried Christian, "it is broad daylight; had we not better start?"

Then, speaking to Fuldrade, who seemed buried in thought —

"Fuldrade, this old gentleman cannot drink our *kirschwasser*, yet I cannot offer him water. Have you anything better?"

Fuldrade took up a milk-pail, and, with an intelligent glance at Christian, went out.

"Wait a moment," she said; "I shall be here directly."

She rapidly tripped over the wet meadow; the drops of rain, collecting in the large leaves, poured about her feet in little crystal streams. At her approach to the cave the finest cows arose up as if to greet their young mistress. She patted them all, and, having seated herself, began to milk one, a fine white cow, which, standing motionless, with eyes half-closed, seemed grateful for the preference.

When her pail was full Fuldrade made haste back, and, presenting it to Bernard, said, smiling —

"Drink as much as you like; that is the way we drink milk warm from the cow in the country."

Which was done at once, the good man thanking her many times, and praising the excellence of this frothy milk, flavoured, as it were, with the wild aromatic plants of the Schnéeberg, Fuldrade seemed pleased with his eulogiums, and Christian, who had slipped on his blouse, standing behind them, staff in hand, waited for the end of these compliments before he cried —

"Now, master, en route! We have plenty of water now to turn the mill for six weeks without stopping, and I must be back by nine o'clock."

And they started, following the gravelly road under the hill.

"Adieu!" said Maître Bernard to the young girl, who gently bowed her head without speaking; "farewell! And may God make you always happy!"

The next day, about six in the evening, Bernard Hertzog, having returned to Saverne, was seated before his writing-desk, and describing in his chapter upon the antiquities of the Dagsberg, his discovery of the Merovingian arms in the woodman's hut in the Nideck. Then he went on to prove that the name of Tribocci, or Triboques, was derived from the German *drei büchen* — that is, three beeches. As a convincing proof, he referred to the three trees and the three toads of Nideck, which latter our kings have converted into three *fleurs-de-lis*.

All the antiquaries of Alsace envied him this admirable and interesting discovery. On both banks of the Rhine he was known as doctor, doctissimus, eruditus Bernardus, under which triumphal titles he dilated with honest pride, while he tried to bear his honours with becoming gravity.

And now, my dear friends, if you are curious to know what became of old Irmengarde, refer to the second volume of Bernard Hertzog's *Archeological Annals*, where under date July 16, 1836, you will find the following statement:

"The old teller of legends, Irmengarde, surnamed '*The Soul of the Ruins*,' died last night in the hut of the woodman Christian. Wonderful to relate, in the very same hour, almost the same minute, the principal tower of Nideck fell, and was washed away by the waterfall below.

"Such is the end of the most ancient monument known of Merovingian architecture, of which Schlosser, the historian, says," etc., etc.

THE QUEEN OF THE BEES

"As you go from Motiers-Navers to Boudry, on your way to Neufchatel," said the young professor of botany, "you follow a road between two walls of rocks of immense height; they reach a perpendicular elevation of five or six hundred feet, and are hung with wild plants, the mountain basil (thymus alpinus), ferus (polypodium), the whortleberry (vitis idoea), ground ivy, and other climbing plants producing a wonderful effect.

"The road winds along this defile; it rises, falls, turns, sometimes tolerably level, sometimes broken and abrupt, according to the thousand irregularities of the ground. Grey rocks almost meet in an arch overhead, others stand wide apart, leaving the distant blue visible, and discovering sombre and melancholy-looking depths, and rows of firs as far as the eye could reach.

"The Reuss flows along the bottom, sometimes leaping along in waterfalls, then creeping through thickets, or steaming, foaming, and thundering over precipices, while the echoes prolong the tumult and roar of its torrents in one immense endless hum. Since I left Tubingen the weather had continued fine; but when I reached the summit of this gigantic staircase, about two leagues distant from the little hamlet of Novisaigne, I suddenly noticed great grey clouds begin passing overhead, which soon filled up the defile entirely; this vapour was so dense that it soon penetrated my clothes as a heavy dew would have done.

"Although it was only two in the afternoon, the sky became clouded over as if darkness was coming on; and I foresaw a heavy storm was about to break over my head.

"I consequently began looking about for shelter, and I saw through one of those wide openings which afford you a perspective view of the Alps, about two or three hundred yards distant on the slope leading down to the lake, an ancient-looking grey châlet, moss-covered, with its small round windows and sloping roof loaded with large stones, its stairs outside the house, with a carved rail, and its basket-shaped balcony, on which the Swiss maidens generally hang their snowy linen and scarlet petticoats to dry.

"Precisely as I was looking down, a tall woman in a black cap was folding and collecting the linen which was blowing about in the wind.

"To the left of this building a very large apiary supported on beams, arranged like a balcony, formed a projection above the valley.

"You may easily believe that without the loss of a moment I set off bounding through the heather to seek for shelter from the coming storm, and well it was I lost no time, for I had hardly laid my hand on the handle of the door before the hurricane burst furiously overhead; every gust of wind seemed about to carry the cottage bodily away; but its foundations were strong, and the security of the good people within, by the warmth of their reception, completely reassured me about the probability of any accident.

"The cottage was inhabited by Walter Young, his wife Catherine, and little Raesel, their only daughter.

"I remained three days with them; for the wind, which went down about midnight, had so filled the valley of Neufchatel with mist, that the mountain where I had taken refuge was completely enveloped in it; it was impossible to walk twenty yards from the door without experiencing great difficulty in finding it again.

"Every morning these good people would say, when they saw me buckle on my knapsack —

"'What are you about, Mr. Hennetius? You cannot mean to go yet; you will never arrive anywhere. In the name of Heaven stay here a little longer!'

"And Young would open the door and exclaim —

"'Look there, sir; you must be tired of your life to risk it among these rocks. Why, the dove itself would be troubled to find the ark again in such a mist as this.'

"One glance at the mountain side was enough for me to make up my mind to put my stick back again in the corner.

"Walter Young was a man of the old times. He was nearly sixty; his grand head wore a calm and benevolent expression — a real Apostle's head. His wife, who always wore a black silk cap, pale and thoughtful, resembled him much in disposition. Their two profiles, as I looked at them defined sharply against the little panes of glass in the chalet's windows, recalled to my mind those drawings of Albert Durer the sight of which carried me back to the age of faith and the patriarchal manners of the fifteenth century. The long brown rafters of the ceiling, the deal table, the ashen chairs with the carved backs, the tin drinking-cups, the sideboard with its old-fashioned painted plates and dishes, the crucifix with the Saviour carved in box on an ebony cross, and the worm-eaten clock-case with its many weights and its porcelain dial, completed the illusion.

"But the face of their little daughter Raesel was still more touching. I think I can see her now, with her flat horsehair cap and watered black silk ribbons, her trim bodice and broad blue sash down to her knees, her little white hands crossed in the attitude of a dreamer, her long fair curls — all that was graceful, slender, and ethereal in nature. Yes, I can see Raesel now, sitting in a large leathern armchair, close to the blue curtain of the recess at the end of the room, smiling as she listened and meditated.

"Her sweet face had charmed me from the first moment I saw her and I was continually on the point of inquiring why she wore such an habitually melancholy air, why did she hold her pale face down so invariably, and why did she never raise her eyes when spoken to?

"Alas! The poor child had been blind from her birth.

"She had never seen the lake's vast expanse, nor its blue sheet blending so harmoniously with the sky, the fishermen's boats which ploughed its surface, the wooded heights which crowned it and cast their quivering reflection on its waters, the rocks covered with moss, the green Alpine plants in their vivid and brilliant colouring; nor had she ever watched the sun set behind the glaciers, nor the long shades of evening draw across the valleys, nor the golden broom, nor the endless heather — nothing. None of these things had she ever seen; nothing of what we saw every day from the windows of the chalet.

"'What an ironical commentary on the gifts of Fortune!' thought I, as I sat looking out of the window at the mist, in expectation of the sun's appearing once more, 'to be blind in this place! Here in presence of Nature in its sublimest form, of such limitless grandeur! To be blind! Oh, Almighty God, who shall dare to dispute Thy impenetrable decrees, or who shall venture to murmur at the severity of Thy justice, even when its weight falls on an innocent child? But to be thus blind in the presence of Thy grandest creations, of creations which ceaselessly renew our enthusiasm, our love, and our adoration for Thy genius, Thy power, and Thy goodness; of what crime can this poor child have been guilty thus to deserve Thy chastisement?'

"And my reflections continually reverted to this topic.

"I asked myself, too, what compensation Divine pity could make its creature for the deprival of its greatest blessing, and, finding none, I began to doubt its power.

"'Man, in his presumption,' said the royal poet, 'dares to glorify himself in his knowledge, and judge the Eternal. But his wisdom is but folly, and his light darkness.'

"Oh that day one of Nature's great mysteries was revealed to me, doubtless with the purpose of humbling my vanity, and of teaching me that nothing is impossible to God, and that it is in His power only to multiply our senses, and by so doing gratify those who please Him."

Here the young professor took a pinch from his tortoiseshell snuffbox, raised his eyes to the ceiling with a contemplative air, and then, after a short pause, continued in these terms:

"Does it not often happen to you, ladies, when you are in the country in fine weather in summer, especially after a brief storm, when the air is warm, and the exhalations from the ground filling it with the perfume of thousands of plants, and their sweet scent penetrates and warms you; when the foliage from the trees in the solitary avenues, as well as from the bushes, seems to lean over you as if it sought to take you in its arms and embrace you; when the minutest flowers, the humble daisy, the blue forget-me-not, the convolvulus in the hedgerows raise their heads and follow you with a longing look — does it not happen to you to experience an inexpressible sensation of languor, to sigh for no apparent reason, and even to feel inclined to shed tears, and to ask yourselves, 'Why does this feeling of love oppress me? why do my knees bend under me? whence these tears?'

"Whence indeed, ladies? Why from life, and the thousands of living things which surround you, lean to you, and call to you to stay with them, while they gently murmur, 'We love you; love us, and do not leave us.'

"You can easily imagine, then, the deep enthusiastic feeling and the religious sentiment of a person always in a similar state of ecstasy. Even if blind, abandoned by his friends, do you think there is nothing to envy in his lot? or that his destiny is not infinitely happier than our own? For my own part I have not the slightest doubt of it.

"But you will, doubtless, say such a condition is impossible — the mind of man would break down under such a load of happiness. And, moreover, whence could such happiness be derived? What organs could transmit, and where could it find, such a sensation of universal life?

"This, ladies, is a question to which I can give you no answer; but I ask you to listen and then judge.

"The very day I arrived at the chalet I had made a singular remark — the blind girl was especially uneasy about the bees.

"While the wind was roaring without Raesel sat with her head on her hands listening attentively.

"'Father,' said she, 'I think at the end of the apiary the third hive on the right is still open. Go and see. The wind blows from the north; all the bees are home; you can shut the hive.'

"And her father having gone out by a side door, when he returned he said —

"'It is all right, my child; I have closed the hive.'

"Half an hour afterwards the girl, rousing herself once more from her reverie, murmured —

"'There are no more bees about, but under the roof of the apiary there are some waiting; they are in the sixth hive near the door; please go and let them in, father.'

"The old man left the house at once. He was away more than a quarter of an hour; then he came back and told his daughter that everything was as she wished it — the bees had just gone into their hive.

"The child nodded, and replied —

"'Thank you, father.'

"Then she seemed to doze again.

"I was standing by the stove, lost in a labyrinth of reflections; how could that poor blind girl know that from such or such a hive there were still some bees absent, or that such a hive had been left open? This seemed inexplicable to me; but having been in the house hardly one hour, I did not feel justified in asking my hosts any questions with regard to their daughter, for it is sometimes painful to talk to people on subjects which interest them very nearly. I concluded that Young gave way to his daughter's fancies in order to induce her to believe she was of some service in the family, and that her forethought protected the bees from several accidents. That seemed the simplest explanation I could imagine, and I thought no more about it.

"About seven we supped on milk and cheese, and when it was time to retire Young led me into a goodsized room on the first floor, with a bed and a few chairs in it, panelled in fir, as is generally the case in the greater number of Swiss châlets. You are only separated from your neighbours by a deal partition, and you can hear every footstep and nearly every word.

"That night I was lulled to sleep by the whistling of the wind and the sound of the rain beating against the windowpanes. The next day the wind had gone down and we were enveloped in mist. When I awoke I found my windows quite white, quite padded with mist. When I opened my window the valley looked like an immense stove; the tops of a few fir-trees alone showed their outlines against the sky; below, the clouds were in regular layers down to the surface of the lake; everything was calm, motionless, and silent.

"When I went down to the sitting-room I found my hosts seated at table, about to begin breakfast.

"'We have been waiting for you,' cried Young gaily.

"'You must excuse us,' said the mother; 'this is our regular breakfast hour.'

"'Of course, of course; I am obliged to you for not noticing my laziness.'

"Raesel was much more lively than the preceding evening; she had a fresh colour in her cheeks.

"'The wind has gone down,' said she; 'the storm has passed away without doing any harm.'

"'Shall I open the apiary?' asked Young.

"'No, not yet; the bees would lose themselves in this mist. Besides, everything is drenched with rain; the brambles and mosses are full of water; the least puff of wind would drown many of them. We must wait a little while. I know what is the matter: they feel dull, they want to work; they are tormented at the idea of devouring their honey instead of making it. But I cannot afford to lose them. Many of the hives are weak — they would starve in winter. We will see what the weather is like tomorrow.'

"The two old people sat and listened without making any observations.

"About nine the blind girl proposed to go and visit her bees; Young and Catherine followed her, and I did the same, from a very natural feeling of curiosity.

"We passed through the kitchen by a door which opened on to a terrace. Above us was the roof of the apiary; it was of thatch, and from its ledge honeysuckle and wild grapes hung in magnificent festoons. The hives were arranged on three shelves.

"Raesel went from one to the other, patting them, and murmuring —

"'Have a little patience; there is too much mist this morning. Ah! The greedy ones, how they grumble!'

"And we could hear a vague humming inside the hive, which increased in intensity until she had passed.

"That awoke all my curiosity once more. I felt there was some strange mystery which I could not fathom, but what was my surprise, when, as I went into the sitting-room, I heard the blind girl say in a melancholy tone of voice —

"'No, father, I would rather not see at all today than lose my eyes. I will sing, I will do something or other to pass the time, never mind what; but I will not let the bees out.'

"While she was speaking in this strange manner I looked at Walter Young, who glanced out of the window and then quietly replied —

"'You are right, child; I think you are right. Besides, there is nothing to see; the valley is quite white. It is not worth looking at.'

"And while I sat astounded at what I heard, the child continued —

"'What lovely weather we had the day before yesterday! Who would have thought that a storm on the lake would have caused all this mist? Now one must fold up its wings and crawl about like a wretched caterpillar.'

"Then again, after a few moments' silence —

"'How I enjoyed myself under the lofty pines on the Grinderwald! How the honey-dew dropped from the sky! It fell from every branch. What a harvest we made, and how sweet the air was on the shores of the lake, and in the rich Tannemath pastures — the green moss, and the sweet-smelling herbs! I sang, I laughed, and we filled our cells with wax and honey. How delightful to be everywhere, see everything, to fly humming about the woods, the mountains, and the valleys!'

"There was a fresh silence, while I sat, with mouth and eyes open, listening with the greatest attention, not knowing what to think or what to say.

"'And when the shower came,' she went on, 'how frightened we were! A great humble-bee, sheltered under the same fern as myself, shut his eyes at every flash; a grasshopper had sheltered itself under its great green branches, and some poor little crickets had scrambled up a poppy to save themselves from drowning. But what was most frightful was a nest of warblers quite close to us in a bush. The mother hovered round about us, and the little ones opened their beaks, yellow as far as their windpipes. How frightened we were! Good Lord, we were frightened indeed! Thanks be to Heaven, a puff of wind carried us off to the mountain side; and now the vintage is over we must not expect to get out again so soon.'

"On hearing these descriptions of Nature so true, at this worship of day and light, I could no longer entertain the least doubt on the subject.

"'The blind girl sees,' said I to myself; 'she sees through thousands of eyes; the apiary is her life, her soul. Every bee carries a part of her away into space, and then returns drawn to her by thousands of invisible threads. The blind girl penetrates the flowers and the mosses; she revels in their perfume; when the sun shines she is everywhere; in the mountain side, in the valleys, in the forests, as far as her sphere of attraction extends.'

"I sat confounded at this strange magnetic influence, and felt tempted to exclaim —

"'Honour, glory, honour to the power, the wisdom, and the infinite goodness of the Eternal God! For Him nothing is impossible. Every day, every instant of our lives reveals to us His magnificence.'

"While I was lost in these enthusiastic reflections, Raesel addressed me with a quiet smile.

"'Sir,' said she.

"'What, my child?'

"'You are very much surprised at me, and you are not the first person who has been so. The rector Hegel, of Neufchatel, and other travellers have been here on purpose to see me: they thought I was blind. You thought so too, did you not?'

"'I did indeed, my dear child, and I thank the Lord that I was mistaken.'

"'Yes,' said she, 'I know you are a good man — I can tell it by your voice. When the sun shines I shall open my eyes to look at you, and when you leave here I will accompany you to the foot of the mountain.'

"Then she began to laugh most artlessly.

"'Yes,' said she, 'you shall have music in your ears, and I will seat myself on your cheek; but you must take care — take care. You must not touch me, or I should sting you. You must promise not to be angry.'

"'I promise you, Raesel, I promise you I will not,' I said with tears in my eyes, 'and, moreover, I promise you never to kill a bee or any other insect except those which do harm.'

"'They are the eyes of the Lord,' she murmured. 'I can only see by my own poor bees, but He has every hive, every ant's nest, every leaf, every blade of grass. He lives, He feels, He loves, He suffers, He does good by means of all these. Oh, Monsieur Hennetius, you are right not to pain the Lord, who loves us so much!'

"Never in my life had I been so moved and affected, and it was a full minute before I could ask her —

"'So, my dear child, you see by your bees; will you explain to me how that is?'

"'I cannot tell, Monsieur Hennetius; it may be because I am so fond of them. When I was quite a little child they adopted me, and they have never once hurt me. At first I liked to sit for hours in the apiary all alone and listen to their humming for hours together. I could see nothing then, everything was dark to me; but insensibly light came upon me. At first I could see the sun a little, when it was very hot, then a little more, with the wild vine and the honeysuckle like a shade over me, then the full light of day. I began to emerge from myself; my spirit went forth with the bees. I could see the mountains, the rocks, the lake, the flowers and mosses, and in the evening, when quite alone, I reflected on these things. I thought how beautiful they were, and when people talked of this and that, of whortleberries, and mulberries, and heaths, I said to myself, 'I know what all these things are like — they are black, or brown, or green.' I could see them in my mind, and every day I became better acquainted with them, thanks to my dear bees; and therefore I love them dearly, Monsieur Hennetius. If you knew how it grieves me when the time comes for robbing them of their wax and their honey!'

"'I believe you, my child — I believe it does.'

"My delight at this wonderful discovery was boundless.

"Two days longer Raesel entertained me with a description of her impressions. She was acquainted with every flower, every Alpine plant, and gave me an account of a great number which have as yet received no botanical names, and which are probably only to be found in inaccessible situations.

"The poor girl was often much affected when she spoke of her dear friends, some little flowers.

"'Often and often,' said she, 'I have talked for hours with the golden broom or the tender blue-eyed forget-me-not, and shared in their troubles. They all wished to quit the Earth and fly about; they all complained of their being condemned to dry up in the ground, and of being exposed to wait for days and weeks ere a drop of dew came to refresh them.'

"And so Raesel used to repeat to me endless conversations of this sort. It was marvellous! If you only heard her you would be capable of falling in love with a dogrose, or of feeling a lively sympathy and a profound sentiment of compassion for a violet, its misfortunes and its silent sufferings.

"What more can I tell you, ladies? It is painful to leave a subject where the soul has so many mysterious emanations; there is such a field for conjecture; but as everything in this world must have an end, so must even the pleasantest dreams.

"Early in the morning of the third day of my stay a gentle breeze began to roll away the mist from off the lake. I could see its folds become larger every second as the wind drove them along, leaving one blue corner in the sky, and then another; then the tower of a village church, some green pinnacles on the tops of the mountains, then a row of firs, a valley, all the time the immense mass of vapour slowly floated past us; by ten it had left us behind it, and the great cloud on the dry peaks of the Chasseron still wore a threatening aspect; but a last effort of the wind gave it a different direction, and it disappeared at last in the gorges of Saint-Croix.

"Then the mighty nature of the Alps seemed to me to have grown young again; the heather, the tall pines, the old chestnut-trees dripping with dew, shone with vigorous health; there was something in the view of them joyous, smiling, and serious all at once. One felt the hand of God was in it all — His eternity.

"I went downstairs lost in thought; Raesel was already in the apiary. Young opened the door and pointed her out to me sitting in the shade of the wild vine, with her forehead resting on her hands, as if in a doze.

"'Be careful,' said he to me, 'not to awake her; her mind is elsewhere; she sleeps; she is wandering about; she is happy.'

"The bees were swarming about by thousands, like a flood of gold over a precipice.

"I looked on at this wonderful sight for some seconds, praying the Lord would continue His love for the poor child.

"Then turning round —

"'Master Young,' said I, 'it is time to go.'

"He buckled my knapsack on for me himself, and put my stick into my hand.

"Mistress Catherine looked on kindly, and they both accompanied me to the threshold of the châlet.

"'Farewell!' said Walter, grasping my hand; 'a pleasant journey; and think of us sometimes!'

"'I can never forget you,' I replied, quite melancholy; 'may your bees flourish, and may Heaven grant you are as happy as you deserve to be!'

"'So be it, M. Hennetius,' said good Dame Catherine; 'amen; a happy journey, and good health to you.'

"I moved off.

"They remained on the terrace until I reached the road.

"Thrice I turned round and waved my cap, and they responded by waving their hands.

"Good people; why cannot we meet with such every day?'

"Little Raesel accompanied me to the foot of the mountain, as she had promised. For a long time her musical hum lightened the fatigue of my journey; I seemed to recognise her in every bee which came buzzing about my ears, and I fancied I could hear her say in a small shrill tone of voice —

"'Courage, M. Hennetius, courage; it is very hot, is it not? Come, let me give you a kiss; don't be afraid; you know we are very good friends.'

"It was only at the end of the valley that she took leave of me, when the sound of the lake drowned her gentle voice; but her idea followed me all through my journey, nor do I think it will ever leave me."

THE INVISIBLE EYE

CHAPTER I

When I first started my career as an artist, I took a room in the roof-loft of an old house in the Rue des Minnesängers, at Nuremberg.

I had made my nest in an angle of the roof. The slates served me for walls, and the roof-tree for a ceiling: I had to walk over my straw mattress to reach the window; but this window commanded a magnificent view, for it overlooked both city and country beyond.

The old second-hand dealer, Toubec, knew the road up to my little den as well as I knew it myself, and was not afraid of climbing the ladder. Every week his goat's head, surmounted by a rusty wig, pushed up the trapdoor, his fingers clutched the edge of the floor, and in a noisy tone he cried —

"Well, well, Master Christian, have we anything new?"

To which I answered —

"Come in: why the deuce don't you come in? I'm just finishing a little landscape, and want to have your opinion of it."

Then his long thin spine lengthened itself out, until his head touched the roof; and the old fellow laughed silently.

I must do justice to Toubec: he never bargained with me. He bought all my pictures at fifteen forms apiece, one with the other, and sold them again at forty. He was an honest Jew.

This kind of existence was beginning to please me, and I was every day finding in it some new charm, when the city of Nuremberg was agitated by a strange and mysterious event.

Not far from my garret-window, a little to the left, rose the auberge of the Boeuf-gras, an old inn much frequented by the country-people. The gable of this auberge was conspicuous for the peculiarity of its form: it was very narrow, sharply pointed, and its edges were cut like the teeth of a saw; grotesque carvings ornamented the cornices and framework of its windows. But what was most remarkable was that the house which faced it reproduced exactly the same carvings and ornaments; every detail had been minutely copied, even to the support of the signboard, with its iron volutes and spirals.

It might have been said that these two ancient buildings reflected one another; only that behind the inn grew a tall oak, the dark foliage of which served to bring into bold relief the forms of the roof, while the opposite house stood bare against the sky. For the rest, the inn was as noisy and animated as the other house was silent. On the one side was to be seen, going in and coming out, an endless crowd of drinkers, singing, stumbling, cracking their whips; over the other, solitude reigned.

Once or twice a day the heavy door of the silent house opened to give egress to a little old woman, her back bent into a half-circle, her chin long and pointed, her dress clinging to her limbs, an enormous basket under her arm, and one hand tightly clutched upon her chest.

This old woman's appearance had struck me more than once; her little green eyes, her skinny, pinched-up nose, her shawl, dating back a hundred years at least; the smile that wrinkled her cheeks, and the lace of her cap hanging down upon her eyebrows — all this appeared strange, interested me, and made me strongly desire to learn who this old woman was and what she did in her great lonely house.

I imagined her as passing there an existence devoted to good works and pious meditation. But one day, when I had stopped in the street to look at her, she turned sharply round and darted at me a look the horrible expression of which I know not how to describe, and made three or four hideous grimaces at me; then dropping again her doddering head, she drew her large shawl about her, the ends of which trailed after her on the ground, and slowly entered her heavy door.

"That's an old madwoman," I said to myself; "a malicious, cunning old madwoman! I ought not to have allowed myself to be so interested in her. But I'll try and recall her abominable grimace — Toubec will give me fifteen forms for it willingly."

This way of treating the matter was far from satisfying my mind, however. The old woman's horrible glance pursued me everywhere; and more than once, while scaling the perpendicular ladder of my lodging-hole, feeling my clothes caught in a nail, I trembled from head to foot, believing that the old woman had seized me by the tails of my coat for the purpose of pulling me down backwards.

Toubec, to whom I related the story, far from laughing at it, received it with a serious air.

"Master Christian," he said, "if the old woman means you harm, take care; her teeth are small, sharp-pointed, and wonderfully white, which is not natural at her age. She has the Evil Eye! Children run away at her approach, and the people of Nuremberg call her Fledermausse!"

I admired the Jew's clear-sightedness, and what he had told me made me reflect a good deal; but at the end of a few weeks, having often met Fledermausse without harmful consequences, my fears died away and I thought no more of her.

One night, when I was lying sound asleep, I was awoken by a strange harmony. It was a kind of vibration, so soft, so melodious, that the murmur of a light breeze through foliage can convey but a feeble idea of its gentle nature. For a long time I listened to it, my eyes wide open, and holding my breath the better to hear it.

At length, looking towards the window, I saw two wings beating against the glass. I thought, at first, that it was a bat imprisoned in my chamber; but the moon was shining clearly, and showed the wings of a magnificent night-moth, transparent as lace. At times their vibrations were so rapid as to hide them from my view; then for a while they would lie in repose, extended on the glass pane, their delicate articulations made visible anew.

This vaporous apparition in the midst of the universal silence opened my heart to the tenderest emotions; it seemed to me that a sylphid, pitying my solitude, had come to see me; and this idea brought the tears into my eyes.

"Have no fear, gentle captive — have no fear!" I said to it; "your confidence shall not be betrayed. I will not retain you against your wishes; return to Heaven — to liberty!"

And I opened the window.

The night was calm. Thousands of stars glittered in space. For a moment I contemplated this sublime spectacle, and the words of prayer rose naturally to my lips. But then, looking down, I saw a man hanging from the iron stanchion which supported the sign of the Boeuf-gras; the hair in disorder, the arms stiff, the legs straightened to a point, and throwing their gigantic shadow the whole length of the street.

The immobility of this figure, in the moonlight, had something frightful in it. I felt my tongue grow icy cold, and my teeth chattered. I was about to utter a cry; but by what mysterious attraction I know not, my eyes were drawn towards the opposite house, and there I dimly distinguished the old woman, in the midst of the heavy shadow, squatting at her window and contemplating the hanging body with diabolical satisfaction.

I became giddy with terror; my strength deserted me, and I fell down in a heap insensible.

I do not know how long I lay unconscious. On coming to myself I found it was broad day.

Mingled and confused noises rose from the street below. I

looked out from my window.

The burgomaster and his secretary were standing at the door of the Boeuf-gras; they remained there a long time. People came and went, stopped to look, then passed on their way. At length a stretcher, on which lay a body covered with a woollen cloth, was brought out and carried away by two men.

Then everyone else disappeared.

The window in front of the house remained open still; a fragment of rope dangled from the iron support of the signboard. I had not dreamed — I had really seen the night-moth on my window-pane — then the suspended body — then the old woman!

In the course of that day Toubec paid me his weekly visit.

"Anything to sell, Master Christian?" he cried.

I did not hear him. I was seated on my only chair, my hands upon my knees, my eyes fixed on vacancy before me. Toubec, surprised at my immobility, repeated in a louder tone, "Master Christian! — Master Christian!" then, stepping up to me, tapped me smartly on the shoulder.

"What's the matter? — what's the matter? Are you ill?" he asked.

"No — I was thinking."

"What the deuce about?"

"The man who was hung —"

"Aha!" cried the old broker; "you saw the poor fellow, then? What a strange affair! The third in the same place!"

"The third?"

"Yes, the third. I ought to have told you about it before; but there's still time — for there's sure to be a fourth, following the example of the others, the first step only making the difficulty."

This said, Toubec seated himself on a box and lit his pipe with a thoughtful air.

"I'm not timid," said he, "but if anyone were to ask me to sleep in that room, I'd rather go and hang myself somewhere else! Nine or ten months back," he continued, "a wholesale furrier, from Tubingen, put up at the Boeuf-gras. He called for supper, ate well, drank well, and was shown up to bed in the room on the third floor which they call the 'green chamber.' The next day they found him hanging from the stanchion of the sign.

"So much for number one, about which there was nothing to be said. A proper report of the affair was drawn up, and the body of the stranger buried at the bottom of the garden. But about six weeks afterwards came a soldier from Neustadt; he had his discharge and was congratulating himself on his return to his village. All the evening he did nothing but empty mugs of wine and talk of his cousin, who was waiting his return to marry him. At last they put him to bed in the green chamber, and the same night the watchman passing along the Rue des Minnesängers noticed something hanging from the signboard-stanchion. He raised his lantern; it was the soldier, with his discharge-papers in a tin box hanging on his left thigh, and his hands planted smoothly on the outer seams of his trousers, as if he had been on parade!

"It was certainly an extraordinary affair! The burgomaster declared it was the work of the devil.

The chamber was examined; they replastered its walls. A notice of the death was sent to Neustadt, on the margin of which the clerk wrote — "Died suddenly of apoplexy."

"All Nuremberg was indignant against the landlord of the Boeuf-gras, and wished to compel him to take down the iron stanchion of his signboard, on the pretext that it put dangerous ideas in people's heads. But you may easily imagine that old Nikel Schmidt didn't listen with the ear on that side of his head.

"'That stanchion was put there by my grandfather,' he said; 'the sign of the Boeuf-gras has hung on it from father to son, for a hundred and fifty years; it does nobody any harm, it's more than thirty feet up; those who don't like it have only to look another way."

"People's excitement gradually cooled down, and for several months nothing happened. Unfortunately, a student from Heidelberg, on his way to the University, came to the Boeuf-gras and asked for a bed. He was the son of a pastor.

"Who could suppose that the son of a pastor would take into his head the idea of hanging himself to the stanchion of a public-house sign, because a furrier and a soldier had hung themselves there before him? It must be confessed, Master Christian, that the thing was not very probable — it would not have appeared more likely to you than it did to me. Well —"

"Enough! enough!" I cried; "it is a horrible affair. I feel sure there is some frightful mystery at the bottom of it. It is neither the stanchion nor the chamber —"

"You don't mean that you suspect the landlord? — as honest a man as there is in the world, and belonging to one of the oldest families in Nuremberg?"

"No, no! Heaven keep me from forming unjust suspicions of anyone; but there are abysses into the depths of which one dares not look."

"You are right," said Toubec, astonished at my excited

manner; "and we had much better talk of something else. By the way, Master Christian, what about our landscape, the view of Sainte-Odile?"

The question brought me back to actualities. I showed the broker the picture I had just finished.

The business was soon settled between us, and Toubec, thoroughly satisfied, went down the ladder, advising me to think no more of the student of Heidelberg.

I would very willingly have followed the old broker's advice, but when the devil mixes himself up with our affairs he is not easily shaken off.

CHAPTER II

In solitude, all these events came back to my mind with frightful distinctness.

The old woman, I said to myself, is the cause of all this; she alone has planned these crimes, she alone has carried them into execution; but by what means? Has she had recourse to cunning only or really to the intervention of the invisible powers?

I paced my garret, a voice within me crying, "It is not without purpose that Heaven has permitted you to see Fledermausse watching the agony of her victim; it was not without design that the poor young man's soul came to wake you in the form of a night-moth! No! All this has not been without purpose. Christian, Heaven imposes on you a terrible mission; if you fail to accomplish it, fear that you yourself may fall into the toils of the old woman! Perhaps at this moment she is laying her snares for you in the darkness!"

During several days these frightful images pursued me without cessation. I could not sleep; I found it impossible to work; the brush fell from my hand, and, shocking to confess, I detected myself at times complacently contemplating the dreadful stanchion. At last, one evening, unable any longer to bear this state of mind, I flew down the ladder four steps at a time, and went and hid myself beside Fledermausse's door, for the purpose of discovering her fatal secret.

From that time there was never a day that I was not on the watch, following the old woman like her shadow, never losing sight of her; but she was so cunning, she had so keen a scent that without even turning her head she discovered that I was behind her, and knew that I was on her track. But nevertheless, she pretended not to see me — went to the market, to the butcher's, like a simple housewife; only she quickened her pace and muttered to herself as she went.

At the end of a month I saw that it would be impossible for me to achieve my purpose by these means, and this conviction filled me with an inexpressible sadness.

"What can I do?" I asked myself. "The old woman has discovered my intentions and is thoroughly on her guard. I am helpless. The old wretch already thinks she sees me at the end of the cord!"

At length, from repeating to myself again and again the question, "What can I do?" a luminous idea presented itself to my mind.

My chamber overlooked the house of Fledermausse, but it had no dormer window on that side.

I carefully raised one of the slates of my roof, and the delight I felt on discovering that by this means I could command a view of the entire antique building can hardly be imagined.

"At last I've got you!" I cried to myself; "you cannot escape me now! From here I shall see everything. You will not suspect this invisible eye — this eye that will surprise the crime at the moment of its inception! Oh, Justice! It moves slowly, but it comes!"

Nothing more sinister than this den could be imagined — a large yard, paved with moss-grown flagstones; a well in one corner, the stagnant water of which was frightful to behold; a wooden staircase leading up to a railed gallery, to the left; on the first floor, a drain-stone indicated the kitchen; to the right, the upper windows of the house looked into the street. All was dark, decaying, and dank-looking.

The sun penetrated only for an hour or two during the day the depths of this dismal sty; then the shadows again spread over it — the light fell in lozenge shapes upon the crumbling walls, on the mouldy balcony, on the dull windows.

Oh, the whole place was worthy of its mistress!

I had hardly made these reflections when the old woman entered the yard on her return from market. First, I heard her heavy door grate on its hinges, then Fledermausse, with her basket, appeared. She seemed fatigued — out of breath. The border of her cap hung down upon her nose, as, clutching the wooden rail with one hand, she mounted the stairs.

The heat was suffocating. It was exactly one of those days when insects of every kind — crickets, spiders, mosquitoes — fill old buildings with their grating noises and subterranean borings.

Fledermausse crossed the gallery slowly, like a ferret that feels itself at home. For more than a quarter of an hour she remained in the kitchen, then came out and swept the stones a little, on which a few straws had been scattered; at last she raised her head, with her green eyes carefully scrutinised every portion of the roof from which I was observing her.

By what strange intuition did she suspect anything? I know not; but I gently lowered the uplifted slate into its place, and gave over watching for the rest of that day.

The day following Fledermausse appeared to be reassured. A jagged ray of light fell into the gallery; passing this, she caught a fly, and delicately presented it to a spider established in an angle of the roof.

The spider was so large that, in spite of the distance, I saw it descend, then gliding along one thread, like a drop of venom, seize its prey from the fingers of the dreadful old woman and remount rapidly. Fledermausse watched it attentively; then her eyes half-closed, she sneezed, and cried to herself in a jocular tone —

"Bless you, beauty! — bless you!"

For six weeks I could discover nothing as to the power of Fledermausse: sometimes I saw her peeling potatoes, sometimes spreading her linen on the balustrade. Sometimes I saw her spin; but she never sang, as old women usually do, their quivering voices going so well with the humming of the spinning-wheel. Silence reigned about her. She had no cat — the favourite company of old maids; not a sparrow ever flew down to her yard, in passing over which the pigeons seemed to hurry their flight. It seemed as if everything feared her look.

The spider alone took pleasure in her society.

I now look back with wonder at my patience during those long hours of observation; nothing escaped my attention, nothing was indifferent to me; at the least sound I lifted my slate. Mine was a boundless curiosity stimulated by an indefinable fear.

Toubec complained.

"What the devil are you doing with your time, Master Christian?" he would say to me. "Formerly, you had something ready for me every week; now, hardly once in a month. Oh, you painters! As soon as they have a few kreutzer before them, they put their hands in their pockets and go to sleep!"

I myself was beginning to lose courage. With all my watching and spying, I had discovered nothing extraordinary. I was inclining to think that the old woman might not be so dangerous after all — that I had been wrong, perhaps, to suspect her. In short, I tried to find excuses for her.

But one fine evening while, with my eye to the opening in the roof, I was giving myself up to these charitable reflections, the scene abruptly changed.

Fledermausse passed along her gallery with the swiftness of a flash of light. She was no longer herself: she was erect, her jaws knit, her look fixed, her neck extended; she moved with long strides, her grey hair streaming behind her.

"Oh, oh!" I said to myself, "something is going on!"

But the shadows of night descended on the big house, the noises of the town died out, and all became silent. I was about to seek my bed, when, happening to look out of my skylight, I saw a light in the window of the green chamber of the Boeuf-gras — a traveller was occupying that terrible room!

All my fears were instantly revived. The old woman's excitement explained itself — she scented another victim!

I could not sleep at all that night. The rustling of the straw of my mattress, the nibbling of a mouse under the floor, sent a chill through me. I rose and looked out of my window — I listened.

The light I had seen was no longer visible in the green chamber.

During one of these moments of poignant anxiety — whether the result of illusion or reality — I fancied I could discern the figure of the old witch, likewise watching and listening.

The night passed, the dawn showed grey against my window-panes, and, slowly increasing, the sounds and movements of the reawakened town arose. Harassed with fatigue and emotion, I at last fell asleep; but my repose was of short duration, and by eight o'clock I was again at my post of observation.

It appeared that Fledermausse had passed a night no less stormy than mine had been; for, when she opened the door of the gallery, I saw that a livid pallor was upon her cheeks and skinny neck.

She had nothing on but her chemise and a flannel petticoat; a few locks of rusty grey hair fell upon her shoulders. She looked up musingly towards my garret, but she saw nothing — she was thinking of something else.

Suddenly she descended into the yard, leaving her shoes at the top of the stairs. Doubtless her object was to assure herself that the outer door was securely fastened. She then hurried up the stairs, three or four at a time. It was frightful to see! She rushed into one of the side rooms, and I heard the sound of a heavy box-lid fall. Then Fledermausse reappeared in the gallery, dragging with her a life-size dummy — and this figure was dressed like the unfortunate student of Heidelberg!

With surprising dexterity the old woman suspended this hideous object to a beam of the overhanging roof, then went down into the yard to contemplate it from that point of view. A peal of grating laughter broke from her lips — she hurried up the stairs, and rushed down again, like a maniac; and every time she did this she burst into fresh fits of laughter.

A sound was heard outside the street door; the old woman sprang to the dummy, snatched it from its fastening, and carried it into the house; then she reappeared and leaned over the balcony, with outstretched neck, glittering eyes, and eagerly listening ears. The sound passed away — the muscles of her face relaxed, she drew a long breath. The passing of a vehicle had alarmed the old witch.

She then, once more, went back into her chamber, and I heard the lid of the box close heavily.

This strange scene utterly confounded all my ideas. What could that dummy mean?

I became more watchful and attentive than ever. Fledermausse went out with her basket, and I watched her to the top of the street; she had resumed her air of tottering age, walking with short steps, and from time to time half-turning her head so as to enable herself to look behind out of the corners of her eyes. For five long hours she remained abroad, while I went and came from my spying-place incessantly, meditating all the while — the sun heating the slates above my head till my brain was almost scorched.

I saw at his window the traveller who occupied the green chamber at the Boeuf-gras; he was a peasant of Nassau, wearing a three-cornered hat, a scarlet waistcoat, and having a broad laughing countenance. He was tranquilly smoking his pipe, unsuspicious of anything wrong.

About two o'clock Fledermausse came back. The sound of her door opening echoed to the end of the passage. Presently she appeared alone, quite alone in the yard, and seated herself on the lowest step of the gallery-stairs. She placed her basket at her feet and drew from it first several bunches of herbs, then some vegetables — then a three-cornered hat, a scarlet velvet waistcoat, a pair of plush breeches, and a pair of thick worsted stockings — the complete costume of a peasant of Nassau!

I reeled with giddiness — flames passed before my eyes.

I remembered those precipices that drew one towards them with irresistible power — wells that have had to be filled up because of persons throwing themselves into them — trees that have had to be cut down because of people hanging themselves upon them — the contagion of suicide and theft and murder, which at various times has taken possession of people's minds, by means well understood; that strange inducement which makes people kill themselves because others kill themselves. My hair rose upon my head with horror!

But how could this Fledermausse — a creature so mean and wretched — have made discovery of so profound a law of nature? How had she found the means of turning it to the use of her sanguinary instincts? This I could neither understand nor imagine. Without more reflection, however, I resolved to turn the fatal law against her, and by its power to drag her into her own snare. So many innocent victims called for vengeance!

I hurried to all the old clothes-dealers in Nuremberg; and by the evening I arrived at the Boeuf-gras with an enormous parcel under my arm.

Nikel Schmidt had long known me. I had painted the portrait of his wife, a fat and comely dame.

"Master Christian!" he cried, shaking me by the hand, "to what happy circumstance do I owe the pleasure of this visit?"

"My dear Mr Schmidt, I feel a very strong desire to pass the night in that room of yours up yonder."

We were on the doorstep of the inn, and I pointed up to the green chamber. The good fellow looked suspiciously at me.

"Oh! don't be afraid," I said, "I've no desire to hang myself."

"I'm glad of it! I'm glad of it! for, frankly, I should be sorry — an artist of your talent. When do you want the room, Master Christian?"

"Tonight."

"That's impossible — it's occupied."

"The gentleman can have it at once, if he likes," said a voice behind us; "I shan't stay in it."

We turned in surprise. It was the peasant of Nassau; his large three-cornered hat pressed down upon the back of his neck, and his bundle at the end of his travelling-stick. He had learned the story of the three travellers who had hanged themselves.

"Such a chamber!" he cried, stammering with terror; "it's — it's murdering people to put them into such! — you — you deserve to be sent to the galleys!"

"Come, come, calm yourself," said the landlord; "you slept there comfortably enough last night."

"Thank Heaven! I said my prayers before going to rest, or where should I be now?"

And he hurried away, raising his hands to Heaven.

"Well," said Master Schmidt, stupefied, "the chamber is empty, but don't go into it to do me an ill turn."

"I might be doing myself a much worse one," I replied.

Giving my parcel to the servant-girl, I went and seated myself among the guests who were drinking and smoking.

For a long time I had not felt more calm, more happy to be in the world. After so much anxiety, I saw approaching my end — the horizon seemed to grow lighter. I know not by what formidable power I was being led on. I lit my pipe, and with my elbow on the table and a jug of wine before me, and sometimes rousing myself to look at the woman's house, I seriously asked myself whether all that had happened to me was more than a dream. But when the watchman came, to request us to vacate the room, graver thoughts took possession of my mind, and I followed, in meditative mood, the little servant-girl who preceded me with a candle in her hand.

CHAPTER III

We mounted the windowless flight of stairs to the third storey; arrived there, she placed the candle in my hand and pointed to a door.

"That's it," she said, and hurried back down the stairs as fast as she could go.

I opened the door. The green chamber was like all other inn bedchambers; the ceiling was low, the bed was high. After casting a glance round the room, I stepped across to the window. Nothing was yet noticeable in Fledermausse's house, with the exception of a light which shone at the back of a deep obscure bedchamber — a nightlight, doubtless.

"So much the better," I said to myself as I reclosed the window-curtains; "I shall have plenty of time."

I opened my parcel, and from its contents put on a woman's cap with a broad frilled border; then, with a piece of pointed charcoal, in front of the glass, I marked my forehead with a number of wrinkles. This took me a full hour to do; but after I had put on a gown and a large shawl, I was afraid of myself; Fledermausse herself was looking at me from the depths of the glass!

At that moment the watchman announced the hour of eleven. I rapidly dressed the dummy I had brought with me like the one prepared by the old witch. I then drew apart the window-curtains.

Certainly, after all I had seen of the old woman — her infernal cunning, her prudence, and her dress — nothing ought to have surprised even me; yet I was positively terrified.

The light, which I had observed at the back of her room, now cast its yellow rays on her dummy, dressed like the peasant of Nassau, which sat huddled up on the side of the bed, its head dropped upon its chest, the large three-cornered hat drawn down over its features, its arms pendant by its sides, and its whole attitude that of a person plunged in despair.

Managed with diabolical art, the shadow permitted only a general view of the figure, the red waistcoat and its six rounded buttons alone caught the light; but the silence of night, the complete immobility of the figure, and its air of terrible dejection, all served to impress the beholder with irresistible force; even I myself, though not in the least taken by surprise, felt chilled to the marrow of my bones. How, then, would a poor countryman taken completely off his guard have felt? He would have been utterly overthrown; he would have lost all control of will, and the spirit of imitation would have done the rest.

Scarcely had I drawn aside the curtains than I discovered Fledermausse on the watch behind her windowpanes.

She could not see me. I opened the window softly, the window over the way softly opened too; then the dummy appeared to rise slowly and advance towards me; I did the same, and seizing my candle with one hand, with the other threw the casement wide open.

The old woman and I were face to face; for, overwhelmed with astonishment, she had let the dummy fall from her hands. Our two looks crossed with an equal terror.

She stretched forth a finger, I did the same; her lips moved, I moved mine; she heaved a deep sigh and leant upon elbow, I rested in the same way.

How frightful the enacting of this scene was I cannot describe; it was made up of delirium, bewilderment, madness. It was a struggle between two wills, two intelligences, two souls, one of which sought to crush the other; and in this struggle I had the advantage. The dead were on my side.

After having for some seconds imitated all the movements of Fledermausse, I drew a cord from the folds of my petticoat and tied it to the iron stanchion of the signboard.

The old woman watched me with open mouth. I passed the cord round my neck. Her tawny eyeballs glittered; her features became convulsed —

"No, no!" she cried, in a hissing tone; "no!"

I proceeded with the impassibility of a hangman.

Then Fledermausse was seized with rage.

"You're mad! You're mad!" she cried, springing up and clutching wildly at the sill of the window. "You're mad!"

I gave her no time to continue. Suddenly blowing out my light, I stooped like a man preparing to make a vigorous spring, then seizing my dummy slipped the cord about its neck and hurled it into the air.

A terrible shriek resounded through the street; then all was silent again.

Perspiration bathed my forehead. I listened a long time. At the end of an hour I heard far off — very far off — the cry of the watchman, announcing that midnight had struck.

"Justice is at last done," I murmured to myself; "the three victims are avenged. Heaven forgive me!"

I saw the old witch, drawn by the likeness of herself, a cord about her neck, hanging from the iron stanchion projecting from her house. I saw the thrill of death run through her limbs and the moon, calm and silent, rose above the edge of the roof and shed its cold pale rays upon her dishevelled head.

As I had seen the poor young student of Heidelberg, I now saw Fledermausse.

The next day all Nuremberg knew that "the Bat" had hung herself. It was the last event of the kind in the Rue des Minnesängers.

THE MURDERER'S VIOLIN

Karl Hâfitz had spent six years in mastering counterpoint. He had studied Haydn, Glück, Mozart, Beethoven, and Rossini; he enjoyed capital health, and was possessed of ample means which permitted him to indulge his artistic tastes — in a word, he possessed all that goes to make up the grand and beautiful in music, except that insignificant but very necessary thing — inspiration!

Every day, fired with a noble ardour, he carried to his worthy instructor, Albertus Kilian, long pieces harmonious enough, but of which every phrase was "cribbed." His master, Albertus, seated in his armchair, his feet on the fender, his elbow on a corner of the table, smoking his pipe all the time, set himself to erase, one after the other, the singular discoveries of his pupil. Karl cried with rage, he got very angry, and disputed the point; but the old master quietly opened one of his numerous music-books, and putting his finger on the passage, said:

"Look there, my boy."

Then Karl bowed his head and despaired of the future.

But one fine morning, when he had presented to his master as his own composition a fantasia of Boccherini, varied with Viotti, the good man could no longer remain silent.

"Karl," he exclaimed, "do you take me for a fool? Do you think that I cannot detect your larcenies? This is really too bad!"

And then perceiving the consternation of his pupil, he added — "Listen. I am willing to believe that your memory is to blame, and that you mistake recollection for originality, but you are growing too fat decidedly; you drink too generous of wine, and, above all, too much beer. That is what is shutting up the avenues of your intellect. You must get thinner!"

"Get thinner!"

"Yes, or give up music. You do not lack science, but ideas, and it is very simple; if you pass your whole life covering the strings of your violin with a coat of grease, how can they vibrate?"

These words penetrated the depths of Hâfitz's soul.

"If it is necessary for me to get thin," exclaimed he, "I will not shrink from any sacrifice. Since matter oppresses the mind, I will starve myself."

His countenance wore such an expression of heroism at that moment that Albertus was touched; he embraced his pupil and wished him every success.

*   *   *

The very next day Karl Hâfitz, knapsack on his back and baton in hand, left the Hotel of the Three Pigeons and the brewery sacred to King Gambrinus, and set out upon his travels.

He proceeded towards Switzerland.

Unfortunately, at the end of six weeks he was much thinner, but inspiration did not come any the more readily for that.

"Can anyone be more unhappy than I am?" he said. "Neither fasting nor good cheer, nor water, wine, or beer can bring me up to the necessary pitch; what have I done to deserve this? While a crowd of ignorant people produce remarkable works, I, with all my scicnce, all my application, all my courage, cannot accomplish anything. Ah! Heaven is not good to me; it is unjust."

Communing thus with himself, he took the road from Brück to Freibourg; night was coming on; he felt weary and footsore. Just then he perceived by the light of the moon an old ruined inn half-hidden in trees on the opposite side of the way; the door was off its hinges, the small windowpanes were broken, the chimney was in ruins. Nettles and briars grew around it in wild luxuriance, and the garrett window scarcely topped the heather, in which the wind blew hard enough to take the horns off a cow.

Karl could also perceive through the mist that a branch of a fir-tree waved above the door.

"Well," he muttered, "the inn is not prepossessing, it is rather ill-looking indeed, but we must not judge by appearances."

So, without hesitation, he knocked at the door with his stick.

"Who is there? What do you want?" called out a rough voice within.

"Shelter and food," replied the traveller.

"Ah ha! very good."

The door opened suddenly, and Karl found himself confronted by a stout personage with square visage, grey eyes, his shoulders covered with a great-coat loosely thrown over them, and carrying an axe in his hand.

Behind this individual a fire was burning on the hearth, which lighted up the entrance to a small room and the wooden staircase, and close to the flame was crouched a pale young girl clad in a miserable brown dress with little white spots on it. She looked towards the door with an affrighted air; her black eyes had something sad and an indescribably wandering expression in them.

Karl took all this in at a glance, and instinctively grasped his stick tighter.

"Well, come in," said the man; "this is no time to keep people out of doors."

Then Karl, thinking it bad form to appear alarmed, came into the room and sat down by the hearth.

"Give me your knapsack and stick," said the man.

For the moment the pupil of Albertus trembled to his very marrow; but the knapsack was unbuckled and the stick placed in the corner, and the host was seated quietly before the fire ere he had recovered himself.

This circumstance gave him confidence.

"Landlord," said he, smiling, "I am greatly in want of my supper."

"What would you like for supper, sir?" asked the landlord.

"An omelette, some wine, and cheese."

"Ha, ha! you have got an excellent appetite, but our provisions are exhausted."

"You have no cheese, then?"

"No."

"No butter, nor bread, nor milk?"

"No."

"Well, good heavens! what *have* you got?"

"We can roast some potatoes in the embers."

Just then Karl caught sight of a whole regiment of hens perched on the staircase in the gloom of all sorts, in all attitudes, some pluming themselves in the most nonchalant manner.

"But," said Hâfitz, pointing at this troop of fowls, "you must have some eggs surely?"

"We took them all to market this morning."

"Well, if the worst comes to the worst you can roast a fowl for me."

Scarcely had he spoken when the pale girl, with dishevelled hair, darted to the staircase, crying:

"No one shall touch the fowls! No one shall touch my fowls! Ho, ho, ho! God's creatures must be respected."

Her appearance was so terrible that Hâfitz hastened to say:

"No, no, the fowls shall not be touched. Let us have the potatoes. I devote myself to eating potatoes henceforth. From this moment my object in life is determined. I shall remain here three months — six months — any time that may be necessary to make me as thin as a fakir."

He expressed himself with such animation that the host cried out to the girl:

"Genovéva, Genovéva, look! The Spirit has taken possession of him; just as the other was —"

The north wind blew more fiercely outside; the fire blazed up on the hearth and puffed great masses of grey smoke up to the ceiling. The hens appeared to dance in the reflection of the flame while the demented girl sang in a shrill voice a wild air, and the log of green wood, hissing in the midst of the fire, accompanied her with its plaintive sibilations.

Hâfitz began to fancy that he had fallen upon the den of the sorcerer Hecker; he devoured a dozen potatoes and drank a great draught of cold water. Then he felt somewhat calmer; he noticed that the girl had left the chamber, and that only the man sat opposite to him by the hearth.

"Landlord," he said, "show me where I am to sleep."

The host lit a lamp and slowly ascended the worm-eaten staircase; he opened a heavy trapdoor with his grey head and led Karl to a loft beneath the thatch.

"There is your bed," he said, as he deposited the lamp on the floor; "sleep well, and above all things beware of fire."

He then descended, and Hâfitz was left alone, stooping beneath the low roof in front of a great mattress covered with a sack of feathers.

He considered for a few seconds whether it would be prudent to sleep in such a place, for the man's countenance did not appear very prepossessing, particularly as, remembering his cold grey eyes, his blue lips, his wide bony forehead, his yellow hue, he suddenly recalled to mind that on the Golzenberg he had encountered three men hanging in chains, and that one of them bore a striking resemblance to the landlord; that he had also those grave eyes, the bony elbows, and that the great toe of his left foot protruded from his shoe, cracked by the rain.

He also recollected that that unhappy man named Melchior had been a musician formerly, and that he had been hanged for having murdered the landlord of the Golden Sheep with his pitcher, because he had asked him to pay his scanty reckoning.

This poor fellow's music had affected him powerfully in former days. It was fantastic, and the pupil of Albertus had envied the Bohemian; but just now when he recalled the figure on the gibbet, his tatters agitated by the night wind, and the ravens wheeling around him with discordant screams, he trembled violently, and his fears augmented when he discovered, at the farther end of the loft against the wall, a violin decorated with two faded palm-leaves.

Then indeed he was anxious to escape, but at that moment he heard the rough voice of the landlord.

"Put out that light, will you?" he cried; "go to bed. I told you particularly to be cautious about fire."

These words froze Karl; he threw himself upon the mattress and extinguished the light. Silence fell on all the house.

Now, notwithstanding his determination not to close his eyes, Hâfitz, in consequence of hearing the sighing of the wind, the cries of the night-birds, the sound of the mice pattering over the floor, towards one o'clock fell asleep; but he was awakened by a bitter, deep, and most distressing sob. He started up, a cold perspiration standing on his forehead.

He looked up, and saw crouched beneath the angle of the roof a man. It was Melchior, the executed criminal. His hair fell down to his emaciated ribs; his chest and neck were naked. One might compare him to a skeleton of an immense grasshopper, so thin was he; a ray of moonlight entering through the narrow window gave him a ghastly blue tint, and all around him hung the long webs of spiders.

Hâfitz, speechless, with staring eyes and gaping mouth, kept gazing at this weird object, as one might be expected to gaze at Death standing at one's bedside when the last hour has come!

Suddenly the skeleton extended its long bony hand and took the violin from the wall, placed it in position against its shoulder, and began to play.

There was in this ghostly music something of the cadence with which the earth falls upon the coffin of a dearly-loved friend — something solemn as the thunder of the waterfall echoed afar by the surrounding rocks, majestic as the wild blasts of the autumn tempest in the midst of the sonorous forest trees; sometimes it was sad — sad as never-ending despair. Then, in the midst of all this, he would strike into a lively measure, persuasive, silvery as the notes of a flock of gold-finches fluttering from twig to twig. These pleasing trills soared up with an ineffable tremolo of careless happiness, only to take flight all at once, frightened away by the waltz, foolish, palpitating, bewildering — love, joy, despair — all together singing, weeping, hurrying pell-mell over the quivering strings!

And Karl, notwithstanding his extreme terror, extended his arms and exclaimed:

"Oh, great, great artist! oh, sublime genius! oh, how I lament your sad fate, to be hanged for having murdered that brute of an innkeeper who did not know a note of music! — to wander through the forest by moonlight! — never to live in the world again! — and with such talents! O Heaven!"

But as he thus cried out he was interrupted by the rough tones of his host.

"Hullo up there! Will you be quiet? Are you ill, or is the house on fire?"

Heavy steps ascended the staircase, a bright light shone through the chinks of the door, which was opened by a thrust of the shoulder, and the landlord appeared.

"Oh!" exclaimed Hâfitz, "what things happen here! First I am awakened by celestial music and entranced by Heavenly strains; and then it all vanishes as if it were but a dream."

The innkeeper's face assumed a thoughtful expression.

"Yes, yes," he muttered, "I might have thought as much. Melchior has come to disturb your rest. He will always come. Now we have lost our night's sleep; it is no use to think of rest any more. Come along, friend; get up and smoke a pipe with me."

Karl waited no second bidding; he hastily left the room. But when he got downstairs, seeing that it was still dark night, he buried his head in his hands and remained for a long time plunged in melancholy meditation. The host relighted the fire, and taking up his position in the opposite corner of the hearth, smoked in silence.

At length the grey dawn appeared through the little diamond-shaped panes; then the cock crowed, and the hens began to hop down from step to step of the staircase.

"How much do I owe you?" asked Karl, as he buckled on his knapsack and resumed his walking-staff.

"You owe us a prayer at the chapel of St Blaise," said the man, with a curious emphasis — "one prayer for the soul of Melchior, who was hanged, and another for his *fiancée*, Genovéva, the poor idiot."

"Is that all?"

"That is all."

"Well, then, good-bye — I shall not forget."

And, indeed, the first thing that Karl did on his arrival at Freibourg was to offer up a prayer for the poor man and for the girl he had loved, and then he went to the Grape Hotel, spread his sheet of paper upon the table, and, fortified by a bottle of "rikevir," he wrote at the top of the page *The Murderer's Violin*, and then on the spot he traced the score of his first original composition.

THE SPIDER OF GUYANA

The mineral waters of Spinbronn, in Hundsruck, a few leagues from Pirmesans, formerly enjoyed an excellent reputation, for Spinbronn was the rendezvous of all the gouty and rheumatic members of the German aristocracy. The wild nature of the surrounding country did not deter the visitors, for they were lodged in charming villas at the foot of the mountain. They bathed in the cascade that fell in large sheets of foam from the summit of the rocks, and drank two or three pints of the water every day. Dr. Daniel Haselnoss, who prescribed for the sick and those who thought they were, received his patients in a large wig, brown coat, and ruffles, and was rapidly making his fortune.

Today, however, Spinbronn is no longer a favorite watering place. The fashionable visitors have disappeared; Dr. Haselnoss has given up his practice; and the town is only inhabited by a few poor, miserable woodcutters. All this is the result of a succession of strange and unprecedented catastrophes, which Councillor Bremen, of Pirmesans, recounted to me the other evening.

"You know, Mr. Fritz," he said, "that the source of the Spinbronn flows from a sort of cavern about five feet high, and from ten feet to fifteen feet across; the water, which has a temperature of 67° centigrade, is salty. The front of the cavern is half hidden by moss, ivy, and low shrubs, and it is impossible to find out the depth of it, because of the thermal exhalations that prevent any entrance.

"In spite of that, it had been observed for a century that the birds of the locality — hawks, thrushes, and turtledoves — were engulfed in full flight, and no one knew of what mysterious influence it was the result. During the season of 1801, for some unexplained reason, the source became more abundant, and the visitors one evening, taking their constitutional promenade on the lawns at the foot of the rocks, saw a human skeleton fall from the cascade.

"You can imagine the general alarm, Mr. Fritz. It was naturally supposed that a murder had been committed at Spinbronn some years before, and that the victim had been thrown into the source. But the skeleton, which was blanched as white as snow, only weighed twelve pounds; and Dr. Haselnoss concluded that, in all probability, it had been in the sand more than three centuries to have arrived at that state of desiccation.

"Plausible as his reasoning was, it did not prevent many visitors leaving that same day, horrified to have drunk the waters. The really gouty and rheumatic ones, however, stayed on, and consoled themselves with the doctor's version. But the following days the cavern disgorged all that it contained of detritus; and a veritable ossuary descended the mountain — skeletons of animals of all sorts, quadrupeds, birds, reptiles. In fact, all the most horrible things that could be imagined.

"Then Haselnoss wrote and published a pamphlet to prove that all these bones were relics of the antediluvian world, that they were fossil skeletons, accumulated there in a sort of funnel during the universal Deluge, that is to say, four thousand years before Christ; and, consequently, could only be regarded as stones, and not as anything repulsive.

"But his work had barely reassured the gouty ones, when one fine morning the corpse of a fox, and then of a hawk, with all its plumage, fell from the cascade. It was impossible to maintain that these had existed before the Deluge, and the exodus became general.

"'How horrible!' cried the ladies. 'That is where the so-called virtue of mineral waters springs from. Better die of rheumatism than continue such a remedy.'

"At the end of a week the only visitor left was a stout Englishman, Commodore Sir Thomas Hawerbrook, who lived on a grand scale, as most Englishmen do. He was tall and very stout, and of a florid complexion. His hands were literally knotted with gout, and he would have drunk no matter what if he thought it would cure him. He laughed loudly at the desertion of the sufferers, installed himself in the best of the villas, and announced his intention of spending the winter at Spinbronn."

Here Councillor Bremen leisurely took a large pinch of snuff to refresh his memory, and with the tips of his fingers shook off the tiny particles, which fell on his delicate lace jabot. Then he went on.

"Five or six years before the revolution of 1789, a young doctor of Pirmesans, called Christian Weber, went to St. Domingo to seek his fortune. He had been very successful and was about to retire when the revolt of the negroes occurred. Happily he escaped the massacre and was able to save part of his fortune. He traveled for a time in South America, and about the period of which I speak, returned to Pirmesans and bought the house and what remained of the practice of Dr. Haselnoss. Dr. Christian Weber brought with him an old negress called Agatha, a very ugly old woman, with a flat nose, and enormous lips. She always enveloped her head in a sort of turban of the most startling colors and wore rings in her ears that reached to her shoulders. Altogether she was such a singular-looking creature that the mountaineers came from miles around just to look at her.

"The doctor himself was a tall, thin man, invariably dressed in a blue swallow-tailed coat and leather breeches. He talked very little, his laugh was dry and nervous, and his habits most eccentric. During his wanderings, he had collected a number of insects of almost every species, and he seemed to be much more interested in them than in his patients. In his daily rambles among the mountains he often found butterflies to add to his collection, and these he brought home pinned to the lining of his hat.

"Dr. Weber, Mr. Fritz, was my cousin and my guardian, and directly he returned to Germany, he took me from school and settled me with him at Spinbronn. Agatha was a great friend of mine, though at first she frightened me, but she was a good creature, knew how to make the most delicious sweets, and could sing the most charming songs.

"Sir Thomas and Dr. Weber were on friendly terms and spent long hours together talking of subjects beyond my comprehension — of transmission of fluids, and mysterious things they had observed in their travels. Another mystery to me was the singular influence that the doctor appeared to have over the negress, for though she was generally particularly lively, ready to be amused at the slightest thing, yet she trembled like a leaf if she encountered her master's eyes fixed upon her.

"I have told you that birds, and even large animals, were engulfed in the cavern. After the disappearance of the visitors, some of the old inhabitants remembered that about fifty years before a young girl, Loisa Muller, who lived with her grandmother in a cottage near the source, had suddenly disappeared. She had gone out one morning to gather herbs and was never seen or heard of again, but her apron had been found a few days later near the mouth of the cavern. From that it was evident to all that the skeleton about which Dr. Haselnoss had written so eloquently was that of the poor girl, who had, no doubt, been drawn into the cavern by the mysterious influence that almost daily acted upon more feeble creatures. What that influence was nobody could tell. The superstitious mountaineers believed that the devil inhabited the cavern, and terror spread throughout the district.

"One afternoon in the month of July, my cousin was occupied in classifying his insects and rearranging them in their cases. He had found some curious ones the night before, at which he was highly delighted. I was helping by making a needle red-hot in the flame of a candle.

"Sir Thomas, lying back in a chair near the window and smoking a big cigar, was regarding us with a dreamy air. The commodore was very fond of me. He often took me driving with him and used to like to hear me chatter in English. When the doctor had labeled all his butterflies, he opened the box of larger insects.

"'I caught a magnificent horn-beetle yesterday,' he said, 'the *lucanus cervus* of the Hartz oaks. It is a rare kind.'

"As he spoke I gave him the hot needle, which he passed through the insect preparatory to fixing it on the cork. Sir Thomas, who had taken no notice till then, rose and came to the table on which the case of specimens stood. He looked at the spider of Guyana, and an expression of horror passed over his rubicund features.

"'There,' he said, 'is the most hideous work of the Creator. I tremble only to look at it.'

"And, sure enough, a sudden pallor spread over his face.

"'Bah!' said my guardian, 'all that is childish nonsense. You heard your nurse scream at a spider, you were frightened, and the impression has remained. But if you regard the creature with a strong microscope, you would be astonished at the delicacy of its organs, at their admirable arrangement, and even at their beauty.'

"'It disgusts me,' said the commodore, brusquely. 'Pouff!'

"And he walked away. 'I don't know why,' he continued, 'but a spider always freezes my blood.'

"Dr. Weber burst out laughing, but I felt the same as Sir Thomas and sympathized with him.

"'Yes, cousin, take away that horrid creature,' I cried. 'It is frightful, and it spoils all the others.'

"'Little stupid,' said he, while his eyes flashed, 'nobody compels you to look at them. If you are not pleased you can go.'

"Evidently he was angry, and Sir Thomas, who was standing by the window regarding the mountains, turned suddenly round and took me by the hand.

"'Your guardian loves his spiders, Frantz,' he said, kindly. 'We prefer the trees and the grass. Come with me for a drive.'

"'Yes, go,' returned the doctor, 'and be back to dinner at six.' Then, raising his voice, 'No offense, Sir Thomas,' he said.

"Sir Thomas turned and laughed, and we went out to the carriage.

"The commodore decided to drive himself and sent back his servant. He placed me on the seat beside him, and we started for Rothalps. While the carriage slowly mounted the sandy hill, I was quiet and sad. Sir Thomas, too, was grave, but my silence seemed to strike him.

"'You don't like the spiders, Frantz; neither do I. But, thank Heaven! there are no dangerous ones in this country. The spider your cousin has in his box is found in the swampy forests of Guyana, which is always full of hot vapors and burning exhalations, for it needs a high temperature to support its existence. Its immense web, or rather its net, would surround an ordinary thicket, and birds are caught in it, the same as flies in our spiders' webs. But do not think any more about it; let us drink a glass of Burgundy.'

"As he spoke he lifted the cover of the seat and, taking out a flask of wine, poured me out a full leathern goblet.

"I felt better when I had drunk it, and we continued our way. The carriage was drawn by a little Ardennes pony, which climbed the steep incline as lightly and actively as a goat. The air was full of the murmur of myriads of insects. At our right was the forest of Rothalps. At our left was the cascade of Spinbronn; and the higher we mounted, the bluer became the silver sheets of water foaming in the distance, and the more musical the sound as the water passed over the rocks.

"Both Sir Thomas and I were captivated by the spectacle, and, lost in a reverie, allowed the pony to go on as he would. Soon we were within a hundred paces of the cavern of Spinbronn. The shrubs around the entrance were remarkably green. The water, as it flowed from the cavern, passed over the top of the rock, which was slightly hollowed, and there formed a small lake, from which it again burst forth and descended into the valley below. This lake was shallow, the bottom of it composed of sand and black pebbles, and, although covered with a slight vapor, the water was clear and limpid as crystal.

"The pony stopped to breathe. Sir Thomas got out and walked about for a few seconds.

"'How calm it is,' he said.

"Then, after a minute's silence, he continued: 'Frantz, if you were not here, I should have a bathe in that lake.'

"'Well, why not?' I answered. 'I will take a walk the while. There are numbers of strawberries to be found a little way up that mountain. I can go and get some, and be back in an hour.'

"'Capital idea, Frantz. Dr. Weber pretends that I drink too much Burgundy; we must counteract that with mineral water. This little lake looks inviting.'

"Then he fastened the pony to the trunk of a tree and waved his hand in adieu. Sitting down on the moss, he commenced to take off his boots, and, as I walked away, he called after me: "'In an hour, Frantz.'

"They were his last words.

"An hour after I returned. The pony, the carriage, and Sir Thomas's clothes were all that I could see. The sun was going down and the shadows were lengthening. Not a sound of bird or of insect, and a silence as of death filled the solitude. This silence frightened me. I climbed onto the rock above the cavern and looked right and left. There was nobody to be seen. I called; no one responded. The sound of my voice repeated by the echoes filled me with terror. Night was coming on. All of a sudden I remembered the disappearance of Loisa Muller, and I hurried down to the front of the cavern. There I stopped in affright, and glancing toward the entrance, I saw two red, motionless points.

"A second later I distinguished some dark, moving object farther back in the cavern, farther perhaps than human eye had ever before penetrated; for fear had sharpened my sight and given all my senses an acuteness of perception that I had never before experienced.

"During the next minute I distinctly heard the chirp, chirp of a grasshopper, and the bark of a dog in the distant village. Then my heart, which had been frozen with terror, commenced to beat furiously, and I heard nothing more. With a wild cry I fled, leaving pony and carriage.

"In less than twenty minutes, bounding over rocks and shrubs, I reached my cousin's door.

"'Run, run,' I cried, in a choking tone, as I burst into the room where Dr. Weber and some invited friends were waiting for us. 'Run, run; Sir Thomas is dead; Sir Thomas is in the cavern,' and I fell fainting on the floor.

"All the village turned out to search for the commodore. At ten o'clock they returned, bringing back Sir Thomas's clothes, the pony, and carriage. They had found nothing, seen nothing, and it was impossible to go ten paces into the cavern.

"During their absence Agatha and I remained in the chimney-corner, I still trembling with fear, she, with wide-open eyes, going from time to time to the window, from which we could see the torches passing to and fro on the mountain and hear the searchers shout to one another in the still night air.

"At her master's approach, Agatha began to tremble. The doctor entered brusquely, pale, with set lips. He was followed by about twenty woodcutters, shaking out the last remnants of their nearly extinguished torches.

"He had barely entered before, with flashing eyes, he glanced round the room, as if in search of something. His eyes fell on the negress, and without a word being exchanged between them the poor woman began to cry.

"'No, no, I will not,' she shrieked.

"'But I will,' returned the doctor in a hard tone.

"The negress shook from head to foot as though seized by some invisible power. The doctor pointed to a seat, and she sat down as rigid as a corpse.

"The woodcutters, good, simple people, full of pious sentiments, crossed themselves, and I, who had never yet heard of the hypnotic force, began to tremble, thinking Agatha was dead.

"Dr. Weber approached the negress and passed his hands over her forehead.

"'Are you ready?' he said.

"'Yes, sir.'

"'Sir Thomas Hawerbrook.'

"At these words, she shivered again.

"'Do you see him?'

"'Yes, yes,' she answered, in a gasping voice, 'I see him.'

"'Where is he?'

"'Up there, in the depths of the cavern — dead!'

"'Dead!' said the doctor; 'how?'

"'The spider! oh, the spider!'

'Calm yourself,' said the doctor, who was very pale. 'Tell us clearly.'

"'The spider holds him by the throat — in the depths of the cavern — under the rock — enveloped in its web — *Ah!*"

"Dr. Weber glanced round on the people, who, bending forward, with eyes starting out of their heads, listened in horror.

"Then he continued: 'You see him?'

"'I see him.'

"'And the spider. Is it a big one?'

"'O Master, never, never, have I seen such a big one. Neither on the banks of the Mocaris, nor in the swamps of Konanama. It is as large as my body.'

"There was a long silence. Everybody waited with livid faces and hair on end. Only the doctor kept calm. Passing his hand two or three times over the woman's forehead, he recommenced his questions. Agatha described how Sir Thomas's death happened.

"'He was bathing in the lake of the source. The spider saw his bare back from behind. It had been fasting for a long time and was hungry. Then it saw Sir Thomas's arm on the water. All of a sudden it rushed out, put its claws round the commodore's neck. He cried out, *"Mon Dieu, Mon Dieu!"* The spider stung him and went back, and Sir Thomas fell into the water and died. Then the spider returned, spun its silk round him, and swam slowly, gently back to the extremity of the cavern, drawing Sir Thomas after it by the thread attached to its own body.'

"I was still sitting in the chimney-corner, overwhelmed with fright. The doctor turned to me.

"'Is it true, Frantz, that the commodore was going to bathe?'

"'Yes, cousin.'

"'At what time?'

"'At four o'clock.'

"'At four o'clock? It was very hot then, was it not?'

"'Yes; oh, yes.'

"'That's it. The monster was not afraid to come out then.'

"He spoke a few unintelligible words and turned to the peasants.

"'My friends,' he cried, 'that is where the mass of debris and those skeletons come from. It is the spider that has frightened away your visitors and ruined you all. It is there hidden in its web, dragging its prey into the depths of the cavern. Who can say the number of its victims?'

"He rushed impetuously from the house, and all the woodcutters hurried after him.

"'Bring fagots, bring fagots!' he cried.

Ten minutes later two immense carts, laden with wood, slowly mounted the hill; a long file of woodcutters followed, with hatchets on their shoulders. My guardian and I walked in front, holding the horses by the bridle; while the moon lent a vague, melancholy light to the funereal procession.

At the entrance of the cavern the cortège stopped. The torches were lighted and the crowd advanced.The limpid water flowed over the sand, reflecting the blue light of the resinous torches, the rays of which illuminated the tops of the dark overhanging pines on the rocks above us.

"'It is here you must unload,' said the doctor. 'We must block up the entrance of the cavern.'

"'It was not without a feeling of dread that they commenced

to execute his order. The fagots fell from the tops of the carts, and the men piled them up before the opening, placing some stakes against them to prevent their being carried away by the water. Toward midnight the opening was literally closed by the fagots. The hissing water below them flowed right and left over the moss, but those on the top were perfectly dry.

"Then Dr. Weber took a lighted torch, and himself set fire to the pile. The flames spread from twig to twig and rose toward the sky, preceded by dense clouds of smoke. It was a wild, strange sight, and the woods lighted by the crackling flames had a weird effect. Thick volumes of smoke proceeded from the cavern, while the men standing round, gloomy and motionless, waited with their eyes fixed on the opening. As for me, though I trembled from head to foot, I could not withdraw my gaze.

"We waited quite a quarter of an hour, and Dr. Weber began to be impatient, when a black object, with crooked claws, suddenly approached in the shadow and then threw itself forward toward the opening. One of the men, fearing that it would leap over the fire, threw his hatchet, and aimed at the creature so well that, for an instant, the blood that flowed from its wound half quenched the fire, but soon the flame revived, and the horrible insect was consumed.

"Evidently driven by the heat, the spider had taken refuge in its den. Then, suffocated by the smoke, it had returned to the charge and rushed into the middle of the flames. The body of the horrible creature was as large as a man's, reddish violet in color, and most repulsive in appearance.

"That, Mr. Fritz, is the strange event that destroyed the reputation of Spinbronn. I can swear to the exactitude of my story, but it would be impossible for me to give you an explanation. Nevertheless, admitting that the high temperature of certain thermal springs furnishes the same conditions of existence as the burning climate of Africa and South America, it is not unreasonable to suppose that insects, subject to its influences, can attain an enormous development.

"Whatever may have been the cause, my guardian decided that it would be useless to attempt to resuscitate the reputation of the waters of Spinbronn; so he sold his house and returned to America with his negress and his collection."

THE WHITE AND THE BLACK

I

At that time we passed our evenings at Brauer's alehouse, which opens upon the square of Vieux-Brisach. After eight o'clock there used to drop in, one by one, Frederick Schultz the notary; Frantz Martin the burgomaster; Christopher Ulmett the magistrate; the counsellor Klers; the engineer Rothan; the young organist Theodore Blitz; and some others of the chief townsfolk, who all sat around the same table and drank their foaming *bok-bier* like brothers.

The apparition of Theodore Blitz, who came to us from Jena with a letter of recommendation from Harmosius — his dark eyes, his brown dishevelled hair, his thin white nose, his metallic voice, and his mystic ideas, occasioned us some little disquiet. It used to trouble us to see him rise abruptly and pace two or three times up and down the room, gesticulating the while, mocking with a strange air the Swiss landscapes with which the walls were adorned — lakes of indigo blue, mountains of apple green, paths of brilliant red. Then he would seat himself down again, empty his glass at a gulp, and commence a discussion about the music of Palestrina, about the lute of the Hebrews, about the introduction of the organ into our churches, about the shophar, the sabbatic epochs, etc. He would knit his brows, plant his sharp elbows on the edge of the table, and lose himself in deep thought. Yes, he perplexed us not a little — we others who were grave and accustomed to methodical ideas. However, it was necessary to put up with it; and the engineer Rothan himself; in spite of his bantering spirit, in the end grew calm and no longer continued to contradict the young organist when he was right.

Theodore Blitz was plainly one of those nervously organized beings who are affected by every change of temperature. The year of which I speak was extremely warm; we had several heavy storms towards the autumn, and folk began to fear for the wine harvest.

One evening all our little world was gathered, according to custom, around the table, with the exception of the magistrate Ulmett and the organist. The burgomaster talked about the weather and great hydraulic works. As for me, I listened to the wind gambolling without amongst the plane trees of the Schloss-garten, to the drip of the water from the spouts, and to its dashing against the windows. From time to time one could hear a tile blown off a roof, a door shut with a bang, a shutter beat against a wall. Then would arise the great clamour of the storm, sweeping, sighing, and groaning in the distance, as if all the invisible powers were seeking and calling upon one another in the darkness, while living things hid themselves, sitting in corners, in order to escape a fearful meeting with them.

From the church of Saint-Landolphe nine o'clock sounded, when Blitz hurriedly entered, shaking his hat like one possessed, and saying in his husky voice —

"Surely the Evil One is about his work! The white and the black are having a tussle. The nine times nine thousand nine hundred and ninety thousand spirits of Envy battle and tear themselves. Go, Ahriman! Walk! Ravage! Lay waste! The Amschaspands are in flight! Oromage veils her face! What a time, what a time!"

And so saying he walked round the room, stretching his long skinny limbs, and laughing by jerks.

We were all astounded at such an entry, and for some seconds no one spoke a word. Then, however, the engineer Rothan, led on by his caustic humour, said —

"What nonsense is it that you are singing there, Organist? What do Amschaspands signify to us? or the nine times nine thousand nine hundred and ninety thousand spirits of Envy? Ha! ha! ha! It is really comic. Where on Earth did you pick up such strange language?"

Theodore Blitz stopped suddenly short in his walk and shut one eye, while the other, wide open, shone with a diabolic irony.

When Rothan had finished —

"Oh, engineer," said he; "oh! Sublime spirit, master of the trowel and mortar, director of stones, he who orders right angles, angles acute, angles obtuse, you are right — a hundred times right!"

He bent himself with a mocking air, and went on —

"Nothing exists but matter — the level, the rule, and the compass. The revelations of Zoroaster, of Moses, of Pythagoras, of Odin — the harmony, the melody, art, sentiment, they are all dreams unworthy of an enlightened intellect such as yours. To you belongs the truth, the eternal truth. Ha! ha! ha! I bow myself before you; I salute you; I prostrate myself before your glory, imperishable as that of Nineveh and of Babylon."

Finishing his speech, he made two little turns on his heels, and uttered a laugh so piercing that it was more like the crowing of a cock at daybreak.

Rothan was getting angry, when at that moment the old magistrate Ulmett came in, his head protected by a great otter-skin cap, his shoulders covered by his bottle green greatcoat bordered with fox-skin. His hands hung down beside him, his back was bent, his eyes were half-closed, his big nose was red, and his large cheeks were wet with rain. He was as wet as a drake.

Outside the rain fell in torrents, the gutters gushed over, the spouts disgorged themselves, and the ditches were swollen into little rivers.

"Ah, heavens!" cried the good fellow. "Perhaps it was foolish to come out on such a night, and after such work too — two inquests, verbal processes, interrogatories! The *bok-bier* and old friends, though, would make me swim across the Rhine."

And muttering these words he put off his otter-skin cap and opened his great pelisse to take out his long tobacco pipe and his pouch, which he carefully laid down upon the table. After that he hung his greatcoat and his hat up beside the window, and called out — "Brauer!"

"Well, Magistrate, what do you want?"

"You would do well to put to the shutters. Believe me, this storm will wind up with some thunder."

The innkeeper went out and put the shutters to, and the old magistrate, sitting down in his corner, heaved a deep sigh.

"You know what has happened, burgomaster?" he asked in a solemn voice.

"No. What has occurred, my old Christopher?"

Before he replied — Ulmett threw a glance around the room.

"We are here alone, my friends," said he, "so I am able to tell you. About three o'clock this afternoon someone found poor Gredel Dick under the sluice of the miller at Holderloch."

"Under the sluice at Holderloch?" cried all.

"Yes; a cord round her neck"

In order to understand how these words affected us it is necessary that you should know that Gredel Dick was one of the prettiest girls in Vieux-Brisach; a tall brunette, with blue eyes and red cheeks; the only daughter of an old anabaptist, Petrus Dick, who farmed considerable portions of the Schlossgarten. For some time she had seemed sad and melancholy — she who had beforetime been so merry in the morning at the washing place, and in the evening at the well in the midst of her friends. She had been seen crying, and her sorrow had been ascribed to the incessant pursuit of her by Saphéri Mutz, the postmaster's son — a big fellow, thin, vigorous, with an aquiline nose and curling black hair. He followed her like a shadow, and never let her off his arm at the dances.

There had been some talk about their marriage, but old Mutt, his wife, Karl Bremer his son-in-law, and his daughter Saffayel, were opposed to the match, all agreeing that a "heathen" should not be introduced into the family.

For three days past nothing had been seen of Gredel. No one knew what had become of her. You may imagine the thousand different thoughts which crowded upon us when we heard that she was dead. No one thought any longer of the discussion between Theodore Blitz and the engineer Rothan touching invisible spirits. All eyes were fixed on Christopher Ulmett, who, his large bald head bent, his heavy white eyebrows knit, gravely filled his pipe with a meditative air.

"And Mutt — Saphéri Mutt?" asked the burgomaster. "What has become of him?"

A slight flush coloured the cheeks of the old man as he answered after some seconds of thought —

"Saphéri Mutt? He has gone."

"Gone!" cried little Klers. "Then he acknowledges his guilt?"

"It certainly seems so to me," said the old magistrate simply. "One does not scamper off for nothing. As for the rest, we have searched his father's place, and found all the house upset. The folk seemed struck with consternation. The mother raved and tore her hair; the daughter wore her Sunday clothes and danced about like a fool. It was impossible to get anything out of them. As to Gredel's father, the poor fellow is in the deepest despair. He does not wish to say anything against his child, but it is certain that Gredel Dick left the farm of her own accord on Tuesday last in order to meet Saphéri. That fact is attested by all the neighbours. Now the gendarmes are scouting the country. We shall see, we shall see!"

Then there was a long silence. Outside the rain fell heavily.

"It is abominable!" cried the burgomaster suddenly. "Abominable! To think that every father of a family, even such as bring up their children in the fear of God, are exposed to such misfortunes."

"Yes," replied Ulmett, lighting his pipe. "It is so. They say, no doubt rightly, that Heaven orders all things; but the spirit of darkness seems to me to meddle a good deal more than is necessary in them. For one good fellow how many villains do we find, without faith or law? And for one good action how many evil ones?

I tell you, my friends, if the Evil One were to count his flock —"

He had not time to finish, for at that moment a terrific flash of lightning glared in through the chinks of the shutters, making the lamp burn dim. It was immediately followed by a clap of thunder, crashing, jerky — one of those claps which make you tremble. One might have thought that the world was coming to an end.

The clock of the church of Saint-Landolphe just then struck the half hour. From far, very far off, there came a trembling plaintive voice, crying — "Help, help!"

"Someone cries for help," said the burgomaster.

"Yes," said the others, turning pale, and listening.

While we were all thus in fright, Rothan, curling his lips in a joking fashion, broke out — "Ha! ha! ha! It is Mademoiselle Roesël's cat singing its love story to Monsieur Roller, the young first tenor."

Then dropping his voice and lifting his hand with a tragic gesture, he went on — "The time has sounded from the belfry of the chateau!"

"Ill-luck to those who laugh at such a cry," said old Christopher, rising.

He went towards the door with a solemn step, and we all followed him, even the fat innkeeper, who held his cotton cap in his hand and murmured a prayer very low. Rothan alone did not stir from his seat. As for me, I was behind the others, with outstretched neck, looking over their shoulders.

The glass door was scarcely opened when there came another flash of lightning. The street, with its white flagstones washed by the rain, its flushed gutters, its multitude of windows, its old gables, its signboards, glared out from the night, and then was swallowed up in the darkness.

That glance of the eye allowed me to see the steeple of Saint-Landolphe with its innumerable little carvings all clothed in white light. In the steeple were the bells hanging from black beams, with their clappers, and their ropes hanging down to the body of the church. Below that was a stork's nest, half torn in pieces by the wind, — the young ones with their beaks out, the mother at her wits' end, her wings extended, while the male bird flew about the shining steeple, his breast thrown forward, his neck bent, his long legs thrown out behind as if defying the thunder peals.

It was a strange sight, a veritable Chinese picture — thin, delicate, light, something strange, terrible, upon a black background of clouds broken with streaks of gold.

We stood, with open mouths, upon the threshold of the inn, and asked —

"What did you hear — Ulmett? What can you see — Klers?"

At that moment a lugubrious mewing commenced above us, and a whole regiment of cats set to work springing about in the gutter. At the same time a peal of laughter filled the room —

"Ah well! ah well!" cried the engineer. "Do you hear them? Was I wrong?"

"It was nothing," murmured the old magistrate. "Thank Heaven, it was nothing. Let us go in again. The rain is recommencing."

As we took our places again, he said —

"Is it astonishing, Rothan, that the imagination of a poor old fellow such as myself goes astray at a time when Earth and Heaven confound themselves, while good and bad are struggling together, while such mysterious crimes occur around us even at this day? Is it strange?"

We all took our places with a feeling of annoyance with the engineer, who had alone remained quiet, and had seen us disconcerted. We turned our backs on him as we emptied our glasses without saying a word, while he, his elbow on the edge of the window ledge, hummed between his teeth I know not what military march, the time of which he beat with his fingers on the ledge, without deigning to notice our ill-humour.

So things went on for some minutes, when Theodore Blitz said laughingly —

"Monsieur Rothan triumphs. He does not believe in invisible spirits. Nothing troubles him. He has a good foot, good eyes, and good ear. What more is wanting to convict us of ignorance and folly?"

"Ha," replied Rothan, "I should not have dared to say it, but you express things so well, Monsieur Organist, that one cannot disagree with you, especially in any matter that concerns yourself. As for my old friends Schultz, Ulmett, Klers, and the others, it is different, very different. Any one may at times be led astray by a dream, only one must see that it does not become a custom."

Instead of answering to this direct attack, Blitz, his head bent down, seemed to be listening to some noise without.

"Hush," said he, looking at us. "Hush."

He lifted his finger, and the expression of his face was so striking that we all listened with an indefinable feeling of fear.

The same instant heavy steps were heard in the street without, a hand was laid on the catch of the door, and the organist said to us in a trembling voice — "Be calm — listen and see. Heaven be with us."

The door opened and Saphéri Mutz appeared. Should I live to be a thousand years old the figure of that man will never be erased from my memory. He is there — I see him. He advances reeling, pale — his hair hanging about his face — his eye dull, glassy — his blouse tight to his body — a big stick in his hand. He looks upon us without seeing us, like a man in a dream. A winding track of mud is left behind him. He stops, coughs, and says in a low voice, as if speaking to himself —

"Well! what if they arrest me! What if they kill me! I would rather be here!"

Then, recollecting himself; and looking at us, one after another, he cried with a movement of terror —

"I have spoken! What did I say! Hi! the burgomaster — the magistrate Ulmett."

He made a bound as if he would fly, and I know not what he saw in the darkness of the night without which drove him once more from it into the room.

Theodore Blitz slowly arose. After he had looked at us, he walked up to Mutt, and, with an air of confidence, he asked him in a low voice, pointing to the dark street —

"Is it there?"

"Yes," said the man, in the same mysterious tone.

"It follows you?"

"From Fischbach."

"Behind you?"

"Yes, behind me."

"That is so, it is surely so," said the organist, throwing another look upon us. "It is always thus. Well then, stop here, Saphéri; sit down by the fire. Brauer, go and look for the gendarmes."

At the word gendarmes the wretched fellow grew fearfully pale and seemed to think again of flight, but the same horror beat him back once more, and he sank down at the corner of the table, his head between his hands.

"Oh! had I but known — had I but known!" he moaned.

We were more dead than alive. The innkeeper went out. Not a breath was heard in the room. The old magistrate had put down his pipe, the burgomaster looked at me with a stupefied air. Rothan no longer whistled. Theodore Blitz, sitting at the end of a bench, looked at the rain streaking the darkness.

So we remained for a quarter of an hour, fearful all the time that the man would take it into his head to attempt to fly. But he did not stir. His long hair coiled from between his fingers, and the rain dripped from his clothes onto the floor.

At length the clatter of arms was heard without, and the gendarmes Werner and Keltz appeared upon the step. Keltz, darting a side glance at the man, lifted his great hat, saying —

"Good evening, Monsieur Magistrate."

Then he came in and coolly put the handcuffs on Saphéri's wrists, while Saphéri covered his face with his hands.

"Come, follow me, my son," said he. "Werner, close up."

A third gendarme, short and fat, appeared in the darkness, and all the troop set off. The wretched man made no resistance.

We looked at one another's pale faces.

"Good evening, gentlemen," said the organist, and he went off.

Then each of us, lost in his own thoughts, rose and departed to his home in silence.

As for me, I turned my head more than twenty times before I came to my door, fearful that I should see the other that had followed Saphéri Mutt, ready to lay its hands upon me.

And when at last, thank Heaven, was safe in my room, before I got into bed and blew out my light I took the wise precaution of looking under my bed to convince myself that it was not hidden there. I even said a prayer that *it* would not strangle me during the night. Well, what then?

One is not a philosopher at all times.

II

Until then I had considered Theodore Blitz as a species of visionary imbecile. His maintaining the possibility of holding correspondence with invisible spirits by means of the music composed by all the sounds of nature, by the rustling of the leaves, by the murmur of the winds, by the hum of the insects, had appeared to me very ridiculous, and I was not the only one in that opinion.

It seemed all very well to tell us that if the grave sound of the organ awoke in us religious sentiments, that if martial music swept us on to war, and the simple melodies led us into reveries, it was because the different melodies were the invocation of the genii of the Earth, who came suddenly into our midst, acted on our organs, and made us participants of their own proper essence. All that, however, appeared tome to be very obscure, and I had never doubted that the organist was just a little mad.

Now, however, my opinions changed respecting him. I said to myself that man is not a purely material being, that we are composed of body and soul; that to attribute all to the body, and to endeavour to ascribe all significance to it, is not rational; that the nervous fluid, agitated by the undulations of the air, is almost as difficult to comprehend as the direct action of occult powers; that we know not how it is that even a mere tickling of our ears, regulated by the rules of counter points excites in us a thousand agreeable or terrible emotions, elevates the soul to Heaven, melts us, awakens in us the ardour of life, enthusiasm, love, fear, pity. No, the first theory was not satisfactory. The ideas of the organist appeared to me more sublime, more weighty, more just, and more acceptable, looking at things all round.

Then how could one explain, by means of mere nervous sensation, the arrival of Saphéri Mutt at the inn; how could one explain the terror of the unhappy man, which forced him to yield himself up; and the marvellous foresight of Blitz when he said to us —

"Hush! Listen! He comes! Heaven be with us!"

In the end all my prejudices against an invisible world disappeared, and new facts occurred to confirm me in this fresh manner of thinking.

About five days after the scene I have described, Saphéri Mutt had been transported by the gendarmes to the prison of Stuttgart. The thousand tales which had been set afloat respecting the death of Gredel Dick died away. The poor girl slept in peace at the back of the hill of the Trois-Fontaines, and folk were busied in looking after the wine harvest. One evening about nine o'clock, as I left the great warehouse of the custom-house — where I had been tasting some samples of wine on behalf of Brauer, who had more confidence in my judgment in such a matter than in his own — my head a little heavy, I chanced to direct my steps towards the great Alley des Plantanes, behind the church of Saint-Landolphe.

The Rhine displayed to my right its azure waters, in which some fishermen were letting down their nets. To my left rose the old fortifications of the town. The air began to grow cool; the river murmured its eternal song, the fir trees of the Black Forest were softly ruffled; and as I walked on the sound of a violin fell on my ears.

I listened.

The black-headed linnet never threw more grace, more delicacy, into the execution of his rapid trills, nor more enthusiasm into the stream of his inspiration. It was like nothing I had heard. It had no repose, no measure. It was a torrent of notes, delirious, admirably symphonizing, but void of order or method.

Then, dashing with the thread of the inspiration, came some sharp incisive notes, piercing the ear.

"Theodore Blitz is here," said I to myself; putting aside the high branches of an elder hedge at the foot of a slope.

I looked around me, and my eyes fell upon a horse-pond covered with duck-weed, where the big frogs showed their flat noses. A little farther off rose some stables, with their big sheds, and an old dwelling-house. In the court, surrounded by a wall breast-high in which was a worm-eaten door, walked five or six fowls, and under the great stall ran the rabbits, their croups in the air, their tails up. When they saw me they disappeared under the gate of the grange like shadows.

No noise save the flow of the river and the bizarre fantasy of the violin could be heard.

Where on Earth was Theodore Blitz?

The idea occurred to me that he was perhaps making trial of his music on the family of the Mutzes, and, curiosity impelling me, I glided into a hiding-place beside the wall to see what would happen in the farm.

The windows were all wide open, and in a room on the ground floor, long, with brown beams, level with the court, I perceived a table furnished with all the sumptuousness of a village feast; twenty or thirty covers were there. But what most astonished me was to see but five persons in front of this grand display. There was old Mutt, sombre and thoughtful, clad in a suit of black velvet with metal buttons. His large osseous head, gray, his forehead contracted in fixed thought, his eyes sunken, staring before him. There was the son-in-law, thin, insignificant, the neck of his shirt coming up almost to his ears. There was the mother in a great tulle cap, with a distracted look, the daughter — a rather pretty brunette, in a cap of black taffeta with spangles of gold and silver, her bosom covered with a silk neckerchief of a thousand colours. Lastly, there was Theodore Blitz, his three-cornered hat over his ear, the violin held between his shoulder and chin, his little eyes sparkling, his cheeks standing out in relief from a deep wrinkle, and his elbows thrown out and drawn in, like a grasshopper scraping its shrill aria on the heath.

The shades of the setting sun, the old clock with its delf dial with red and blue flowers, and above all the music, which grew more and more discordant, produced an indefinable impression upon me. I was seized with a truly panic terror. Was it the effect of my having breathed too long the *rudesheim*? Was it the effect of the pale tints of the falling night? I do not know; but without looking farther I glided away as quietly as possible, bending down, creeping by the wall in order to regain the road, when all of a sudden a large dog darted the length of his chain towards me, and made me utter a cry of surprise.

"Tirik!" cried the old postmaster.

And Theodore, perceiving me, jumped out of the room, crying —

"Ah! it is Christian Species! Come in, my dear Christian! You have come most opportunely."

He strode across the court and came and took my hands.

"My dear friend," said he to me, with strange animation. "This is a time when the *black* and the *white* engage with one another. Come in, come in."

His excitement frightened me, but he would accept none of my excuses, and dragged me on without my being able to make any resistance.

"You must know, dear Christian," said he, "that we have this morning baptized an angel of Heaven, the little Nickel Saphéri Bremer. I have celebrated her coming into the world by the chorus of the 'Séraphins.' Nevertheless, you may imagine that three-fourths of those who were invited have not come. Ha! ha! ha! Come in then! You will be welcome."

He pushed me on by the shoulders, and willing or unwilling, I stepped across the threshold. All the members of the Mutt family turned their heads. I should have liked not to have sat down, but those enthusiasts surrounded me. "This will be the sixth!" cried Blitz. "The number six is a good number!"

The old postmaster took my hands with emotion, saying — "Thanks, Monsieur Species, thanks for having come! They say that honest folk fly from us! That we are abandoned alike by God and by man! You will stop to the end?"

"Yes," mumbled the old woman, with a supplicating look. "Surely Monsieur Species will stay to the end. He will not refuse us that?"

Then I understood why the table was set in such grand fashion, and why the guests were so few. All of those invited to the baptism, thinking of Gredel Dick, had made excuses for not coming.

The idea of a like desertion went against my heart.

"Oh, certainly," I said. "Certainly! I will stay — with plea-sure — with great pleasure!"

The glasses were refilled, and we drank of a rough strong wine, of an old *markobrünner*, the austere flavour of which filled me with melancholy thoughts.

The old woman, putting her long hand upon my shoulder, murmured —

"Just a drop more, Monsieur Species, just a drop more."

And I dared not say no.

At that moment Blitz, passing his bow over the vibrating cords, made a cold shudder pass through all my limbs.

"This, my friends," said he, "is Saul's invocation to the Pythoness."

I should have liked to run away, but in the court the dog was lamentably howling, the night was coming on, and the room was full of shadows. The harsh features of old Mutz, his keen eyes, the sorrowful compression of his big jaws, did not reassure one.

Blitz went on scraping, scraping away at that invocation of his, with great sweeps of his arm.

The wrinkle which ploughed itself deep down his left cheek grew deeper and deeper, the perspiration stood on his forehead.

The postmaster filled up our glasses again and said to me in a low imperious voice —

"Your health."

"Yours, Monsieur Mutz," responded I, trembling.

All of a sudden the child in the cradle commenced to cry, and Blitz, with a diabolical irony, accompanied its shrill wailing with piercing notes, saying —

"It is the hymn of life — ha! ha! ha! Really little Nickel sings it as if she were already old — ha! ha! ha!" The old clock at the same time commenced to strike in its walnut-tree case; and when I raised my eyes, astonished by the noise, I saw a little figure advance from the background, bony, bald, hollow-eyed, a mocking smile on its lips — Death, in short. He came out a few steps and set himself to gather, by jerks, some bits of flowers painted in green on the edge of the clock-case.

Then, at the last stroke of the hour, he turned half round and went back to his den as he had come out.

"Why the deuce did the organist bring me here?" said I to myself. "This is a nice baptism! And these are merry folk — ha! ha! ha!"

I filled my glass and drank it in order to gain courage.

"Well, let us go on, let us go on. The die is cast. No one escapes his destiny. I was destined before the commencement of the ages to go this evening to the custom-house; to walk in the alley of Saint-Landolphe; to come in spite of myself to this abominable cutthroat place, attracted by the music of Blitz; to drink *marko-brünner* which smacks of cypress and vervain; and to see Death gathering painted flowers! Well, it is droll — truly droll!"

So I dreamed, laughing at men who, thinking themselves free, are dragged on by threads attached to the stars. So astrologers have told us, and we must believe them.

I laughed then amongst the shadows as the music ceased.

A great silence fell around. The clock alone broke the stillness with its regular tick-tack; outside the moon, slowly rising over the Rhine, behind the trembling foliage of a poplar, threw its pale light over innumerable ripples. I noticed it, and saw a black boat pass along in the moon's reflected light.

On it was a man, all dark like the boat. He had a loose cloak around him, and wore a large hat with wide brim, from which hung streamers.

He went by like a figure in a dream. I felt my eyelids growing heavy.

"Let us drink," cried the organist.

The glasses clattered.

"How well the Rhine sings! It sings the air of Barthold Gouterolf," said the son-in-law, "*ave-ave-stella!*"

No one made reply.

Far off, we could hear the rhythmic beat of two oars. "Today," cried the old postmaster suddenly, in a hoarse voice, "Saphéri makes expiation."

No doubt he had long been thinking of that. It was that which had rendered him so sad. My flesh crept. "He thinks of his son," said I to myself; "of his son who dies today!"

And a cold shiver ran through me.

"His expiation," cried the daughter with a harsh laugh, "yes — his expiation!"

Theodore touched my shoulder, and, bending to my ear, said —

"The spirits are coming — they are at hand!"

"If you speak like that," cried the son-in-law, whose teeth were chattering. "If you speak like that, I shall be off!"

"Go then, go then, coward!" said the daughter. "No one has need of you."

"Very well, I will be off," said he, rising.

And taking his hat off the hook in the wall, he went away

with long strides. I saw him pass rapidly before the windows, and I envied him.

How could I get away?

Something was walking upon the wall in front. I stared — my eyes wide open with surprise, and at length saw that it was a cock. Far off between the old palings the river shone, and its ripples slowly beat upon the sand of the shore. The light upon it danced like a cloud of seagulls with great white wings. My head was full of shadows and weird reflections.

"Listen, Peter," cried the old woman at the end of a moment "Listen, you have been the cause of all that has happened to us."

"I!" cried the old man huskily, angrily. "I! Of what have I been the cause?"

"Yes," she went on. "You never took pity on our lad. You forgave nothing. It was you who prevented his marrying that girl!"

"Woman," cried the old man, "instead of accusing others, remember that his blood is on your own head. During twenty years you have done naught but hide his faults from me. When I punished him for his evil disposition, for his temper, for his drunkenness, you — you would console him, you would weep with him, you would secretly give him money, you would say to him, "your father does not love you; he is a harsh man!" And you lied to him that you might have the greater portion of his love. You robbed me of the confidence and respect that a child should have for those who love him and correct him. So then, when he wanted to marry that girl, I had no power to make him obey me."

"You should have said 'yes!'" howled the woman.

"But," said the old man, "I had rather say no because my mother, my grandmother, and all the men and women of my family would not be able to receive that pagan in Heaven."

"In Heaven," chattered the woman. "In Heaven!" And the daughter added in a shrill voice —

"From the earliest time I can remember, our father has only bestowed upon us blows!"

"Because you deserved them," cried the old man. "They gave me more pain than they did you."

"More pain! ha! ha! ha! more pain!"

At that moment, a hand touched my arm. It was Blitz. A ray of the moon, falling on the windowpanes, scattered its light around. His face was white, and his stretched-out hand pointed to the shadows. I followed his finger with my eyes, for he evidently was directing my attention to something, and I saw the most terrible sight of which I have a memory — a shadow, motionless, appeared before the window, against the light surface of the river. This shadow had a man's shape, and seemed suspended between Heaven and Earth. Its head hung down upon its breast, its elbows stood out square beside the body, and its legs straight down tapered to a point.

As I looked on, my eyes round, wide opened with astonishment, every feature developed in that wan figure. I recognized Saphéri Mutt; and above his bent shoulders I saw the cord, the beam, and the outline of the gibbet. Then, at the foot of this deathly apparition, I saw a white figure, kneeling, with long dishevelled hair. It was Gredel Dick, her hands joined in prayer.

It would seem as though all the others, at the same time, saw that strange apparition as well as myself; for I heard them breathe —

"Heaven! Heaven have mercy on us!"

And the old woman, in a low choking voice, murmured —

"Saphéri is dead!"

She commenced to sob.

And the daughter cried —

"Saphéri! Saphéri!"

Then all disappeared, and Theodore Blitz, taking me by the hand, said —

"Let us go."

We set off. The night was fine. The leaves fluttered with a sweet murmur.

As we went on, horrified, along the great Alley des Plantanes, a mournful voice from far off sang upon the river the old German song —

> *"The grave is deep and silent,*
> *Its borders are terrible!*
> *It throws a sombre mantle*
> *It throws a sombre mantle*
> *Over the kingdom of the dead."*

"Ah!" said Blitz, "if Gredel Dick had not been there we should have seen the *other* — the fearful one take Saphéri. But she prayed for him! The poor soul! she prayed for him. What is *white* remains *white!*"

The voice far off, growing feebler and feebler, answered the murmur of the tide —

"Death does not find an echo
For the song of the thrush,
    The roses which grow on the grave,
    The roses which grow on the grave,
Are the roses of grief."

    The horrible scene which had unfolded itself to my eyes, and that far-off melancholy voice which, growing fainter and fainter, at length died away in the distance, remain with me as a confused mirage of the infinite, of that infinite which pitilessly absorbs us, and engulfs us without possibility of our escape. Some may laugh at the idea of such an infinity, like the engineer Rothan; some may tremble at it, as did the burgomaster, some may groan with a pitiable voice; and others may, like Theodore Blitz, crane themselves over the abyss in order to see what passes in the depths. It all, however, comes to the same thing in the end, and the famous inscription over the temple of Isis is always true —

    I am he that is.
    No one has ever penetrated the mystery which envelops me.
    No one shall ever penetrate it.